Pardon my gender

BOB ARNONE

iUniverse, Inc.
New York Bloomington

Pardon My Gender

This is a work of fiction. All of the characters, names, incidents, organizations, and dialogue in this novel are either the products of the author's imagination or are used fictitiously.

iUniverse books may be ordered through booksellers or by contacting:

iUniverse
1663 Liberty Drive
Bloomington, IN 47403
www.iuniverse.com
1-800-Authors (1-800-288-4677)

Because of the dynamic nature of the Internet, any Web addresses or links contained in this book may have changed since publication and may no longer be valid. The views expressed in this work are solely those of the author and do not necessarily reflect the views of the publisher, and the publisher hereby disclaims any responsibility for them.

ISBN: 978-1-4502-5686-5 (sc)
ISBN: 978-1-4502-5687-2 (hb)
ISBN: 978-1-4502-5688-9 (ebook)

Printed in the United States of America

iUniverse rev. date: 09/13/2010

For my devoted wife Pat, children and grandchildren

PROLOGUE

The nineteenth amendment gave women the right to vote, but seemingly, the men of Happy Hills Country Club, in Huntington Village Long Island, chose to completely ignore what our elected officials considered an inherent right.

Membership at Happy Hills was titled in the name of men and if a couple divorced, the now severed woman was considered ***persona non grata!*** Years of loyalty to the club and long term relationships were not factors and ignored by those in power…the men.

Death of a male member was approached in a kinder and gentler way. The board of directors would vote in deciding whether to allow the surviving spouse to inherit her husbands membership. One could argue it was an a*rbitrary* and *capricious* procedure, but certainly not by the woman whose fate lay in the *whims* of the men controlling the board, led by their infamous president, Mike Grace.

The gentlemen members enjoyed all of the comforts in their country club. They had their own *grill room* in which breakfast was served daily and a varied lunch menu provided in the confines of the **male only room**. Their bar was generous in size, with multiple television screens adorning the walls on three sides. Jars of nuts, pretzels, potato chips and trail mix, sat atop a shelf for their enjoyment.

Women were forbidden entry to the grill room, considered a gentlemen's domain, with the freedoms of exchanging off color jokes or addressing an official in not so flattering terms, who happened to make a controversial call in the sporting event of the day. Yes, one could say…it was their heaven on earth.

Could women enjoy the same comforts in their own grill room? **NOT IN THEIR LIFETIME,** for you see…they didn't have a grill room. If an individual or group of women desired breakfast, it had to be in the main dining room, an expansive like catering hall with varied hours, most of which didn't accommodate golfers who required express type service in order to make their registered tee times.

There was a *half-way house* at the second hole which served coffee, candy and other snacks, but on Tuesdays, **LADIES DAY,** rolls and bagels were delivered early to the men's grill, but more often than not, the *half-way house was skipped*...so the ladies did without.

Women's golf times were restricted, prime one's reserved for the gentlemen of the club. One could only speculate, how in the twenty-first century, the country club could avoid a challenge by the spouses of its members or...The National Organization of Women?

Happy Hills was steep in tradition and more than fifty-years old. The club was initially established as a restricted gentlemen's golf club, spouses strictly prohibited from playing. Over time, the wives of members *were granted* the opportunity to play, but on a limited basis. That tradition is maintained to the present day and fiercely guarded by board of director president, Mike Grace. But history has shown, that a courageous individual comes forward, who believes in a cause for the betterment of a race, gender, nationality or... **the control of their honey pots!**

CHAPTER 1
PARDON MY GENDER

IT WAS SUMMER and the grass glistened from the morning dew while mists of water from sprinkler heads dotting the golf course, burst into a rainbow of colors, the bright celestial body slightly over the horizon, punctuating it's splendor. Suddenly, the peaceful setting was broken by someone yelling, ***"Fore!"*** from behind the golfers standing in the fairway, waiting for the players on the green to walk off before hitting their ball. The players turned away from the warning shouts, lowering their heads while bracing for the incoming ball when it happened. Bill Harper grabbed the back of his leg and crumbled to the ground, his playing partners rushing to his aid. Getting to his feet, Harper brushed off his pants and looked indignantly in the direction of the culprit who had violated a basic etiquette of play.

"Hey jackass, what's the rush?" He shouted out. "There's nowhere to go, you dumb broad. Are you trying to kill us?"

Harper turned to his playing partners. **"Can you see why women don't belong on a golf course?"** He demanded. "They're dangerous and a damn menace."

So began the journey of one man's efforts to reshape the landscape of a country club and whose efforts would unexpectedly draw national attention while pitting husbands against wives, triggering the meaning of never... never...***unleash a woman's wrath!***

At forty-five and a successful New York businessman, still listed in society magazines as one of the city's most eligible bachelors, Bill Harper had been a member of Long Island's Happy Hills Country Club for twenty years. Tall at six-four with a chiseled one-hundred-seventy-five pound frame, Bill was the club champion and the fantasies of many single as well as some of the married women at Happy Hills.

"Calm down Bill," a young woman, wearing a white silk outfit clinging to her slim figure announced as she approached him. "If that's the worst of your injuries, count your blessings."

"Cummings, you sick broad, I should have guessed it was you. I don't understand why the club hasn't banned you and other women golfers years ago." Harper said.

"Oh, ***PARDON MY GENDER***, Bill. I guess your prehistoric thinking would prefer us in the kitchen and making babies," the defiant Nora snapped.

"That would be a good first start," he snarled. "Couldn't you see us in the fairway?"

Red haired and green eyed, Nora was striking in appearance. As the woman's club champion for the past five years, she was a feisty competitor always giving her best and asking for no quarter.

"I saw you," she told him, "but I didn't think I'd reach you. Were you on the hundred yard marker?"

"Yes we were...**but what the hells the difference where we were?"** Harper snarled.

"Well...it means I hit my drive two hundred sixty-five yards. Aren't you impressed?"

"Cummings, what would impress me is if this club banned all women from the course. Now take your skinny butt back to the tee box and if one more ball comes close to us before we finish...I'll personally break every club in your bag!"

"Oh get a life Bill," she called over her shoulder as she rejoined her group. "You come near my bag and you'll never be able to bend over for a putt again...because your driver will be where the sunshine don't reach."

"Nora, was he hurt?" One of her partners asked.

"Nah, I missed." Nora told her. "The ball should have hit him where he thinks so he'd have a greater appreciation for women."

When Nora approached the elevated tee box, she paused before hitting her ball. She stood tall, her eyes scanning the beauty of the golf course, as a hawk in the distance was majestically riding the wind then gliding to one of the resident trees. A gentle summer breeze carried the aroma of lilac, as she closed her eyes, exhilarated and marveling at nature's bounty. She swelled with emotion, a tear gathering momentum, slowly descended down, disappearing with a touch.

It was a well designed course, with elevations allowing one to view it's striking array of two hundred year oaks and one hundred fifty foot whispering pine trees. Several of the fairways were gently turned, challenging a player's skill but considered fair by it's members. Great pains were taken to accentuate the perimeters of the putting greens, dotting them with lush and colorful plantings of the season, several of which were visible from the higher elevation tee boxes. It was not surprising, that Happy Hills had an extensive waiting list seeking membership, of course ...**none of whom were women**.

Nora took a deep breath, then hit her ball. She was still bothered by the crusty attitude of Bill, a man of means and good looks, she couldn't figure him out. It was rumored when her husband Nick, died of a heart attack at age thirty-six, it was Bill, who provided one of the dissenting votes, Nora, barely admitted to the club by a six to five approval. She concluded he was part of the *good old boys*, entrenched with the idea that women at Happy Hills were simply tolerated and should remain a silent minority.

What Nora couldn't have predicted, was the coming turn of events in which she and Bill would be drawn into a personal battle, challenging her physical skills and friendships, as well as revealing demons of her deceased husband, while fending off unlikely suitors pursuing the beautiful woman.

CHAPTER 2
THE FUSE IS LIT

"DID YOU HEAR what happened out on the course today?" Bill Harper asked the country club pro. "That crazy bastard Cummings, hit into our group on the twelfth hole and nailed me."

"Are you okay?" Asked the head pro.

"I'm fine, but she could have caused some serious damage. The woman has no common sense and I really think she should be suspended to teach her a lesson." Harper insisted.

"Why don't I have a talk with her, Mr. Harper?" Dave suggested. "I'm sure it wasn't intentional. Suspending her seems a bit harsh."

"Intentional or not, she's a menace." Bill grumbled. "And if you don't do something about it, I'll bring it up to the board and also discuss your lack of action. So listen up," he added, glaring at the pro. "Don't wait too long to do it."

Shortly thereafter, Nora walked into the pro-shop to buy a glove and browse through some of the newly stocked items. She couldn't resist touching several tops, feeling for softness and then placing the item against herself while assessing how it looked in the dressing mirror. She placed a white blouse and yellow cashmere sweater on the counter.

"Hello Mrs. Cummings."

"Hey Dave, what's happening?" Nora said, as she turned to try on a blue wind breaker that caught her eye.

"Mrs. Cummings, I heard about the incident at the twelfth hole today. What happened?"

"Oh, it was no big deal," as she slipped on the jacket. "I hit Harper with my ball," she said, casually returning to the mirror. "It was an accident, pure and simple. When I went over to apologize, he called me a jackass. The conversation went south after that."

"Mr. Harper's not letting go of this and he's recommending disciplinary action to the board."

Nora placed the jacket on the counter. "Dave, ever since my husband died, Harper has been on my case and it's not just me. He hates the idea of women in the club."

"That may be so, but he's bringing this to the board and I can't stop him. I suggest you talk to him before he makes this a bigger issue than it deserves."

"Dave, the man is in love with himself, he won't listen to me."

"There must be something you can think of to calm him down?" Dave suggested.

"I suppose I could start a petition for women golfers to play after nine at night, he'd love that." Nora bristled, but recognizing Dave's disappointment in her remark. "Look, I know he's put you in a difficult position. I'll try to approach him, but I can guarantee whatever I say will go on deaf ears. The man is in a world of his own and it just frustrates me having one set of rules for the men and one for the women. It tries my patience."

"I understand, but please, just cool your heels when you talk to him." Dave pleaded.

Nora grinned. "I'll wear my sneakers Dave," she said. "And that's a promise."

She might have made light of it with the club pro, but Bill Harper's complaint would metastasize into a serious problem, one with far reaching implications, and...not just for Nora.

CHAPTER 3
THE LOCKER

"HEY NORA, I HEARD you almost gave Bill a third nut today. Tell me all the juicy details," asked Cathy Daley, as she approached her friend in the ladies locker room.

Cathy had been a friend since high school. When Nora's husband died, it was Cathy, who helped her cope with her grief. Now, the feisty and outspoken brunette, devoted to Nora, didn't hesitate to place herself in harms way of those who spoke out against her friend.

"There's nothing to tell." Nora said, sipping on her ice tea. "I accidentally hit into Bill's group and he had a baby over the whole thing."

"I'm your best friend and I'm telling you he's trouble. If he had his way, none of us would be here." Cathy grumbled.

"I know, I'm just fed up with the board thinking of us as second class citizens to the men. It frustrates the hell out of me." Nora said, slipping out of her golf clothes and into a white terrycloth robe.

"Hey, Nora." Marion Blake called out, a frequent locker room critic, whose husband was a board member and had voted against Nora remaining in the club when Nick died. "You're making it difficult for the rest of us around here. You and Nick knew the rules when you joined the club," she snapped. "Your bitching now about the club makes life around here a bit edgy. Why don't you back off? You're only giving the men a reason to toughen the rules for women golfers."

"That won't ever happen to you, will it Marion." Nora snapped. "I hear your husband wears the skirt in the family. Unless...he's thinking about getting rid of some excess baggage?"

"You know something Nora, you're a bitch," the matronly blonde said.

"Why don't you just resign from the club? You're not welcome here." Blake demanded.

"You're not talking for everyone here!" An angry Cathy, told the fifty-eight year old, facing up to a woman who, although taller than her, was not a particularly attractive person.

"I'm not speaking to you Cathy." Marion snapped, brushing her blonde hair vigorously.

"You'd better keep your friend in check. Club champion or not, she's on thin ice. Why don't you find yourself a good man, Nora. Perhaps that's what's missing in your life?" Marion snipped.

"You and your little clique can continue bending over for your husbands, I'm sure they'll eventually realize you're not worth the price." Nora hissed.

"Well I never." Marion howled.

"Maybe that's the problem, Marion." Nora snapped.

"Don't pay any attention to her." Cathy said, as Marion marched back to her locker, muttering under her breath. "She's not happy unless she's talking about somebody. The real problem is she doesn't know that she and her friends are in the minority. Most of the other women feel the same as you and I do, they're just not as vocal."

Nora shrugged, closing her locker door. The conversation had come to a halt, other members careful not to be drawn into the fray.

"It's best they're not, Cathy. They have husbands to contend with. Speaking about husbands, how does Fred feel about women at the club?"

"You have to ask?" Cathy responded…in a surprised tone. "He's one of the board members who voted to keep you in the club. You know how he adored Nick, they were like brothers. Fred was like a kid who lost their puppy when Nick passed."

"I know he did, Cathy. But deep down, how do you think he feels?"

"Like most of the married men here who try to keep their wives happy, especially the older members. Not all of the wives play golf. They're content to enjoy the social aspects of the club. But if it came down to a vote, most of them would stick together."

"I don't think they can legally kick us out." Nora said, retrieving her bag from her locker.

"Probably not." Cathy admitted, as she sat on a bench across from her friend. "But, they can tighten the rules to the point where we wouldn't want to stay."

"Maybe **I should** try to make peace with the jerk?" Nora conceded.

"I suppose there's no harm in trying. How about tonight, at the fourth of July dance? After a couple of drinks it should be easy." Cathy suggested, sipping on an Avian.

"Easy for you to say." Nora snipped. "You didn't hit him."

"I'd hit ten men with a golf ball if I could hit one as far as you can." Cathy said with a grin.

Nora smiled. She realized how much she depended upon her friend's wry humor. "I'm going to hit the showers and try to figure out how I'm going to approach Bill," she said. "My skin crawls just thinking about apologizing to him."

"Think about it this way, you have something he doesn't have and that's **the *power of a* woman**. Haven't you looked at yourself in the mirror lately? If I were a man…I'd jump your bones myself!" Cathy whispered, not wanting to add fodder for Marion.

Nora slapped her friend's shoulder. She couldn't help from being amused. Cathy had always been outrageous, but she had given Nora something to think about. Perhaps, just perhaps, she had gone too far. Could she sway the handsome champion, or would they clash, blinded by self-pride?

CHAPTER 4
THE NINETEETH HOLE

OVER DRINKS AT THE CLUBHOUSE, Bill explained the incident on the golf course to board president Mike Grace, a burly man with thick eyebrows, bushy hair and a craggy face that gave him a formidable look.

"Didn't she see you guys waiting to hit to the green?" Mike asked in his gravelly voice.

"She did, but I don't think she cared. She said it was the best drive of her life. Sounds like the familiar golf excuse for being in a hurry." Bill said, sipping on a *martini.*

"How long of a drive was it?"

"I don't know, she said it was two-hundred-sixty-five-yards plus, but who gives a damn.

Nora should have waited until we moved to the green. It's not as though she's a novice. She's the women's club champion for Christ sake. What pisses me off is the arrogance of the woman. Nick was such a nice guy, but she's just a stubborn broad who needs to be bridled."

"Easy Bill, maybe it was just an accident?" Mike said, then reaching for the dish of peanuts.

"Listen, I don't believe she intentionally meant to hit me. It could have been any of the three other players. It's this whole woman issue. This club was established on the foundation of being a refuge for men. It's the main reason I joined and stayed. But through the years, it's changed. Now we have more women golfers than ever before and they think they have the same rights as the men." Bill hesitated, as a group of fellow golfers crowded into the room and began to clamor for drinks.

"The fact is they don't have the same rights." Mike reminded him, moving his chair closer to Bill. "I'll grant you, I've been frustrated myself having to play behind four women, but under their current time restrictions it doesn't happen too often."

"Here's your *martini,* Mr. Harper," the server said, placing down a coaster.

The two men waited before continuing. It was as they all knew, a mistake to talk about club problems in front of the staff.

"It's too often as far as I'm concerned." Bill went on, after their lunch order was taken and they were alone again. "Several members feel the same and there's been a lot of talk about leaving here and joining Old Oaks Country Club. The club I belong to in Palm Beach, restricts women membership, it's a pure delight. Look, they have their exclusive clubs. I wouldn't think of joining an all female organization, would you?"

"No, but that's different, Bill. The wives enjoy the social aspects of our club." Mike said.

"So, why couldn't we have two memberships, golfing for men and social for the women?"

"I wouldn't have the support of the board for a drastic move like that. Besides, I can guarantee it would bring about a legal challenge and NOW would be at our gates picketing the club."

Bill, looked at him quizzically, shaking his head and reaching for his *martini.* It was clear he didn't think his proposal was viable and knew, Mike was right. But...perhaps there was a compromise.

"There's another way, Mike. Suppose we tighten the noose by applying additional restrictions to the women golfers?" Bill said, with a wry smile.

Mike appeared to be willing to listen, which was, as Bill knew all to well, rarely the case.

"You do realize you're opening a can of worms here." Mike said, signaling for another round of drinks.

"It would stop the bleeding and the talk about members leaving." Bill suggested.

"I need some time to think about this." Mike, frowned. "I want some feed back from the other board members at the dance tonight."

"Good idea. I'm sure they feel as I do and support whatever is proposed." Bill said, then raising his glass. ***"Here's to clearer fairways and long pants."***

The two collaborators were smiling now, but...would not be prepared for the unexpected fireworks at the evenings gala event, the indoor heat, more intense than the outdoor fireworks display.

CHAPTER 5
THE DANCE

WHEN NORA CUMMINGS entered the crowded ballroom of the Happy Hills Country Club that evening, she paused for a moment, as she usually did, to take in the ambiance. John Lennon's lyrics echoed, as waiters and waitresses bustled in and out of the kitchen. Large panes of glass at the rear of the room were accented with green velvet drapes that looked out over a spectacular scene of the summer tinged trees lining the golf course. Apple logs crackled in the fireplace to the right of the entry, while to the left, was a horseshoe mahogany bar whose backdrop was a mirrored wall, glittering the glasses and bottles just below.

The room décor sparkled in colonial regalia celebrating the birth of independence, each table displaying a grouping of small American flags surrounding a centerpiece of colorful flowers. Table utensils and cloth napkins were adorned with red, white and blue markings.

"Hey Nora." Cathy's husband called out. "You look spectacular!"

"Thanks Fred."

She was dressed to kill, her hair in a French twist and wearing a red Dior dress which clung to her shapely body, exposing a tantalizing glimpse of her cleavage. Her long, white, graceful neck, was adorned with a thirty-two karat diamond necklace and matching dangling earrings which sparkled in cadence with her every move.

"So, I see you're fully equipped for battle." Cathy remarked in a low voice, as Fred pulled out Nora's chair.

"When I'm on the course, I'm out to win. This situation is no different." Nora told her friend, grinning.

"What's your strategy?"

"Damn if I know." Nora said.

"Speak of the devil, look who's coming," Cathy hissed.

"Ladies." Bill Harper said, smiling as he continued past their table, a flustered Nora, turning towards Cathy's husband Fred, as though engaging him in conversation.

"Nora, why don't you and I powder our nose?" Cathy said, reaching for her hand. They walked to the lobby when she turned to her friend. "That's prime beef that just greeted us. You said you didn't have a plan. Well, I have one for you. There's a full moon tonight. Why don't you take him outside and ***flash him!*** Maybe if he sees one of your boobies he'll forget what happened?" Cathy suggested, with a big grin.

"If he was the last man on earth and we were on a deserted island, I'd die before I'd let him touch me." Nora assured her. Pride not revealing, even to her best friend, that she found Bill, a very sexy man, who on more than one occasion…was part of her nocturnal fantasies.

"Lady, if you were on that island with him…I'd suggest a paper bag on his head so you won't know it's him." Cathy snapped.

"You're so bad!" Nora giggled, placing her hand on her friend's shoulder. "Let's get back to the table."

"I thought I lost you two." Fred remarked, as he reached for another chair. "I couldn't help overhearing you girls before," he said. "I must say, your situation is more dire than you imagine."

Fred was forty-five and good looking. He was a muscular fellow whose brown eyes matched his hair. As a board member, he had supported Nora's continued membership in the club because of his longtime friendship with her deceased husband.

"Bill met with Mike Grace this afternoon. He wants to tighten the rules for the women golfers." Fred revealed.

"Don't worry, Fred, we can take anything he can dish out." Nora insisted.

"That's very brave of you," he assured her. "But, I don't think you realize the seriousness of the situation. Bill's trying to force as many women as possible to **quit playing** golf at the club."

Nora was astonished at Fred's revelation and her reaction was immediate.

"That pompous ***worm of a man*!"** She exclaimed while starting to rise. "I'm going to his table," she hissed. "He can't make the rules at this club. Who does he think he is?"

Cathy put out a restraining hand. "Think twice before you go charging over to his table," she warned. "It won't do any good to make a scene, not here, not now."

"There's nothing to think twice about. He lit the fuse, I'll give him the fireworks." Nora told her, storming over to Bill's table, with Cathy close behind. It was clear to everyone who saw them, that a confrontation was about to take place.

The other two couples at Nora's table, looked at Fred for direction. He smiled, then shaking his head in disbelief. They all rose, hurrying to avoid missing the unscheduled drama about to unfold. They would not be disappointed and in for a shock that would have far reaching repercussions between the two combatants, triggering a road to unimaginable consequences.

CHAPTER 6
THE CHALLENGE

"WELL, WELL, look who's here folks." Bill said as Nora approached his table. "It's the lady who's bent on killing any golfer who gets in her way."

The other members at his table laughed, infuriating Nora. Everyone in the room was watching her, but she didn't care, her focus was clear and her intent resolute.

"You self-indulging, poor excuse of a man." Nora scowled. ***"Get over yourself!"***

Marion Blake, who had managed to look even more unattractive than usual, wearing a tight fitting, purple silk gown, that was far from flattering, exposing waves of indulging after dinner desserts, rose from her chair.

"Nora Cummings," she puffed. "You're making a fool of yourself!"

"Sit down Marion and enjoy your *Shirley Temple.*" Nora demanded.

"May I suggest you go back to your table, have a few drinks and think about joining another club." Bill remarked smugly. "Frankly, your welcome here is about finished."

"I have a better idea, you pompous jerk." Nora huffed. "I challenge you to a thirty-six-hole two day golf match. You win and I'll resign from the club."

Cathy, as well as several other members couldn't believe what they had just heard. She knew her friend had a bit of a fiery temper at times, but this was too insane, even for Nora.

"I must admit, you're a beautiful woman Nora, but I think you've been standing in the sun too long. What's the catch?" Bill demanded, momentarily unnerving Nora, in alluding to her beauty. "Not that you have a snowballs chance in hell of winning," turning to other members at his table and shaking his head in scorned disbelief.

"I win…and the rules around here change." Nora told him, fire in her eyes and hands on hips. "Men and women have equal status, a grillroom for the ladies and no more restrictive tee times. And that's not all of it. The board of directors must consist of an equal number of women and men. Any member who resigns from the club within five years of me beating your sorry butt, forfeits their initiation bond, which I believe is thirty-thousand dollars."

Nora could see from the way they looked at one another, her proposal had taken them by surprise. It wasn't a whimsical thought, sputtered out in the heat of their exchange, but a well choreographed position culminating over time. Women at Happy Hills had learned long ago not to be so aggressive and as long as Nick had been alive, she had kept her thoughts on this subject to herself, not wanting to embarrass him. But now, it was all or nothing as far as she was concerned.

"Well gentlemen." Bill said to several of the board members at his table. "Are you going to back your club champion?" Without hesitation, they all agreed, several smiling at what they considered to be a predicable outcome. "Nora, there's your answer. When do you propose this...slaughter take place?"

She hesitated, her heart beating faster from the adrenalin rush, as she contemplated the time she needed to prepare. "One month from tomorrow, August 8th and Sunday the 9th." Nora said briskly.

Little did she realize, her challenge would unleash an event that would be monumental in scope, the topic of discussion in the days ahead and would pit husbands against wives.

"May I suggest something to you, Nora?" Bill said, grinning. "Enjoy the rest of the evening, particularly since this is the last social event before our match and the last you'll be able to attend."

Nora glared at him. Granted she had caused this scene, but he asked for it. Now, he was all but threatening her. **How dare he!**

"And may I suggest something to you." Nora said in response. "Enjoy your steak, I understand protein is important for a man of your age. The last lady I played golf with said you were having problems shooting straight, or was it...shooting at all?"

Bill bristled, as Nora returned to her table, accompanied by cries of support from some of the other women. **"Go get him Nora!** We're behind you."

But Cathy, was frowning. "Are you out of your mind?" She asked her, as Nora slid gracefully into her seat. "How do you intend to beat him? He's the men's golf champion you crazy broad, he's going to kill you." Cathy said, giggling aloud.

Nora staring at her friend, burst into laughter, both friends placing their hands on the others shoulder. Soon, the entire table was in laughter.

"Nora." Cathy began, patting the tears from her eyes, still laughing with little control. "Remind me never to ask you for advice." Cathy then losing it, once again giggling aloud, turned to her husband. "Fred," she mockingly blurted, "If you don't like the rules around our house, I challenge you to an arm wrestle. If I win, you have to do the wash for a year and if I lose, I'll leave." Cathy breaking into full laughter.

"Okay Cathy, I get the point." Nora said laughing. "Enough already!"

But, although it seemed amusing enough now, Nora was aware that in issuing her challenge, she had put a good deal at stake. How would the other women members perceive her dispute with Harper? Sure, it was amusing now, but would they support her or consider she overstepped her bounds, grandstanding with self-pride?

CHAPTER 7
THE PLAN

EVEN WHILE NORA, shared in the fun with Cathy, she knew the challenge given to Bill, in all probability, would be the final curtain for her as a member of the country club. But she was determined not to go down without a fight, and even though she had five weeks to prepare for the match, she intended to be ready. She visited an old friend at his golf club and explained the challenge made to Bill.

"You've really stuck your neck out on this one." George Harris, a teaching professional and a long time friend, told her.

"George, you're my only hope. Nick said you're the best teaching pro on Long Island. I need your help to prepare for this match. I want you to work with me every day at my club."

"Nora, I'm flattered, but I just can't drop everything," he protested. "I have teaching lessons practically every day."

"You're only a half hour away. Calculate a number that would compensate you for the lessons you'd have to cancel. I'll pay and add an additional twenty-five percent."

"Nora, the extra money isn't necessary. Nick was a friend. Let me sleep on it and I'll call you tomorrow?"

George was fifty-eight and still an attractive man. He was a slim six-two and had a well tanned face as a backdrop to his silver hair and blue eyes. He was deliberate in his mannerisms, choosing his words carefully, his speech tone low, sometimes barely audible. His teaching lessons with Nick, resulted in a special friendship, yet, his hidden feelings for Nora, would soon betray him.

"I'm counting on you George." Nora told him, placing her arm on his shoulder, her eyes pleading for his help, a subtle whiff of her perfume, heightening the teaching pro's senses.

"I'm late for my next lesson," he said, smacking his lips. "I promise to call you." Then turned to greet an awaiting student, his gait showing a noticeable limp.

As Nora left for the parking lot, she retrieved her cell phone from her bag and called Cathy.

"What are you doing?" She asked, when her friend answered.

"Taking the ice pack off my head."

"Did you hurt yourself?"

"No, but after last night, I came home and had two stiff drinks. They were toasts to your chutzpah my friend, and now I'm paying the consequences."

"Well, I have the perfect solution." Nora told her.

"Take three aspirins, get in the shower and meet me at the mall in an hour in front of Macy's. Shopping is always a woman's cure for pain. We'll do Macy's and the rest of the stores, then have lunch."

"Nora, promise me something?" Cathy said. "If I die before you, please place this on my head-stone. ***'Here lies the friend of the craziest woman in the world?"***

"I promise, you nut," she told her. "Now go take a shower."

Nora was concerned about her friend. Cathy seemed to be drinking more and more these days. And she wasn't the only one of the women at the club to do so. Still, she told herself, there was no time to think about that now. From here on in, she had to focus on defeating Bill Harper.

CHAPTER 8
THE MALL

NORA AND CATHY HAD LIVED as neighbors in Jamaica Estates, New York and attended the same schools through high school. Although they enrolled at different colleges, Nora in Boston and Cathy in Virginia, they had remained close friends. They wrote regularly and saw one another during holidays and summer breaks, cementing a friendship that began in grammar school. Cathy was the freckled face girl who always seemed to be the object of a joke or prank and Nora, always there to defend her. One particular memory was held dear by Cathy. On that day, Nora had told her, the only reason she was teased about her freckles was because others were jealous.

"Jealous of me? Why?" Cathy would ask.

"Because," Nora explained. "You have the most beautiful freckles in the whole wide world."

In her senior year at college, Nora met Nick at a basketball game while both were attending Boston University and were engaged within a year. They had a great deal in common, being the only child and raised by affluent parents. Nick came from a prominent Boston family whose father was a leading litigator. Nora's father was the principal of a well regarded securities firm on Wall Street.

While Nick attended law school, Nora completed her master's degree in special education. They were married within six months, both barely twenty-five, the ceremony held at *St. Patrick's Cathedral* and the reception at the *Waldorf Astoria*, Cathy, Nora's maid-of-honor.

When Nick graduated from law school, he joined his father's firm and was made partner by the time he was twenty-nine. When the firm expanded their operations to New York City, he was asked to be the lead attorney.

Nora and Nick lived in a fashionable east side apartment, a wedding gift from their parents. Although wanting to start a family, Nora's attempts to become pregnant were unsuccessful, then being told, she would never be able to conceive. It was a bitter disappointment, feeling deprived of her natural right as a woman. However, Nick was a supportive husband, although feeling helpless to change the hand nature had dealt his wife. He constantly assured her, their love for one another was all that mattered. After several discussions on the subject, both agreed a surrogate or adoption wasn't an option, at least for them. Nora, a devote Catholic, felt ***'The hand of God,'*** would somehow intervene.

Both were active athletes. Sharing a love of golf, they joined the Happy Hills Country Club in Huntington, Long Island, playing mostly on weekends and holidays. They were fond of working out, Nick running an occasional marathon, Nora biking in Central Park. They appeared in excellent health and therefore it came as a shock, when Nora received a phone call one day at one-thirty in the afternoon, the caller I.D. indicating it was Nick, but hearing the voice of his friend Jerry, instead.

* * *

"Something's happened to Nick," he said. "He was working out on the treadmill, and..."

"Jerry, talk to me. Was there an accident?" Nora demanded. "Is he in the hospital?"

"Nora, I'm sorry...Nick...he didn't make it to the hospital."

"What do you mean? Is he still in the gym? Jerry, put Nick on the phone. I want to talk to him," the frantic Nora demanded.

"Nora...Nick...is dead."

"No, no, Jerry. He can't be, tell me it's not true!" She screamed out, putting her hand over her mouth. "Tell me it's not true," she demanded, falling to her knees, sobbing and repeating her plea to the caller over and over.

"He was only thirty-six, Cathy. How can this happen?" Nora asked, as the mourners paid their last respects.

"Honey, there's no rhyme or reason for these things." Cathy said, placing her arm around her friend. "We take for granted that we'll be here forever, then out of the blue, something like this hits us smack in the face and we suddenly realize how frail life can be."

"It's not fair...it's just not fair," the grieving widow said, patting her eyes with a tissue.

Six months had passed since her husband died. Nora was financially secure, a substantial life insurance policy on Nick's life, provided her with several options, one of which was moving to the suburbs of Long Island. Influenced by her friend, Nora purchased a home near Cathy, on Huntington's north shore, a stone's throw away from Happy Hills Country Club.

* * *

"Hi Cathy." Nora greeted her friend in front of Macy's. "Do we eat first or shop till we drop?"

"Let's eat and then shop." Cathy pleaded. "I'm starving."

"How's Friday's?"

"Good by me," said her freckled faced friend.

Within ten minutes, they were seated at a table by the window, both ordering a garden salad and unsweetened ice tea.

"So, have you had time to think about what club we're going to join?" Cathy began.

"What are you talking about?"

"I'm talking about the way you kicked Bill's butt last night." Cathy snipped.

"Cathy, if Bill beats me it's because he's a better player than me."

"***He is a better player*!"** Cathy told her friend, laughing out loud.

"I thought you were my best friend?" Nora hissed, leaning her head to one side, her expression one of animated distain.

"I am, but if you were stepping off the curb and a truck was heading right for you, I'd grab you, wouldn't I?" Cathy asked, raising her hands up in a pantomime expression.

"I know what Bill can do as a golfer, but if you insist on telling me that I'm going to lose, I won't have a chance."

"**How in hell do you expect to beat him?** He's drives the ball a ton and is usually on the green in two?"

"I know Cathy, that's why I've asked George Harris, to work with me every day before the match."

"George? Boy, you really like to play with fire." Cathy said, shaking her head side to side.

"What are you talking about?" Nora asked with a quizzical look.

"Don't you know, that George has had a crush on you for years?" Cathy revealed to her friend.

"Get out of town! George? He's never made a pass. Besides, he's twenty years older than me."

Cathy smirked. "It was only his friendship with Nick, that kept him in check. Do you think that thing between his legs knows there's an age difference? It has a mind of it's own, you know. I'm just warning you, that coaching won't be the only thing on his mind when he tells you he'll do it. Because he will, you know. It's a sure thing."

No sooner did Cathy, finish speaking, Nora's cell phone rang. And sure enough…it was George.

"I didn't think I'd hear from you until tomorrow." Nora said, turning her back to Cathy, who had spread her arms at one hundred and eighty degrees while tilting her head with an, **'I told you so'** expression."

"Nora, I initially told myself, that it wasn't a good idea to say yes to your proposal. But, considering our past friendship, I'm going to accept with certain conditions. First, there'll be no debating my instructions."

"I can deal with that." Nora told him.

"I'm going to lay out a six hour daily regime, which will include practice time with me and drills to be done on your own. And Nora, I won't accept any payment," the pro demanded.

"George, I can't agree to that." Nora protested. "It would disturb me, in knowing that I'm preventing you from earning a living."

"Listen," he started. "Did Nick ever discuss with you about him lending me five-thousand dollars three years ago?"

"No George." Nora admitted. "He never mentioned it to me."

"That would be just like Nick." George said. "You see, my son Jimmy, got into a jam with some girl and got her pregnant. She didn't want the baby and so, I needed the money to fix the problem. Nick gave it to me with no strings attached. You'd think a single thirty-year-old would have used better judgment in this day and age, but ever since his mother died, he changed. Joan was devoted to Jimmy, there wasn't anything she wouldn't have done for him.

Six months before Nick died, I met him at his office in the city to pay him back. He refused to take the money. I knew you guys were more than comfortable, but how many people in the same situation would give a pass on five thousand dollars?"

The waiter briefly interrupted the conversation, placing their salads on the table, giving Nora, time to pause.

It always touched her when someone talked of Nick's generosity. He had been, she reminded herself, the ultimate decent man and Nora doubted she would ever find anyone like him.

"So you can understand, why I couldn't accept your money now, can't you?" George continued. "I can easily rearrange my schedule and my assistants will shoulder some of the load, so I won't lose money," he assured her.

It made sense, Nora told herself. If George, could feel he was repaying a favor, then so be it. Making no more protest, she arranged to meet him at seven-thirty the next morning and assured him as well, she would clear it with her club's pro.

"Don't say a word about this to me," she warned Cathy, putting her cell phone away. "If you do, I'll tell your husband...how you stare at that young pool boy every Tuesday afternoon."

"I never do any such thing!" Cathy sputtered. "Why, he's only twenty-five. How? Now that's plain blackmail, Nora Cummings."

"You're turning red faced." Nora teased her. "Did I hit a nerve?"

"Well, he might as well be naked, cleaning a pool in a skimpy bathing suit," she huffed, stabbing at her salad with her fork. "Don't tell me you haven't taken a peek now and then. Besides, there's no harm in looking...is there?" Cathy asked, looking for some form of absolution from her friend.

Nora tried to change the subject, but with no success. She knew from experience that once Cathy decided to talk about sex there was no stopping her.

"You know what I think Nora," she finally said..."I think you need some serious bed time. When's the last time you got your **wah wah** to meet an eligible **pepperoni?** Don't let it rust out girl! I'd lend you Fred, but the man's out of bullets. You ought to do something to get smiling again."

"Cathy!" Nora exclaimed, grinning. "People will hear you. Besides, perhaps I'm not interested in getting serious with anyone," the blushing friend snipped.

"Good for you!" A silver haired woman at the table next to them said. "Personally, I think a good vibrator is a simpler conclusion and you don't have to serve breakfast in the morning."

Both women smiled at the pleasant woman, turned to each other, then raising their eyes and grinning from ear to ear.

"You know what I think, Nora?" Cathy continued, when a few other customers who had heard the exchange stopped laughing. "We should do this more often. Just get away and leave all the problems behind us."

"Depends on what kind of problems you're talking about?"

"I just get bored." Cathy told her. "I feel life is passing me by like a run-a-way freight train, that something is missing and I can't pin point what it is. Don't you ever feel that way?"

"I'm too busy to think about it. Between golf and my charity work, it seems like I'm always running. Sounds like you're the one that needs some serious bed time."

"More ice tea?" Asked the waiter? Then grinning, he turned to Cathy, bending at the waist and speaking softly, he said, "I get off in a half-hour and I'm sure we'd both be smiling in the morning?"

Cathy couldn't believe the nerve of the young waiter, but kept her cool. "Bend down you hunk, I want to whisper something in your ear."

Anxious and still grinning, he complied. Cathy grabbed his crotch with one hand and ear with the other, then squeezing tightly, she proclaimed, "From what I feel here, there's not enough beef to satisfy a frog in heat. Now get out of my face," releasing the young server, who placed both hands on his privates, slowly walking away and grimacing in pain.

"See what you started." Nora jabbed.

"Just a boy in heat," countered her friend, stabbing at her salad.

As they finished their meal, Nora was concerned about Cathy's comments. It was obvious she was unhappy and having trouble in her relationship with Fred. And as much as she loved her friend, she didn't know what she could do about it.

Little did she realize, the scope of Cathy's troubles and the far reaching affect it would have on the friendship she held so dear.

CHAPTER 9
THE SPA

AFTER SHOPPING for a couple of hours, the two friends decided to see if the spa at the mall had openings for massages. Finding they could be accommodated, they were soon side-by-side on two tables while their bodies were gently pressed into submission by the hands of the masseuse.

"Maybe you need to get more involved." Nora suggested. "You know, I've never asked why you and Fred never had children."

"When we first got married it seemed like the thing to do." Cathy said, her voice slightly muffled. "But whenever I brought the subject up, Fred would tell me that we'd talk about it later. After a few years, I suppose I just became accustomed to a life without the responsibility. Then, I saw some of our mutual friends wither from kids and the thought of being like them frightened me. It takes an unselfish person to have children. You should know, you and Nick made a life without them."

The subject of why children were not part of Nora's life had never been discussed with Cathy. The charities dear to Nora, revolved around children, a clear footprint to her past.

"Nick and I wanted to have kids," she said, "but…I couldn't. He wanted to adopt and I didn't. I won't tell you it didn't put a strain on our marriage, but I couldn't get over the issue of raising a child that wasn't biologically from the both of us. I can't tell you…how often I regret, in not going surrogate. At least part of him would be with me. Have you and Fred ever discussed adoption?"

"No, we didn't. You know…it seems strange you and I have never talked about this before, as close as we are." Cathy said.

"Some things are best left unsaid, until the time is right." Nora explained, as she gently closed her eyes, the rhythmic hands of the masseuse, dulling her senses.

"I'm thirty-eight and Fred is forty-five. I can't imagine being fifty-three and having to deal with an adolescent. It's quite possible I'd be using drugs before the kid did. And if I had a daughter who wanted birth control pills before she was forty, I'd have a nervous breakdown. No, a child's not a solution to anything now."

"Why don't you plan a second honeymoon and get away?"

"With Fred, or someone else's husband?" Cathy said, causing Nora to lift her head, gawking at her friend.

"Don't look at me that way. I'm in a funk with Fred. The pilot light is low and the wick seems to be burned out. Fred has a stressful job. It's not easy when you're in sales. Oh, he does just fine money wise." Cathy told her. "It's the guys. Seems like he'd rather be playing golf and cards then spending time with me. When we do have time together, he's always talking about this golf shot or that card hand. I swear, sometimes I feel if I stood naked in front of him, he would say **"NICE PAIR OF HEARTS**."

"Oh come on Cathy." Nora said laughing. "I'm sure you're exaggerating? Have you told Fred how you feel?"

"Sure. And do you know what his response was? 'I'm not an alcoholic, I don't gamble and I don't do drugs. What do you want from me?"

"He has a point." Nora told her. "What did you say?"

"I said I'd rather have him be a drunken card player and doing drugs, if that would make him pay more attention to me." Cathy snipped.

As usual, Nora, thought Cathy was trying to make light of the situation. But she had a hunch just the opposite was true. Something was really wrong with her friend's marriage.

"Maybe you'll have to change the menu to get the attention you're looking for?" She suggested...."and I'm not talking about cooking in the kitchen. I'm talking about what goes on upstairs." Nora said, with a raised eyebrow.

It didn't take long to explain, as explicitly as possible, what she meant.

"You did those things with Nick?" Cathy said, with a look of astonishment, her mouth agape.

CHAPTER 10
TRAINING DAY ONE

THE AROMA OF COFFEE welcomed Nora, as she stretched her arms upward, letting out a loud series of sighs. She always started her mornings with a hearty breakfast and strong coffee. And today was special. It would be her first day of training with George, on this hot July morning.

After showering, Nora browsed through her closet, determining which of her twenty-five or so color coordinated golf outfits to choose. The bright yellow golf shirt and white shorts appealed to her this morning, and after dressing, she ate a breakfast of cereal and berries while watching the local news.

The drive to Happy Hills took approximately fifteen minutes. Nora left her house at eight fifteen allowing enough time to do some stretching before meeting George and arrived at the practice range before him.

She was hitting some balls when she heard, *"Nice tempo."* She turned to find George, leaning on a club, his contagious smile exposing a perfect formation of appendages. The well tanned pro was wearing a powder blue shirt, accenting his parted silver hair and matched his blue eyes. George, a traditionalist, wore white pants rather than shorts in spite of the intense heat.

The practice area was expansive, every seven feet separated by a generous basket of practice balls, tennis courts providing a backdrop of clattering racquets finding their mark.

George wasted no time in establishing his focus. There were no good mornings, or how pretty she looked. He was all business, or least for today. "We have five weeks to prepare for the match." George told her. "What are some of the challenges we face?"

"Well, Bill can hit the ball longer than I can."

"Let's deal with that issue first." George suggested. "He'll be hitting from the blue tees and you'll be hitting from the red. The difference in driving distance won't be as significant as you think."

"Who said Bill, won't insist that we hit from the same tee box?"

"He won't win that argument on pride alone," he told her. "Now, you're approximately the same distance to the green with him. Let's assume you're both on the green in two, who'll win the hole?"

"The one who putts the best?"

"That's right. So, can we conclude his driving distance will be neutralized? Because if we can, what do you think it will take to win the match?" George pressed.

"If he shows up drunk and can't see the hole." Nora said, trying to lighten up the pro.

"Enough with the jokes Nora," the normally soft spoken George, scowled. "I'm not here to be entertained. Again, what do you think it'll take to win this match?" He demanded.

She wondered, what Cathy had been thinking, when she suggested George, had a crush on her. One thing she knew for sure, she'd hate to see him when he was mad. Where's his sense of humor, she thought to herself? But in a way, she guessed she needed him to be tough, in order to have any chance against Harper. George knew the game inside out and had seen both her and Bill play. She needed his advice and was willing to admit that. After all, George was not here to simply please her. It was clear to Nora, he was really concentrating on this.

"Mid-irons and short game will win the match," she replied.

"Right you are." George said. "Now, six strokes separate you and Harper. He's a two handicap and you're an eight. If both of you play to your handicaps you can't win. I can cut two, maybe three strokes off your handicap, which puts you at a five-six. The question now becomes, how do we make up the difference from his two to your five?"

"How do we do that?"

"We have to show him a side of your game he hasn't seen or heard about. We'll be breathing down his neck the entire match, which hopefully will affect the way he plays. Maybe he won't always be on the green in two. We're going to concentrate on your game to the green, chipping, trap play and putting. That means working from the seven iron to your sand wedge. The other factor will be hole-by-hole strategy. Here's a spiral pad, bring it with you everyday. During the match, you'll reference each hole you play. Now let's get to work."

Under George's watchful eye, Nora practiced everything he had suggested all morning. At noon, they went to the dining room where one of the first people they saw was Dave Thompson, the club pro.

"I want to thank you for the courtesy of letting me work with Nora, here at the club." George said, extending his hand.

"Not a problem." Dave assured him. "In fact, you've done us a favor. We haven't had this much excitement in years. The entire membership is buzzing about the match. There's going to be a huge turnout for the event," he added, as Bill Harper approached the table.

"They're coming out to say goodbye to Nora," he said, smirking. "He's not going to help you…no one can." Bill pointing to George.

"Are you worried about little old me?" Nora said, playfully. "George, I see fear in the man's face," mocking her handsome adversary.

"You do have the looks, I'll say that much." Bill said devilishly. "But what makes you think you can win this match?"

Before Nora could answer, George put a restraining hand on her shoulder and stood from his chair, glaring at Bill. "I'll handle this," he said in a measured tone.

"Oh, is Georgee boy fighting your battles now?" Bill said, scornfully.

"I just have one question," a frowning George said, as he stood almost nose to nose from Bill. "Don't you think it imprudent to brow beat an opponent you know doesn't have a chance against you?" Nora's expression, curious at the teaching pro's admission.

"Well, at least someone has some sense." Bill replied, taking a step back. "Why don't you advise your little girl to stay home and avoid her embarrassment?"

"Actually," George said, "that's what I told Nora, but she insists on making a go of it. But here's an idea. Since all of the principals are together, why don't we clarify the rules of the challenge? I understand, it's a two day *match play* contest."

"No, it's not *match play*," countered Bill. "It's *medal play*, whoever has the lowest score at the end of two rounds will be the winner, not a hole by hole winner." Bill, knowing if Nora, imploded at any one hole with a high score, the match would be over in *metal play*. But in *match play*, a high score at any one hole is the loss of that hole alone and could easily be overcome. This would somewhat neutralize Bill and further narrow the gap between he and Nora.

"I understood, it was Nora who challenged you to a two day match?" George said. "That being the case, the assumption indicates *match play* at respective tees, you at the blue and Nora at the red." George continued, weaving a web to which Harper, would have no escape.

"Wait a minute!" Bill protested. "You just went from *match play* versus *medal play* to different tee boxes," his face flushed, veins protruding from is neck.

"Am I to assume Mr. Harper, you wish to cancel the match, thereby forfeiting and losing to the agreed upon terms?" George said calmly, staring directly into Bill's eyes. "I'm sure the membership would be interested in why you decided it too risky to play the match."

"You know what," Bill scowled, "it doesn't make a difference what tees she plays from or whether it's *medal* or *match play,* she's still going to get her pretty little butt kicked."

"You old fox George." Dave Thompson whispered, as Harper stormed angrily out of the dining room. "Nora, you just saw a master of the con at work."

"George, that was amazing!" Nora said with enthusiasm.

As they ate their lunch, it was clear that George felt good about how he had handled the situation. Nora often felt his eyes lingering on her and hoped the attraction he so obviously felt for her, would not stand in the way of their working together.

"Good first day, Nora." George said. "We worked hard and started our strategy."

"Oh, you mean the terms of the match?"

"No, no." George told her, shaking his head. "I mean finding out about the man. If we can rattle him so easily, watch what happens when he turns around and finds you breathing down his neck."

Nora let her admiration of George show in her eyes and saw him flush.

"Well, just make sure you control that feisty temper of yours," the pro demanded, as Nora leaned over and kissed him on the cheek. The minute she did, she regretted it. It would she knew, be a mistake to lead him on in that way. The game was the only thing they should focus on and that's what she intended to do. But George on the other hand, would view it as a sign of affection, dictating his plans for the future.

CHAPTER 11
THE BOARD

"ALL IN FAVOR of presenting the recommended improvements to the full membership, say aye."

With no dissenting votes among the nine members, Mike Grace, president of the board of directors, tapped his gavel and closed the new business matters of the meeting.

The board room was somewhat unremarkable. It was rectangular, housing a long table sitting eight on each side and one at each end. The walls were mahogany and adorned with portraits of past presidents, George Washington at one end and Ronald Reagan on the other, two small American flags book ending each. The floor was covered with a rust wall-to-wall rug accented by a brown border. There were no windows in the room.

"Gentlemen, the last order of discussion, which will be *unofficial* and not part of the minutes, is the up-coming match between Nora Cummings and Bill Harper. Now, we've all had some laughs over drinks, but, I want to clearly spell out the consequences...**if by chance she wins,"** the burly club president said, as he reached for his beer.

"Not a snowball's chance in hell of that happening." Bill Harper declared.

"Are you serious Mike? There's no chance Bill will lose to that broad." Herb Blake chimed in agreement.

"I'll wear a dress for a year if that candy ass beats Bill!" Ralph Cipriano shouted, his pink short sleeve shirt making him a target of innuendo.

"From what I hear Ralph, you might enjoy that," another board member ranked, eliciting laughter from the other members, while Ralph's complexion flushed bright red.

"If she beats you Bill…I'll pay for your dress and mine." Ralph quipped.

"Save your money sweetie." Bill snapped, while the others joined in laughter.

"You know gentlemen, if history has taught us anything, it's that the underdog does win on occasion." Fred Daley said, running one hand through his disheveled brown hair. "We should seriously consider what Mike's suggesting."

"Isn't your wife buddy-buddy with Nora Cummings?"

"What does that have to do with the idea that anything's possible?" Fred demanded, clearly annoyed at Bill's innuendo, then standing and tucking at his beige shorts.

"Well it seems to me we ought to have a united front on this without any weak sisters talking about losing." Bill told him truculently.

"Bill and the rest of you hear me out." Mike interrupted. "There's no need for name calling and fighting amongst ourselves. As president of this board, I'm responsible to all members of the club."

The tone of the conversation was getting intense. Mike had to control the direction of the meeting before it got out of hand.

"Happy Hills is undeniably a men's club and has been for the past fifty years. **It's our get away from the *skirts.*"** Mike continued. "Let's take stock of what we have. We eat alone in the men's grill, smoking our cigars without some broad coughing and telling us how harmful that beautiful smell is to her health. We can curse when we want and the golf course is our toilet. Why in hell do you think it was named, Happy Hills? I agree, there's little chance of Bill losing to Nora. But, if the unthinkable does happen…consider what we're giving up?"

"What are you proposing Mike, that I refuse to play? We'd all be the laughing stock of the club."

"No Bill, not all of us." Mike snapped.

The room became silent. The mood turned somber and clearly doubt was now replacing certainty.

"There's a lot at stake here gentlemen." Fred Daley said, all of the board members turning in his direction. "But I think I have somewhat of a solution," the husky forty-five year old continued.

"What Fred, you want me to beg for Nora's forgiveness for her lack of courtesy on the course?" Bill snarled, clearly suspect of his intentions.

Fred shook his head in disgust, throwing his hands up in frustration.

"Let him speak Bill." Mike demanded.

"If I'm not mistaken." Fred continued. "One of the conditions if you lose was that no member can leave the club for five years without forfeiting their bond."

"So what's your point?" Bill scowled, sensing his support might be withering.

"If you're so sure, Nora doesn't have a chance of beating you..."

"She doesn't!" Bill interrupted, his expression one of distain at the suggestion of losing.

The trap set by Fred Daley was in place. He wasn't in favor of Nora beating Bill, because he enjoyed the men's only environment as much as the other members, but he disliked Harper's brash and cocky attitude.

"I'm glad you're so sure Bill, then you shouldn't object to my proposal."

"Yeah, and what's that?"

"If Nora should win, you personally compensate any member who wishes to leave Happy Hills for their lost bond." Fred Daley said, several of the board members shaking their heads in apparent agreement.

"Are you out of your mind!" Bill cried out, jumping to his feet with clenched fists. "They're two-hundred and fifty members at our club. If they all decided to leave at an average of thirty grand a bond, I'd be on the hook for seven and a half million."

Arms folded, sitting back in his chair, Fred's grin said it all.

"I understand when you sold your investment company, it was reportedly for about one hundred million?" Fred commented, moving forward in his chair, eyebrows raised.

"So what!" Bill snarled. "What's your point?"

"It's this," Fred began, clearly choosing his words with care. "The board members have a responsibility to protect the integrity of the club. If you say you can't lose, it's not an issue. But on the other hand, if you do, you certainly can afford to compensate those who wish to leave Happy Hills. After all, we wouldn't be in this predicament if you accepted Nora's apology and her explanation of an accidental mishap."

Fred leaned back in his chair. He had boxed Bill into a corner. If he didn't accept Fred's challenge, he would have to cancel the match and be ridiculed as long as he remained a member of the club. It was also reasonable, although Bill's calculation for his potential liability was correct, mass exodus of all members was purely hypothetical and unlikely.

"Seems like a fair solution to me," the sixty-two year old, Herb Blake said, prompting the other board members to support Fred's proposal.

Bill could hardly contain himself. He was outraged at the suggestion, feeling betrayed by several of the board members who were elected through his support. Then the trap, skillfully choreographed by Fred, closed.

"Sure it's a reasonable solution...because none of you are on the line for seven and half million." Bill snapped. "But I'm going to show you guys, how much of a better man I am…than all of you put together. I'm going to agree to this ridiculous idea, but I won't forget…that my so called friends, turned their backs on me when I needed them." And with that, Bill kicked back his chair and **STORMED OUT** of the board room.

CHAPTER 12
THE LADIES LUNCHEON

ABOUT THE SAME TIME the board meeting had concluded, the members wives were entering the dining room of the club, each with a pink ribbon attached to their blouse or jacket, indicating their support for the annual breast cancer awareness day. Tablecloths and napkins were pink, as was the rose for each place setting. A glass tubular vase, filled with assorted flowers, adorned the center of all tables.

"Ladies, ladies, please be seated so we can begin our program," the pleasant appearing woman in a pink dress announced. "I'm Sharon Kelly, chairlady for the Happy Hills breast cancer luncheon. For those who are guests of a member, we thank you for your participation. Each and every one of us has a stake in one day seeing a cure for breast cancer. We have a wonderful program scheduled which will include a silent auction and a fifty-fifty drawing. Some of our member volunteers will be visiting your tables and offering chances for your participation in the drawings. Please be as generous as you can. They will also collect personal contributions you wish to make either in your name or that of a loved one."

The women closely followed what Sharon was saying, many of them, no doubt aware, she had a personal battle with the disease.

"Each year we invite a breast cancer survivor or someone currently in treatment to say a few words to our members and guests," she continued. "This year, I have the pleasure of introducing Melissa Allen, *breast cancer survivor*."

Their guest, a graceful woman with long blonde hair, swept back in a chignon, rose and went to the podium. She was showered with polite applause.

"Thank you," she began. "As Sharon said, I'm a breast cancer *survivor* and

I emphasize the word "*survivor*." Five years ago during a regular check-up, my doctor noticed a small lump near my left breast. After extensive testing, including a mammogram and biopsy, it was concluded that I had stage three breast cancer. When I heard the word "*cancer*,**" MY KNEES BUCKLED**. I had visions of leaving my husband and three beautiful daughters, never to do the things Jeff and I had planned, never to see my daughters weddings or my future grandchildren. I was, in plain language, a wreck. I cried for days," she paused, reaching for a glass of water.

"When the crying stopped and reality set in," she continued, "I asked my doctor my alternatives. We discussed various treatments and then I asked what would she do given the same choices? She said…remove the breast, which I must confess, sent a foreboding chill throughout my body. Jeff and I went for a second and third opinion, each coming to the same conclusion. As women, you can imagine how it felt never to be seen whole again in the eyes of your husband, or see yourself in the mirror as you once were. When I shared my feelings with Jeff, he said, 'I know you'll always be whole here,' pointing to my heart. 'I just hope your boyfriend feels the same,' he added, and we both had a good laugh. I won't go into the past five years of my life, but I'd like to leave you with a thought. **NEVER GIVE UP THE FIGHT, NEVER,** for we are the profiles in courage for our children to follow when they face adversity. Thank you and God bless all of you for your support."

When she concluded, the members and their guests rose and loudly applauded for an extended period, her words resonating with all of the women present.

"Boy, talk about the important things in life?" Cathy said, wearing a pink and white print sundress.

"It was certainly a moving presentation." Nora agreed, dressed in a white *Escada* suit, her jacket cropped over a pink blouse.

A story like Melissa's always made an impact with Nora. It was…she thought now, important to remember, there were many things in life more pressing than a golf competition.

"Did you ladies hear about the board meeting last night?" Sharon asked, shaking out her napkin.

"Cathy was just starting to tell me." Nora said.

"I take it, the board voted to make Bill Harper, financially responsible for any member who chooses to leave the club, if Nora, beats him in the match." Sharon said.

"Why, that could be in the millions," someone remarked.

"Lets not think about that now." Nora told them. "What you just heard was inspirational and it empowered women. Let's not let ourselves be drawn down by the men and their schemes."

"My husband set the trap on Bill and he took the bait." Cathy said, irrepressible as usual.

"And my husband voted in favor." Sharon added.

"Everyone on the board voted in favor of Fred's proposal." Cathy declared. "Who wouldn't want the option of leaving and getting back their money?"

Nora came to realize, that she might as well join them, since it was clearly going to be impossible to keep them off the subject. Besides she thought, suddenly elated, she had an idea.

CHAPTER 13
TRAINING DAY TWO

WTH THREATENING SKIES, Nora questioned if the weather would force the cancellation of her practice. She dressed appropriately before leaving for the club. When reaching Happy Hills, she went directly to the practice range to limber up before George arrived. When he did, Nora was anxious to inform him about the turn of events which occurred the night before.

"George, remember you told me we had to make up six strokes with Bill? I think last night we narrowed the gap."

"Well I'll be damned," said George, when Nora went on to tell him about the boards' vote.

"Do you realize what this means?" She asked him, grinning.

"It means every time Bill, hits a drive from the tee box or an iron shot to the green, there'll be more pressure on him and his hands will also be a little tighter on every putt." George gushed.

"Obviously he knows, not everyone's going to leave the club if he loses." Nora said, pushing back her wind blown hair. "But if ten members leave, he's on the hook for three hundred thousand dollars. It's no longer a friendly Saturday game with the boys."

"Let's get to work," said a more serious George. "I don't like the look of that sky."

"Hit your fifty-six-degree wedge twenty-five-yards," he directed, adjusting his wind breaker. "Give me twenty with that club."

"What about hitting it eighty-to-ninety-yards?" She asked.

"Just twenty-five-yards for now," he said. "Remember, we're doing this my way," he said with firm resolve, wanting to give a clear message.

"Okay George." Nora shrugged. "You're the boss."

"How many of the shots you just took were within five feet of the flag?" George asked, when she had finished hitting the twenty wedge shots.

"About eight, why?"

"You're going to continue to hit that wedge twenty-five-yards until you can give me seventy percent of them **within five feet** of the flag." George insisted. "This is where you win and lose matches. You can hit long drives, but if your short game is missing, so will your victories."

It took Nora about an hour to accomplish what George demanded.

"Now give me twenty-five to the **fifty-yard** flag," he told her. "I want seventy percent **within eight feet**," holding on to his hat, as the weather grew more threatening.

This time, it took Nora, an hour and a half to make the grade, as a light drizzle made it difficult to secure a firm grip on her club.

"Now give me twenty five at the **seventy-five-yard** flag." George instructed. "I want sixty-percent **within ten feet**."

"George, I'm tired and getting soaked." Nora protested. "Can we continue this tomorrow morning? It's getting difficult in this drizzle."

"Is that what you're going to say to Harper? I'm tired and it's drizzling. Can't we continue tomorrow?"

"I only meant…" Nora began, feeling piqued by his stern response.

"I know what you're asking. Should I re-think doing this with you? Am I wasting my time and energy? Do you want this Nora, or is it just a lark for you? Is this an ego trip or are you serious about having a chance in winning this match? Do I stay or do I go? Tell me now, I don't want to give you all that I have and have you give me fifty-percent?"

Surprised by his outburst, the soft spoken and mild mannered George, was showing his competitive nature, which only made Nora, more determined then ever.

"How many yards are we at?" She asked sheepishly, her arms and legs discovering a different intensity from past practices.

"Seventy-five," the instructor told her, wiping the brim of his hat.

Two hours later, Nora had satisfied George's requirements and discovered to her surprise, that instead of feeling tired, she had been energized in spite of the conditions. This was going to work after all. George had pushed her to another level of determination and she liked the feeling.

"It's four-thirty." George said, glancing up and then at his watch. "Do you think you can give me another twenty five at the **hundred-yard** flag and **within fifteen feet** before dark?"

"It gets dark about eight and the rain is subsiding," Nora said, reaching for another club from her bag. "If I can't do it before six, I'll mail Harper a surrender letter."

"That's the spirit. I want fifty percent within fifteen feet."

Nora finished the drill in less than an hour and a half, but not without a price. Her clothes were saturated from the misty rain and her right hand had blistered in two places.

"Ten minutes before your surrender deadline," George said, congratulating her. "You cut it close, but you did it."

When she stood on tiptoe and kissed him on the cheek, Nora meant it at first, as a sort of apology for having been so reluctant to follow his directions. But then, as she saw him glance at her shirt, which was wet from the rain and clinging to her breasts, she realized that she must be careful not to give him any false hope. Much as she liked and admired him, he could never be anything more to her, than a man who had been her and Nick's dear friend. She was determined not to give him any reason to think there was any more than a professional arrangement between them.

"See you at nine tomorrow," he said, looking at Nora, in a way that made her remember Cathy's warning.

Nora was walking in the parking lot towards the women's locker room when a black Bentley convertible stopped in front of her path.

"Practicing Nora?" Bill asked, leaning his head out of the window. "Or were you out trying to kill someone else on the course?"

"Look Bill, I'm not in the mood for wise cracks," she barked. "Move your car out of my way."

"Walk around Cummings." Bill demanded.

Nora, shook her head side to side. He really did think he was the cock of the walk and she looked forward to disabusing him of that notion. "Bill, back your car out of the way or I'll put a nine iron through your front windshield," she said evenly.

"You'll have to walk around Nora...**because I'm not moving!"**

"You know Harper, you're stupider than I thought," she told him. "How did you ever get to be the head of a company? I heard about the trap you fell into last night, they really *suckered* you in...Billy Boy. You know, after I kick your butt, I'm going to get as many of my friends to quit the club just to put you on the hook for as much money as possible. Then, after you pay the freight, I'll just get them to rejoin again," Nora threatened.

"You think their husbands would allow that?" He said grinning. "For a real sexy lady, I can't believe you're that naive."

His flattery struck Nora. She flushed, closing her windbreaker, avoiding view of her rain soaked golf shirt. She wondered though, how a person with the physical appeal of Bill, was so stubborn. She was curious about the other side of the man, the suave lover some of his conquests at the club spilled out over a few too many martini's.

"Bill, don't ever question the power of a woman. She can prevent a husband from making a deposit for a long...long...time." Nora said, then reaching for the nine-iron from her bag.

Grinning, Bill put his Bentley in reverse. "I hope you're not part of that group, Nora. It would be such a shame to waste those lovely attributes. Maybe if you used them, you wouldn't be so fixated on issues that are best left to others."

There it was, a glimpse of the other side, and she seemed stunned for the moment, but just for a moment.

I'm here to stay!" She called after him...and she meant it. Never in her life had she wanted to prove herself any more than she did now.

CHAPTER 14
THE MEN'S GRILL

ALL ONE HAD TO DO was to visit the grill room at Happy Hills to conclude it was indeed a male bastion. It was dominated by a U shaped bar, its walls adorned with pictures of famous athletes and celebrities who at one time or another had played there. The ceiling and walls consisted of rich oak wood, highlighted with gold leaf trim with small lions also painted in gold, separating every six feet. A rustic brown rug with the club's emblem in the center, covered the entire floor and was dotted with round tables and low back chairs cushioned with green leather.

Another wall featured a high definition, sixty-inch television set. Coffee, bagels, rolls and danish were always available, along with cashews, pretzels, potato chips and trail mix. A full breakfast could be served any time before noon and thereafter, a generous lunch menu provided. Certainly, the male members of the club never had a concern about the availability of food.

As for the women, they were without a grillroom. Breakfast was not available, although coffee and rolls could be purchased at the end of the first golf hole in the halfway house, but only on Tuesdays, ladies day, if they were delivered at all. The reasoning of not providing breakfast for the women was simple enough. They could only play after twelve noon, except on Tuesday, when they had to play before ten in the morning. With restricted playing times, it didn't make sense to serve breakfast for women at the halfway house while the men were anxiously waiting for them to move along so they could have access to the golf course.

If husbands and wives wanted to have breakfast or lunch together, it had to be in the ballroom dining area of the club. Yes, one could say in the twenty-first century, the men of Happy Hills were under the radar of scrutiny.

"Happy Hills was put on the map by the men of this club." Mike Grace said to Bill Harper, as they turned to see if Tiger Woods would make his putt. "The man's amazing!" Someone cried out from another table as the ball fell in the cup.

"As I was saying." Mike continued, flicking a crumb off his black golf shirt. "All the little perks we have can go down the drain if you don't beat that broad," the five-eight, two hundred pound president scoffed, his thick eyebrows raised.

"Blame yourself." Bill huffed. "You're supposed to be a good friend of mine. How could you let Fred Daley, put me in a corner with his **`You pay the lost bond money for all members who leave if Nora, were to win?`** You're the damn president of the board. Why didn't you shoot it down?" Bill's face flushed with emotion, tugging to open the top button of his blue golf shirt.

"Because I didn't have a chance." Mike told him, rubbing his eyes, singed by drops of perspiration. "Didn't you see how fast the other members jumped on the band wagon?"

"What I saw were a bunch of ***sunshine friends*** duck and run for cover, that's what I saw."

Bill grumbled, his tone bringing attention to members sitting nearby.

Mike took a handkerchief from his pocket, wiping his brow, his sun parched wrinkle lines acting as catch channels, the conversation with his friend getting uncomfortable.

"Bill, do you believe there's anyone here who thinks Nora, has a snowballs chance in hell of beating you? You'll slaughter her." Mike insisted. "Your drives alone will be fifty-yards or more past her."

"That's not going to happen." Bill told him. "I've agreed we'd play from two different tees.

She'll be hitting from the women's tee box and I'll be hitting from the blue tees."

"Why in the hell did you agree to that? The yardage of the golf course from the blue tees is sixty-six-hundred and sixty-yards. The yardage from the ladies tees is only fifty-one-hundred yards. Why would you take away your biggest advantage?" The board chairman scowled.

"George Harris suckered me into it." Bill told him, as he stood, nervously tucking his shirt in his pants. "The son-of-a-bitch threatened to have Nora, withdraw from the match and then blame me for being frightened of being fair."

"Bill, this is starting to make me feel uneasy." Mike told him, frowning. "We'll have to retrieve some of the advantage Mr. Harris thinks he's gained. And I think I know just how to do it. Hey, Dave, come over here." Mike told the club pro, just a few feet away. "Tell me Dave, who gave George Harris, permission to give lessons at our club?"

"He's not giving lessons," the pro said, pushing down the collar of his white shirt, surprised at the question. "He's working with Nora. He's an old friend of the family and I didn't see any harm in making an exception."

"Look Dave." Mike frowned, displeased with the pro's response. "We have rules that have been carefully thought out by the board and they've worked for many years. If we start making exceptions to those rules we'll soon experience chaos, you ought to know that. I think you should explain the boards position on this matter to Mr. Harris and you ought to do it today." Mike demanded.

"But I've already given him permission to work with Nora." Dave protested. "I'll look foolish going against my word."

"Dave, you'll also look foolish when you tell your wife, **THAT YOU'RE LOOKING FOR ANOTHER JOB!**" Mike snarled, with a grim expression and loud enough to gain the attention of other members.

"That's not fair," the club pro objected. "I've been here almost fifteen years and you're willing to let me go on this?"

"You hold your position here at the behest of the board of directors." Mike reminded him.

"And Dave… I'm the ***El Presidente.*** Are we clear?"

"Yes Mr. Grace, very clear."

"I'm glad you see the light. And Dave…I want this to be effective immediately. I don't want to see George, giving lessons to anyone at our club." Mike demanded, then turning away as though dismissing the club pro.

"There's only one problem." Dave told him. "Nora has scheduled George to play with her as a guest twice a week for the next four weeks. She's a member with member privileges. How do you want me to handle that?"

"Tell our starter to give them tees times as late in the day as possible and only when Nora is allowed to play. We don't want a member to abuse our guest policies." Mike said, never turning to address the club pro.

And with that, Dave left the grill room, distressed and disheartened. This was the first time in his tenure at Happy Hills that anyone had threatened him this way.

"Well Bill, that's just step one in getting back some of your advantage." Mike told him when Dave departed. "Not that you need an edge to beat the broad, but an edge is always nice to have."

"All you need are some *Churchill* cigars so you can call Castro to discuss bringing back the casinos to Cuba, ***El Presidente.***" Bill said, grinning. "Let's order lunch…it's on me."

"Bill, what's the sense of having a position of power if you can't use it?"

"You don't have to convince me." Bill assured him. "I've been dealing from the power position for years. When the politicians call me for donations and I'm not talking about the federal limitations, there's always strings, so somewhere down the line when I need a special favor…it's there."

"Isn't power wonderful?" Mike reveled.

After a few more minutes of the *huff and fluff,* Mike turned the conversation to what was at the forefront of everyone's mind.

"You know, Nora has a lot of women rooting for her and from what I hear they'll be quite a contingent out there watching the match. You can turn that to your advantage." Mike told him. "With all of those people watching, she's sure to be a nervous Nelly."

"The bigger the crowd the better. It just might rattle her big time." Bill mused.

"They'll be a bigger contingent of men out there supporting you." Mike reminded him. "Does it mean your putts will be tentative too?"

"Remember Mike…" Bill started, folding his hands behind his head and smiling. "I'm club champion ten years running…I have ice in my veins. Nora should be looking into other clubs she can join, because in five weeks…she'll be history."

"I certainly hope you're right, because if you're not…you're going to be in a whole lot of trouble." Mike told him, reaching for his beer.

CHAPTER 15
GETTING EVEN

THE FIRST PERSON Nora called was Cathy. "That skunk Bill is up to his dirty tricks," she told her. "He got that jelly belly president of ours to stop George from working with me at the club, telling Mike, the rules prohibit another pro from giving lessons at Happy Hills."

"But I thought you cleared it with Dave Thompson?"

"I did!" Nora told her. "But Mike said he bent the rules and told him to rescind his permission. Mike threatened that if he didn't follow his order, he'd be fired. I don't blame Dave, he has his family to think about."

"What bastards!" Cathy scowled. "Nora, we have to do something, we can't let them get away with this."

"Mike and Bill may be flexing their muscles, but I have a plan, Cathy. We women have a power source of our own, you know. And it's been around since Eve convinced Adam to take that first bite of the apple." Nora said.

"I don't get it?" Cathy replied, somewhat confused.

"Cathy, if you and a lot of our friends cooperate, **it's the men who won't be getting it!"**

"Are you thinking what I think you're thinking?" Cathy asked, with a devious smile. **"A no nuggie campaign?"**

"You've got it, Cathy. If those conniving men want to tighten the noose, **we'll shut down the honey pots."**

Well aware of Cathy's feisty personality, Nora would depend upon her friend to lead the charge. Cathy may only have been five-five and a slim one-hundred-fifteen pounds, but in Nora's eyes, she was a giant.

"I love it!" Cathy said. "What do you want me to do?"

"Call all of our friends and ask if they can meet us tomorrow at three in the ladies locker room."

"Nora, if they ask why...I'll tell them we're ***GOING TO WAR!*** But why in the ladies locker room? It might be tight if I get the kind of response I anticipate. Why not in the dining room?"

"I don't want any of the men or staff to hear what we're planning." Nora explained.

"Gotcha." Cathy laughed. "Leave it to me. We'll make these men wish they never tangled with us. I'm with you honey. **WE'RE CLOSING DOWN OUR WAH WAH'S!"**

"That's just the first salvo, Cathy. Wait until you hear what else I have in mind."

"Tell me girl, tell me!" Her brown eyed friend demanded, her enthusiasm bubbling over.

"In due time, Cathy. I'm running late and I have to drive over to George's club for practice. I don't want to lose focus on the match and beating Bill. But I promise you, the point we're going to make...***WILL KNOCK THEIR SOCKS OFF!"***

CHAPTER 16
THE MEETING

BY THE NEXT MORNING, the women's locker room was buzzing. Cathy had succeeded in getting forty-seven women to attend the hastily called meeting and although the quarters were tight they were manageable.

Cathy had used the telephone chain ordinarily used to notify women members about changes in schedule to ensure that everyone would have an opportunity to attend. And by the looks of their faces, they were curious as to exactly why they were there, only told that a rule change mandated by the men was the topic of the meeting.

Nora stood on a bench so everyone could see and hear her. "Ladies, ladies," she called out. "I want to thank you all for coming on such short notice. Cathy, briefly mentioned of a situation that has developed which affects all of us and we need your help.

For years we've been treated as second-class citizens," Nora continued. "Each time we tried to make some strides, the men have shot us down. Now, once again, they're *putting us in our place.* It's high time to let them know, **we're sick and tired of it** and we're not going to stand for their shenanigans any more."

Nora had reservations in asking the women to take the drastic action she was about to propose and hoped she wouldn't make a fool of herself. She would be devastated if the meeting resulted in a repudiation of her cause.

"All of you are friends and aware of my match with Bill Harper, scheduled four weeks from now. George Harris, a long time friend of my late husband Nick and a teaching pro at Long Pond Country Club, agreed to prepare me for the match. However, after receiving permission from our pro Dave Thompson, allowing George to train me here at Happy Hills, the president of our board Mike Grace, at Bill Harper's request, has threatened Dave with the loss of his job unless he rescinds his consent."

"That's just the sort of thing Bill would do!" Someone cried out. "And I'm not surprised that Mike went along with it."

"No offense Nora, but what does this have to do with us? It sounds more personal to me," another of the women cried out.

"Good question." Nora continued. "But that wasn't the only issue. Mike has instructed our starter to further limit our golf tee times."

The room was abuzz with chatter, many of the women voicing their objections aloud.

"And to make matters worse." Cathy said, jumping up beside Nora, hands on her hips. "Coffee will no longer be served at the half-way house on ladies day and the women's member- guest has been cancelled."

"What! How dare they!" Screeched Sylvia Gibbs, the feisty and outspoken wife of Bob, a board member and supporter of Mike's action. To Nora's satisfaction, the women were sufficiently worked up to listen to any plan she might present to them, no matter how outrageous.

"They can't do that!" Said Sharon Kelly, whose husband was also a board member. "Most of us have already invited friends to play. Besides, Gil never mentioned a word about this to me and I'm the ladies golf chairperson. Are you sure Nora? Where did you get this information from?"

Sharon was stout and sixty-two years old. Her brown hair was cropped short with visible white strands, clearly indicating she wasn't at all self-conscious about her age.

"Take my word for it, it's true all right. I don't think it's important for me to reveal who gave me this information." Nora told her.

"Well I'm sorry, but if you want my support for whatever you've planned...**I DO** need to know and I'm sure I'm not alone." Sharon declared.

"Yes Nora! We want to know." Others cried out.

Being pressed for an answer, Nora's betrayal of a friend was not an option in her thoughts.

"Please ladies, you're asking me to violate a trust and I can't do that."

"Then I can't be here." Sharon said, rising from one of the benches and looking around for support.

"Hold your horses Sharon!" Cathy cried out. "I gave the information to Nora and I got it straight from the horses mouth, my husband. Is that good enough for you?"

It was a room now filled with curiosity and doubt, as the women turned to one another sharing points of view.

"Why would Fred, tell you such a thing?" Sharon asked, suspiciously.

"Because, he's the one board member who supports giving us equal treatment." Cathy told her.

"Well I don't know what gives you the nerve to say that!" Sharon exclaimed. "My husband Gil, would have said something to me."

One of the members rose, while clasping her brown skirt. Slightly overweight, the middle aged woman adjusted the white pearls around her neck.

"It's true, Sharon." Tammy Grace, wife of the board president volunteered. "That's the reason I'm here. Mike had the gall to ask me to persuade as many of the women I could to turn their back on Nora."

Sharon sat down with a look of disbelief and shock. If the wife of the board president was repudiating her own husband…then it must be true.

"I've stood by for years saying nothing about the inequities at Happy Hills. I played the dutiful wife, just like many of you have, thinking of this club as being the men's domain. But, Mike and others have pushed too far this time and I'm here to support whatever Nora proposes." Tammy said, giving a thumbs up to Nora before taking her seat.

From the mutterings that Nora could hear, it was clear the statement by Tammy, had solidified the women's support more than anything she or Cathy could have said.

"Let me set the record straight." Nora told them, when silence reigned again. "We're not gathered here because of my match with Bill Harper. We're here to support a plan which will send a clear message to the men, that we're determined to have our rights taken seriously."

"Exactly what are you asking us to do?" Sharon snipped, clearly irritated.

"I'm going to let Cathy, respond to the question." Nora told her.

Cathy stood, looking resolved and ready to echo the rally cry of ***'Enough is enough.'***

"Ladies." She started with an elevated tone. "The men have declared war on us. They may be bigger… they may be stronger, but… we think up here." Cathy said, pointing to her head. "And my friends, you know what head does all of their thinking."

"Where's that?" Inquired the ditzy, but well endowed blonde, Laura Dicks.

"The brain between their legs, you flea brain!" Shouted Sylvia Gibbs.

"The brain between their legs?" Laura repeated, with a blank expression… then uttered…"Oh, Oh!"

"Good girl, Laura. I was beginning to worry that you thought your husbands brain was actually above his shoulders." Sylvia laughed, as did several others.

"Ladies! Ladies!" Cathy shouted, trying to regain their attention. "You all know we have what they want and need."

"What's that?" Laura asked innocently.

Before Cathy could answer, there came a loud response from one of the women in the back.

"Our boobs and our honey pot! You dope." Her response eliciting undercurrents of snickering.

"What?" Laura Dicks repeated, looking confused, Cathy and others shaking their heads.

"Until the men come to their senses, what I'm proposing...**is a ban on sex!"** Cathy declared.

"Is that with our husbands, or all men?" Sylvia asked, resulting in loud laughter from the women in the room.

"Just husbands, Sylvia." Cathy responded, shaking her head.

"You're asking an awful lot. If I don't get my fix a couple of times a week, I'm a bitch-on-wheels." Sylvia told her, smiling and shaking her *Mae West* like body.

"That decoy for a vibrator you call a body massager should do the trick for awhile." Cathy grinned.

The mood was becoming silly, which was more than Nora could have hoped for. Cathy was doing exactly what she expected from her friend.

"Hold on!" Cathy said. **"That's just the first salvo,** there's more."

"You're not going to ask us to stop drinking too, are you?" Sylvia cried out.

"I don't want to kill you Sylvia." Cathy replied. "I just want the bank not to accept any deposits from our husbands."

"But if they don't make deposits...how will they pay the bills?" Laura asked. "And what does banking have to do with any of this?" She innocently continued.

The question by Laura was over-the-top for everyone. The laughter was so loud that the club manager sent the matron to investigate the disturbance in the locker room.

"Ladies, we have to keep it down." Nora warned, telling the matron she could report that everything was fine.

"The next item of war...and don't any of you think that's not what it is... will be our refusal to cook, clean, or go out on the town with our husbands." Cathy detailed.

"That's a tall order." Roz Thomas said. "Some of us have social commitments that can't be broken. And we have kids to feed and clothes to clean."

"Cook and clean for your kids." Cathy told her. "But do nothing for your husband. We have to be firm in our resolve. If we're not, we'll lose this battle and be second class citizens at this club forever."

"My friends, are you ready to use your weapons. Are we united?" Nora asked, making eye contact with several of the women, their mood vital to the success of the endeavor.

The response was half-hearted and somewhat muted.

"Come on!" Cathy told them. "You can do better than that. Are we united?"

A thunderous chorus of **YES**, echoed through the locker room.

"Okay then, **LETS SHOW OUR HUSBAND'S THAT WE MEAN BUSINESS!"** Cathy cried out.

CHAPTER 17
HOME SWEET HOME

WHEN GIL KELLY CAME HOME that night, Sharon was in the kitchen, but there was something different about her smile, something he had never seen before. It was almost as though she were mocking him, although of course that was absurd.

"I just got home myself," she said, as though announcing some sort of victory. "I was having a drink at Sylvia's house," she added, in a tone that sent shivers up his spine.

"But you don't drink." Gil protested, a slender red haired man, who always prided himself on the fact, although Sharon had aged and gained a certain amount of weight, theirs was the kind of marriage in which there were no surprises.

"Well I do now so you'd better get used to it!" She said, pushing him aside and closing the dishwasher door.

"Okay," Gil said. "What's going on Sharon? Is it that time of the month?"

"You jerk! I'm sixty-two years old. It hasn't been that time of the month for years," she protested, leaving the kitchen for the den.

Gil was lost. He rewound his thoughts on what he might have done, or forgotten to do that provoked his wife. Was it our anniversary? Her birthday? He finally surrendered.

"Let's start over," he said. "Whatever I did, I apologize. That goes for anything I ever did to annoy you, or will do in the future. How's that? Does that about cover everything?" The perplexed husband said, fueling his wife's anger.

"You think you're funny, don't you?" Sharon said. "Just wait, you'll be hilarious over the next four weeks."

"What in god's name did I do?" He demanded. "Tell me…so we can deal with it and get this nonsense over with."

"Okay, answer me this. Did you know that Mike Grace cancelled the women's member guest and told our starter Fitzgerald, to push tees times to the end of the day for us?" Sharon snapped.

Gil's expression said it all. He was speechless, placing his hand behind his head and lowering his eyes.

"Just as I thought!" She exclaimed triumphantly. "You didn't tell me and I had to be embarrassed in front of my friends because of you…**you miserable lout of a man!"**

"I was going to tell you, I swear!" He pleaded.

"Well you didn't," she told him. "And frankly, I think you ought to be punished."

"Punished! What are you talking about?"

"I'm talking about you sleeping in the guest room…indefinitely!"

"Are you serious? **Is the whole world going nuts**, first Cummings and now you?"

Sylvia Gibbs was sprawled on the couch in the family room, sipping on her *apple martini* and watching Oprah, when her husband appeared.

"Well, you certainly look relaxed," he said. "Is that your first or second *martini*?"

"I stopped counting, so why don't you?" She snapped.

"Because I made a last minute dinner date for tonight with my boss and his wife and I'd like to have you sober, if that's not too much to ask. We're meeting them at Benny's, seven-thirty."

"No can do sugar," she replied, turning up the volume on the television.

"What are you talking about?" He demanded.

Sylvia mischievously grinned at him. "There's going to be a lot of no-can-do's over the next few weeks."

"TURN THAT THING DOWN!" He bellowed. "Are you drunk?"

"Not yet, but give me a little while longer. I'm sure by the time you get home from dinner, I will be," she said turning away, showing her distain at his demand and continued sipping on her *martini*.

"YOU HAVE TO GO!" He insisted. "It's my boss and his wife. What will they think?"

"Tell them you lost me, Bob. I don't give a damn what you tell them," she snapped.

"Alright Sylvia, what's going on?"

"My girlfriends at the club have decided to go on strike," she told him cheerfully, as Oprah leaned closer to Tom Cruise and smiled sympathetically. "And as a member of their union, I won't cross the picket line."

"WHAT THE HELL ARE YOU TALKING ABOUT?" He yelled, grabbing the remote off the table and switching the television off. "What strike?"

"Oh, good going slick. That'll score you some points." Sylvia said, fixing the pillow on the couch.

"Okay, I'm sorry." Bob said, lowering his tone and turning the television back on.

"Good, now you're making some headway. Seems your friends on the board have decided to put the squeeze on the women in the club." Sylvia told him, pouring herself another drink. "Oh, and talking about squeezes, they'll be none of those for quite a while. You might want to read the directions for the body massager, it's a real trip. And please, use it only on the odd days because I've got it reserved for the even ones. Now give me that remote before things really get ugly around here."

When Jerry Dicks arrived home, he expected to find his wife waiting for him as usual with a cold beer in hand, popped and ready…there was no one in sight.

"Laura," he called out. "Where's my sexy kitten?"

When there was no reply, he peeked through the curtain of the sliding door leading to the back of the house and saw his wife pruning roses.

"How come my sex kitten didn't have my beer ready for me?" He said from the opened doorway. "You know how much I look forward to a cold one when I come home."

Laura smiled and clipped off another rose. "Sorry dear, they'll be no more beer waiting for you and **no more deposits in the honey bank."**

"Honey bank? Kitten, that doesn't sound like you, what's going on?"

"We girls are united. Cathy told me **my wah wah and boobs are off limits** to you and our boyfriends."

"Cathy who?" He asked…"and ***WHAT*** **BOYFRIENDS?"**

"We're firm in our position until you men recognize our rights at Happy Hills."

"I still want the answer to my question," he growled. **"ARE YOU TELING ME YOU HAVE A BOYFRIEND?"**

"No," she admitted. "But if I did, my boobs would be off limits to him too, so don't feel bad. Or maybe, I didn't get that right. It's so hard to remember everything they said."

"Kitten, let's go to dinner and talk about this. I'm sure we can work it out?" Jerry pleaded.

"I can't lover, I have to go to Sylvia's house. She's going to lend me her massager and show me how to use it."

"What! Why would you need a massager when you have me?"

"Because my bank is closed for deposits until Cathy, tells me it's OK."

"Please kitten, I really need you tonight."

"Well, maybe you could use Sylvia's massager." Laura suggested. "Although, I don't know exactly how you could," she said, holding the pruning shears upright and against her cheek.

"Oh please! Lord help me!" Jerry cried out.

It wasn't long before the telephones lines were ablaze with the men of Happy Hills, or should it be said, the men of **UNHAPPY HILLS.** They were all saying much the same thing, what was happening to them and how they could deal with it.

That evening, the board president's phone rang off the hook, until finally out of sheer desperation, Mike Grace turned off his phone and joined his wife in the living room.

"Tammy," you were at the meeting with the women at the club today. I don't know what's going on but my phone hasn't stopped ringing with stories of wives going on strike."

"Seems you men have stepped over the line this time. When you push too hard there's usually a reaction," she said, turning the page to the book she was reading, **Deadly Imposter.**

"Stepped over what line? What the hell are you talking about?"

"Oh Mike, spare me the innocence." Tammy said, then standing with her hands on her hips and clearly confronting him. "You know damn well what I mean. Canceling the ladies member guest and telling Fitzgerald to give us late tee times. I've never interfered with your business at the club, but you've gone too far this time."

Clearly agitated, the burly board president paced the floor before answering his wife.

"This is that bitch, Nora Cummings' fault. If her husband Nick was alive, he'd put her in her place."

"Oh, do you mean that's where you've put me all these years?" Tammy demanded.

"At least you had the intelligence to know your place," he told her.

"Mike, you're an ass!" She said, then heading for the front door.

"Tammy Grace!" He bellowed, his bushy eyebrows perked and eyes glaring. **"I ORDER YOU TO COME BACK HERE! DON'T YOU DARE WALK OUT THAT DOOR!"**

They've had their battles before, but this time was different. He lied to her, something they promised never to do.

"I'M GOING TO RUIN THAT WOMAN," he screamed, as the door slammed closed, his wife defiantly leaving.

"I'M GOING TO RUIN HER IF IT'S THE LAST THING I EVER DO!" Mike shouted, raising his right hand, his fist clenched.

CHAPTER 18
THE DAY AFTER

AT LUNCH TIME the next day, the men's grill was abuzz with members telling stories about their wives' bizarre behavior. Then, there was a general outcry from the crowd.

"IT'S ALL YOUR FAULT, MIKE!" Someone cried out. "Why didn't you let well enough alone?"

"Did you have to cancel the women's member guest?" Another disgruntled husband demanded.

"QUIET DOWN! QUIET DOWN!" Mike yelled. "I know what you went through last night. Tammy pulled the same crap with me."

The outcry from the members of the board was continuous and unyielding, each shouting out their wife's objections and refusal to provide for their husbands basic needs.

"Quiet down!" Mike demanded once again, shouting over their objections. "Forget about sex for a minute. The important thing is we can't let these women beat us."

"It's your wife's fault!" Jerry Dicks shouted, shaking his finger in Fred Daley's face. "She and Nora cooked this idiot idea up between them."

Fred smiled, waving both hands and scoffing at the suggestion.

"Oh, so you think that's funny, do you?" Jerry demanded, clenching his fist, standing in a threatening manner.

"STOP IT RIGHT THERE!" Mike snarled, getting between them. "Guys, we can't fight each other. We have something special here at Happy Hills and have for fifty years. Do you want to give it all up for a couple of trouble makers who are inciting our wives to a hopeless rebellion?"

"Well, what are you proposing?" Asked Bob Gibbs. "We have to do something, my wife Sylvia was worse than a farting gorilla."

"WE HAVE TWO CHOICES." Mike told them. "Either we stand firm or we surrender. This is war gentleman and I assure you if we stand together they won't have a chance to continue this ridiculous behavior. I have a plan men, that will beat them into submission. We'll meet again here in the men's grill at four."

"What are you thinking?" Gil Kelly asked.

"Not until this afternoon." Mike said firmly. "I want everyone to hear what I have in mind, but first, I have to make a few calls. But I promise you this, no one will be disappointed."

CHAPTER 19
TRAINING DAY FIVE

"TODAY, we're going to focus purely on strategy." George told Nora, as they approached the first tee the next morning. "I want you to play your game so I can observe how you think on the golf course. I'll be making comments and suggestions hole by hole. So let's begin, why are you teeing your ball there?"

Nora gave him an odd look. She hadn't taken a swing, yet the criticism started. Does he intend to change everything about my game? She asked herself.

"I always tee the ball from here," she told him. "Why?"

George took a tee from his pocket and placed it ten feet to the left of where Nora had hers. "Come here," he said, waving his hand. "Look down the fairway and tell me what you see?"

She reluctantly followed his command, determined to understand the advantage she apparently was missing…then…

"Oh, I see what you mean." Nora said. "I can see more of the fairway from here."

She was judgmental and felt stupid. George was her only hope if she was to have a chance of winning her match against Harper.

"Too many players just walk up to the tee box and place their tee down haphazardly," he told her. "You have to see where the markers are located on the tee box and then choose the spot that gives you the best vision of the hole. Keep your drives in the fairway and you'll avoid second shots from the rough. Once in the thick grass, chances are you won't get to the green in two. Now you're forced to lay up out from the rough and hope to one putt to save par. It all starts with keeping the ball in the fairway with your drive."

Nora felt confident she was beginning to narrow the gap between her and Bill. George had the knowledge to save her strokes. But a lingering question remained. Would it be enough to overcome the *monumental task* of beating her rival?

When Nora's tee shot from the fifth hole settled amongst a group of trees on the left, she and George, walked down the fairway to the ball which had settled ten feet behind two trees with a narrow opening to the green, one hundred-fifty-yards away.

"I presume your going for the green?" George asked, Nora taking a seven iron from her bag. "How about this? I'm going to put five balls here. I'll bet you don't hit more than one of the five balls out and the one you do, won't make the green."

Nora was determined to prove him wrong, even though she knew, golfers often made amateurish mistakes in trying for the impossible shot, resulting in a disastrous score, one that could lose a match.

She hit her first ball hoping it would pass through the narrow opening of the two trees. Instead, the ball hit a tree and bounced back into the woods. The same thing happened to the second, third and fifth shots. Nora did manage to get her fourth ball through the small opening, but as George predicted, it stopped short of the putting green.

"Okay!" Nora said, reluctant to admit defeat, but convinced she had learned a valuable lesson.

"Are you really convinced?" George asked her. "Or are you just frustrated you couldn't prove me wrong?"

"I guess a little bit of both." Nora conceded.

That was the one thing about George, he was insightful and she didn't mind. After all, winning was the name of the game.

"You know why Tiger Woods is the greatest golfer of modern times?" George asked.

"He has more talent than everyone else who plays the game." Nora answered.

"Yes of course, the talent is there, but he also has uncanny control of his emotions. Sure, you'll see him occasionally get ticked at a bad shot, but by the time he's ready for the next one, he's forgotten it. All the great golfers know there's very little that separates them from the rest of the heap. But they also know it's the little things on the course that makes or breaks them."

Nora understood the wisdom in what George had said. Oddly, she had never thought about it before. He had so much to teach her and not just about shots. His philosophy of golf was just as important.

"You know what makes a great poker player?" George went on. "It's the ability to know the odds of every possible hand dealt to him and to read the players who oppose him. Once he knows the odds, all emotions are thrown out. You need to take that to the golf course. Your play was to chip out to the fairway, get to the green in three and hope to one putt. If you two putt, your maximum score is a five instead of a six or more. Remember Nora, we want to eliminate strokes, not add additional ones."

"George, I hear you loud and clear." Nora said. "I really do appreciate your patience."

"The challenge is to avoid competing against the strengths of Bill and concentrate on the weakness in your thinking," he told her. "We have to out think him at every hole. There can't be one moment in this match you throw caution to the wind and let emotion dictate your decisions. Now chip these out to the fairway."

After Nora successfully chipped out all five balls, she turned to George and smiled. "Coming to you for help was a great idea. I'm going to pick your brain like it's never been picked before."

"Let's go to the next hole," said a pleased, George...who had more than helping Nora's golf game on his mind.

CHAPTER 20
THE COUNTER ASSAULT

"GUYS, I KNOW it's been tough at home, but we have few choices to consider." Mike said when the men gathered again that afternoon. This time, it wasn't just board members in the grill room, but several of the male members who's wives protested their displeasure also attended.

"Do we surrender the castle or do we resist with camouflage like the chameleon?" Mike asked the anxious gathering.

"What do we mean, Mike?" Jerry Dicks asked. **"You said you had a plan?"**

"I do." Mike assured him. "You'll have your drink waiting for you when you get home and Bob will have Sylvia eating out of the palm of his hand. And all of you will get back your honey pots, I promise you."

"Mike, tell us how?" Someone called out

"MEN, WE'RE GOING TO COUNTER ATTACK!" Mike told them, his rugged looking face showing serious intent, raising his fist in a victory salute.

"I have a friend who owns an escort service. He owes me big time for keeping his butt out of jail and he's going to provide a lady for each of you every day for two hours. A woman will be at your home from five to seven in the evening, wearing a sexy maid uniform. She'll serve the food you've ordered and make you a drink of your choice. Believe me, in no time your wives will be running back to you better than ever." The president assured the men, several of whom looked at one another, smiling at the potential benefits of Mike's proposal.

"**Wow!** That plan seems awfully expensive," one of the members observed. "How much is it going to cost us, Mike?"

"The girls are on me! What do you think of that?"

"That's a generous offer, but it's going to cost you a bundle, Mike." Ralph said. "Why would you do this?"

"Why...you ask?" Mike leaned forward, draping his arms over the makeshift podium, perspiration generously dripping down, staining his gray golf shirt.

"I'll tell you why, Ralph. I love Happy Hills. This club is my sanctuary. It's my real home, with you guys, the card room and our great golf course. When you want a golf game, do you ask your wife or call one of the guys? When you want a card game, do you ask your wife or your golfing buddies? When you want to have a drink, watch a ball game and chew the fat, do you ask your wife or call your friends? **This club is ours and not the women's!** Do you want to give all of that up? Do you!" Mike bellowed, hoping to arouse their emotions.

"NO! NO!" The members responded.

"Three cheers for Mike!" Someone cried out.

"Thank you men. We must stand together." Mike declared. "This is our club and the membership is in our names, not the skirts. No giving in unless there's complete and unconditional surrender by the women. But...be ready," he warned them. "They're going to get mad, mighty mad. Then, they'll get worried. Why? Because we're taking away from them the most important thing in their life."

"What's that Mike?" Someone asked.

"Their natural instinct as women to serve us men. You must be cool. Smile as if nothing is wrong. If they ask what's with the maid, simply say... she's here to serve your needs."

"ARE YOU READY MEN? Mike asked enthusiastically.

"Yes! Yes!" Was the battle cry of acceptance.

"All right then, your maids will start serving you tomorrow." Mike assured them.

As the members filed out of the room, several of them stopped to shake the crafty president's hand, Bill and Herb remaining behind.

"That was quite a performance, Mike." Bill said, with a wide grin. "I didn't think you had it in you."

"I'll do anything to stop a group of broads from trying to disrupt what this club stands for and you'd better do your part to do the same." Mike demanded.

"It's in the bag." Bill assured him.

"I hope so, because all of this stems from your disagreement with Nora."

"This is going to cost you a bundle." Herb said to Mike.

"No Herb, it's going to cost him a bundle." Mike said, pointing to Bill.

"What the hell are you talking about, Mike?" Bill snapped.

"As I said, this whole problem was started by you and it's only fair that you pay." Mike demanded.

"Yeah, and if I refuse?" Bill snarled.

Their resolve was being tested, but who would be the first to capitulate?

"Then…I'll ask you to resign and give the reason…you were simply afraid to face the thought of losing to Nora."

"You wouldn't!"

"You bet your ass I would!" Mike forcibly replied with raised eyebrows.

"I thought we were friends?" Bill protested, standing from his chair, his face flushed.

"We are, but there's always a cost to friendship. I know you feel the same way about this club as I do. You can afford to solve the problem YOU created."

Mike stood, placing his arm around Bill's shoulder.

"You and I have to do whatever it takes to keep Happy Hills intact. You have the money and I have the political office. Between the two of us we can beat these broads." Mike insisted.

The two stared at one another…silently…for what seemed an eternity. It looked to Herb like the beginning of the gunfight at the OK Corral.

"This plan of yours had better work, or it will cost you more than the money I lose!" Bill threatened, brushing Mike's hand from his shoulder.

"It'll work, Bill. Trust me, it'll work. We'll have those women begging to go back to the way things were and blaming Nora and her friends for all of the problems."

Bill shook his head and slowly walked out of the men's grill, reflecting on the rising cost of his feud with Nora.

Mike snipped off the tip to a cigar, placing it in his mouth. He lit the *Romeo & Juliet Churchill*, taking three big puffs, then leaned back in his chair, smiling.

"Mike, that was brilliant." Herb said, tipping his glass of beer.

"As they say, there's many ways to skin a cat." Mike told him.

Herb wasn't particularly an avid supporter of Mike. Yes, he didn't like Nora, mostly because his wife didn't. But Herb was the **BRUTUS IN WAITING**. He knew Mike's term as president of the board ended in nine months and this situation with the women would help to elect him to another term or make the political ground fertile for himself. He was aware, Mike knew of his ambitions to be board president. But he also knew, he was a convenient pawn for him. Herb was well liked by the other board members and was able to get them in line when needed. As for Mike, he followed the concept of **keeping your friends close and your enemies closer**. But in the end…would it lead to his downfall?

CHAPTER 21
THE MAID'S NIGHT IN

LAURA DICKS was in the kitchen preparing a salad when the doorbell rang. Her husband Jerry, was in the den watching the evening news, wondering who could be at the door, having forgotten about Mike's plan of the daily two-hour maid service. Suddenly, it came to him. He leaped from his chair, newspapers tossed aside and eager to greet the sexy maid hired to make his wife jealous. But, he had no idea what was about to follow and would get more than he had bargained for.

"Hello, can I help you?" Laura asked the gorgeous five-foot-five blonde in a skimpy maid uniform, standing in the doorway.

"Yes, I'm here for Jerry's ***pleasure,"*** the blonde replied. "Oops! I'm sorry. I'm here to serve Jerry. My name is *Candy*."

It was clear her approach had been studiously scripted by her employer, but it had an intimate ring about it, which sent Jerry scampering to the door and his wife standing with a bewildered look of confusion.

"Hi, I'm Jerry," he said clearing his throat. "I assume…you're…Candy. Please, come in and I'll show you around."

Laura stood frozen in the doorway, totally mystified, her eyes flittering, her husband and the scantly dress woman walking past as though she was completely transparent. Jerry was tickled that Candy, was so similar in appearance to his wife and made this situation even more ironic. Showing her to the kitchen, Jerry explained, he had forgotten to order food and asked if she wouldn't mind cooking up some scrambled eggs.

"Just make yourself at home," he said, loud enough for his wife to hear. "Candy, I'll be in the den having a beer. Let me know when dinner is ready… you sweet thing."

"Okay, Jerry. Would you prefer dinner in the kitchen or the dining room?"

"It's cozier in the kitchen. In fact, why don't you make enough **for TWO?"**

When Laura heard her husband suggest dinner for '*two,*' she enjoyed a momentary respite. Perhaps, she thought to herself, this was going to be an intimate dinner her husband had planned in order to make amends. But the brief moment of jubilation came to an abrupt end when Jerry said, ***"This way you can join me,*** *Candy.*"

"Sounds scrumptious Jerry," she replied, bustling about the kitchen as though it were her own.

"Jerry Dicks, can you tell me what's going on here?" Laura demanded.

"It's nothing. I'm just caring for my needs while my wife is on strike."

"Okay Jerry. **I'm no longer on strike,"** she grimly said.

At that moment, Mike Grace was a genius. His plan had worked, **Laura was beaten.** But, Jerry's moment of joyous victory would soon be deflated... when he reached to embrace his wife.

"Get away from me you gigolo!" She hissed.

"But I thought you said you're no longer on strike?"

"Oh, I'm not on strike anymore," she flippantly assured her husband. "But now...**WE'RE AT WAR!** You'd better tell your friend, Sandy..."

"It's Candy." Jerry said in a conciliatory tone.

"Just tell that *lollipop* in my kitchen, she had better clean up after herself." Laura demanded, taking her coat out of the closet.

"Honey, where are you going?" Jerry asked contritely.

"How could you do this to me?" Laura said, tears streaming down her cheeks. And...as she stormed out of the house, Candy called out...***"Dinner's ready."***

When the doorbell rang at the home of Sylvia and Bob Gibbs, their dog Sparky began barking. Sylvia was drinking her usual pre-dinner martini in the living room while Bob was reading Sport's Illustrated. He assumed it had to be the gal from the escort service, but perhaps it was the dinner he had ordered from Gino's.

"I'll get it," he said to his wife, eagerly anticipating her reaction to Mike's special delivery, one he would infinitely regret.

"Hello. I'm Sophia, your maid," said a beautiful brunette in an Italian accent, as she did a slow curtsey, revealing her well developed bosom.

"Please, come in Sophia." Bob said, his plump face wreathed in a smile.

"Am I drunk already?" Sylvia asked, appearing from behind her husband. "Do I see an underdressed prostitute standing at my front door? And lady, if you don't holster those things, my dog *Sparky* over there is going to have a field day nibbling on those babies. He's one oversexed animal."

Sophia instinctively covered her breasts with both hands, her face wrenched in imaginary pain, as she stepped back and away from the dog.

"Sparky's harmless, he won't bother you Sophia." Bob assured her, then glaring at his wife.

Sylvia was tipsy, but not tipsy enough to surmise what was happening. But she was determined not to let her husband see her squirm, after all, this was her home.

"That's no way to talk to my guest." Bob demanded.

"I'll say it once again," she told him. "That's an underdressed prostitute in my home."

Shaking his head, Bob looked at the scantly dressed maid, eliciting a wry smile from her, who wasn't sure who to fear, the dog...or Sylvia.

"Please, forgive my wife for her crudeness." Bob said. "I'm afraid she's had a few too many."

"That's okay Bobby." Sophia told him. "I go in the kitchen to prepare dinner for you."

"Wait a minute, Italian lady." Sylvia said, slurring her words. "Let me ask you a question. Do you do women too? Because I'll pay you double what he's giving you and I guarantee you'll have a better time with me than him. **He's got a blank pistol, lady!** You're wasting your time. **He couldn't satisfy a mouse in heat**. So what do you say, Sophia baby?"

"Sylvia, what's wrong with you?" Bob snarled.

"You have a great looking woman in our house, dressed like that and you ask me what's wrong? I think I'll go down to the Sly Cat and finish my drinking with some sane people. You coming Sophia?"

"Lady, you're my kind of woman!" Sophia said, her accent miraculously vanishing.

"Bob, don't wait up for us. I have a feeling we're going to have a **rip roaring time."**

And with that...both women disappeared into the night, leaving Bob staring at Sparky, the dog turning his head to one side, as if to say...and they call us stupid? And that was the way it went all evening. Mike Grace's ill-conceived plan was a total failure. The next day he was deluged with calls from members with desperate pleas to find a solution to a problem taking the shape of a run-a-way freight train. Mike was beside himself. He called Herb Blake, asking him to quell the troops and to arrange another meeting for three o'clock in the men's grill. He then called the bartender at the club, asking him to prepare sandwiches and to have plenty of liquor available.

Unbeknown to Mike and the other members, Cathy Daley had scheduled a meeting of the women for two o'clock the same afternoon, this time in the dining room. There were no more secrets to be kept. It was an open conflict between the wives and their husbands. The mood at Happy Hills would be very somber, until one way or another...**someone was declared a victor**.

CHAPTER 22
TIT FOR TAT

"I GUESS ALL OF YOU have the same stories to tell about last night?" Cathy began. "But let's take them one at a time. Laura, do you want to share with us what happened at your house last night?"

"Yes, I do. My Jerry, hired a maid to cook for him last night. She actually looked a lot like me."

"You mean there's two of you in this world?" Someone called out, eliciting hardy laughter from several of the women.

"Come on ladies." Nora pleaded. "Go on Laura."

"As I was saying, he had this maid come to our house." Laura sputtered. "She hardly had any clothes on except for a small black skirt and a see-through blouse. When she bent down you could see, well...you know, everything. Cooks don't dress like that and the maids I've seen in hotels wear more clothes than she did. I don't understand why this is all happening? Jerry and I were very happy and now...he's brings home a girl that looks like me but isn't me. I'm really confused, Cathy. I know you said we have to stick together and close our honey pots, but, I don't want my Jerry...**looking for someone else's wah wah."** Laura concluded, amid giggles and snide comments.

"Look ladies," Sylvia interjected. **"We know what those bastards are up to** and if they succeed, we're going to lose this battle of wits. The day I can't out-think my husband Bob... is the day I call for the maid sent to our house last night and take up a new lifestyle."

"Hear! Hear! Sylvia. It would serve the bastard right!" One of the women cried out.

"How did you handle it last night?" Sharon wanted to know.

"My initial reaction was to throw the bimbo out the front door." Sylvia told them, pausing to take a sip of her martini. "But I held my wits and played the game. I offered her twice what she was getting paid from Bob to go out drinking with me. Needless to say, she was as loyal as a husband after sex. **Let me tell you gals how to go on the offensive.** I have a friend who owns a lady's-only strip joint. I'm sure I can get her to help us out. Your husbands will drop dead, when they see these gorgeous hunks in their ***"bikini"*** bathing suits serving you breakfast in the morning. It will probably cost us a couple of hundred each, but it'll be worth seeing our husbands jaws fall to the floor. Are you game, ladies?"

"WE'RE IN!" Several of the women enthusiastically called out.

Nora was keeping a low profile. She didn't want to appear the instigator with nothing to lose. But her efforts would soon fail.

"Nora Cummings," a petite brunette in a yellow sundress called out, leaping to her feet.

"Yes Roz, what is it?"

"Nora, this whole business started because of you. I have three kids who watched their mother ignore their father last night. They asked me if I was mad at their daddy. I can't have another man come in my house to serve me breakfast. My husband is a good man. Happy Hills is his club, not mine. I DON'T EVEN PLAY GOLF FOR CHRIST SAKES!"

"I'm with Roz," another member announced. "This is getting out of hand. Nora doesn't have a husband and she has nothing to lose."

Nora rose, hands on hips, anticipating the question but hoping it wouldn't become an issue.

Her initial reaction was one of anger, feeling the comment was an affront to her deceased husband and her own integrity. But, the question did hit home. She paused, self-interrogating her motives and asking, would she have pressed Harper, if Nick were alive? She lowered her hands from her hips, releasing the tension and taking a more conciliatory posture.

"Look, I understand your concerns. If you don't want to be part of this, that's okay. They'll be no hard feelings and that goes for anyone else who feels their marriage would be in jeopardy, the last thing I want to have happen. So please, anyone who wants to leave can do so, we'll understand."

"Do you mean that Nora?" Roz said. "Because I simply can't go along with something like this. I'm sorry," she added, as she and seven other women left the dining room.

"What Nora just said is important." Cathy told them. "No repercussions for those who left."

The mood turned somber and it was time to regain the momentum originally established… then…

"I hope the guys serving breakfast tomorrow aren't jailbait?" Sharon called out.

"I'll make sure they all have their drivers license as proof of age." Sylvia joked, reaching for her martini, unsuspectingly providing the renewed momentum needed.

"Then it's time for some ***TIT-FOR-TAT.*"** Cathy told them. "I can't wait to see my husband's face in the morning and it's been a long time since I said that."

As the women filed out of the dining room into the parking lot, they passed the men on their way to attend their three o'clock meeting in the grillroom. The ladies lifted their heads high in defiance as they passed their husbands, which they hoped spoke volumes of their cause. It was, if the men had only known, the beginning of the end.

CHAPTER 23
MUTINY IN THE RANKS

THE HEAVY RAIN pelted the skylights in the men's grill, as members waited for their president to make an appearance. The atmosphere was as hostile as the weather. Mike Grace removed his hat and raincoat before walking to the podium, but members wasted little time in their attack.

"You told us your plan was fool proof and our wives would fold like tents!" Jerry said accusingly.

"What do you have to say now, Mike?" Another disgruntled member asked, while a number of the other men nodded vigorously to show their agreement. The tone was getting ugly.

"Men, men!" Mike called out. "Don't you know what they're doing? They're testing your resolve. They believe you'll fold. We can't let that happen."

"What's this *'WE?"* Bob frowned. "This all started because of you, Mike."

Sensing he had a mutiny on his hands, Mike turned to Herb Blake, hoping he could defuse the situation.

"Guys, guys!" Herb cried out. "Quiet down! We're going to take a twenty-minute pause. Grab a sandwich and order a drink. We'll get back to solving the problem after the break."

Reassured, at least for the moment, the disgruntled members crowded around the buffet table, helping themselves to sandwiches and ordering drinks. Herb was trusted by the members. He was seen as a *square shooter*, many supporting him as Mike's eventual successor. He saw his opportunity to solidify his stature with them and perhaps bail Mike out at the same time. But…not without a price.

"Good job, Herb. That was quick thinking." Mike said gratefully.

His eyebrow raised and a faint grin, Herb had more in mind then gratitude.

"Mike, you can only hold these guys together for so long, you know. What are you going to tell them?"

"We have to sell them on the idea, that in time, the women will fold." Mike said, reaching in his pocket for a cigar. "I have an idea that should quiet things down, but I'm going to need your help?"

"Mike, this time...my help is going to cost you." Herb warned him.

Mike lit his *Romeo & Juliet* cigar, taking three hearty puffs, while peering at Herb.

"I want you to announce...that you're not running for the board when your term expires nine months from now." Herb demanded.

"What!" Mike scowled. "I'll do no such thing."

"Then you're on your own!" Herb said, as he rose to join the other members.

"Sit down!" Mike demanded, putting a hand on Herb's arm.

"There's no negotiation on the matter." Herb scowled, moving away from Mike's grip.

"We've been friends for a long time." Mike reminded him.

"That's a laugh. **We've never been friends!"** Herb said, sarcastically. "You've used me whenever it was convenient for you to keep the guys in check, like you're doing now, or when you needed to get the board to agree on a new rule you wanted passed. But friends? NEVER."

Mike took a long puff on his cigar while calculating his next move. "OK Herb, we'll do it your way. But if you want my endorsement as board chairman, you'll have to..."

"Mike." Herb interrupted. **"I don't want your endorsement**. After this fiasco, it would be the kiss of death."

But the sly fox that he was, Mike had no intention of letting Herb, determine his future at Happy Hills. Instead, he encouraged everyone to keep drinking until their belligerence had turned to good fellowship. Then, and only then, did he tell Herb, it was time for him give them the ***"Let's-stand-behind-Mike-speech."*** And although Herb, suspected Mike had something up his sleeve, he did just that.

The room was full of anticipation as Herb, approached the podium.

"Guys, I know you're upset about what transpired in your homes last night, but I think in all fairness to Mike, we should give him the opportunity to tell us what he's proposing to do next."

Grumblings were heard from several of the members as Mike, stepped to the podium.

"Thank you, Herb." Mike started. "I said to you before we undertook our plan, there would be a reaction by the women. I think everyone can testify to that. So Jerry, let me ask you something. Didn't you anticipate Laura, seeing that woman, whatever her name was, in a skimpy uniform or did you expect her to appear invisible?"

"It was Candy. So what are you getting at?"

"Well, what did you expect Laura to say? 'What a wonderful surprise dear, *are we doing a threesome tonight?"* Mike asked, lowering his head to one side and leaning forward on the podium.

"Well, no, but I didn't expect to feel so rotten about it either." Jerry replied

Mike then turned to Bob Gibbs, who was sitting by the window nursing a gin and tonic. "And did you Bob, expect your Sylvia to say, *'It's about time you spiced things up?"*

"Of course not." Bob admitted.

"How about you, Gil. Did you expect Sharon to come out of the closet at age sixty-two and suggest you keep your maid full time for enjoyment?" Mike jabbed.

The laughter grew louder and louder, as Gil, shook his head in agreement and grinned. It was clear, finally the light bulb had been turned on.

"I think you understand now, don't you." Mike said smugly. He had them, he thought to himself, making eye contact with several members as though he were sitting beside them.

"I'm telling you we'll beat these broads!" Mike went on. "But it won't be easy. And I never said it would be. You have to expect the unexpected. They had a meeting just before ours. You know they're up to something. We have the advantage here. Do you want to surrender to them?"

"No!" Someone cried out.

"Will we stand strong?" Mike demanded, playing the room to his concerto.

"Yes!" Was their enthusiastic reply. He relit his cigar, puffing away, trying not to look self-satisfied. He had them back and without surrendering to Herb's threats.

"I promise you men, we'll beat them, and before my term expires you'll have this club back where it belongs… to us! And I swear to you…during my next term as your president, Happy Hills will be better than ever."

"Three cheers for Mike," the members shouted. "Three cheers for Mike."

The board president looked at Herb, contemptuously. He had outfoxed him and was glad of it. Herb was an amateur compared to Mike, and he had to be realizing he was had. Of course, Herb still had a chance to beat Mike, if the members lost their battle with the wives. But Mike was about to deliver his *COUP DE GRACE.*

"We know to expect something tomorrow or the day after." Mike began. "But whatever it is...maintain your cool. In the meantime, let's throw the women off balance. I'll reinstate their member-guest and tell our starter to give them back their tee times. They'll feel like they've won. They'll back away from this nonsense until Bill's match with Nora. But remember, don't react to whatever tricks they have up their sleeves. If you do, we'll lose our edge. If you want your honey pots back, you'll have to put some sugar in front of them."

"I'm afraid I might lose it if they decide to bring a man in the house to get even." Jerry said.

"Okay, let's suppose the worse case scenario." Mike suggested. "You wake up in the morning and there's a half naked man serving your wife breakfast?"

"I'll kill the bastard!" Jerry shouted, his anger at the image triggering his outburst.

"No you won't!" Mike told him. "Because that's what they'll expect."

"What do you want me to do, join them for breakfast?"

"No, Jerry. I want you to kiss your wife on the cheek and after shaking the hand of the guy who made breakfast, say goodbye." Mike said with composure.

"Are you nuts, Mike?"

"Jerry, think of it this way. When we had the maids come in to make the wives jealous, did we have intentions of doing anything sexual with them? Of course we didn't. Does that help you get the picture?"

It was clear, Jerry got the meaning, grinning at Mike's analogy.

"You've got my word, I'll be the perfect gentleman to her friend." Jerry responded... but would he?

"Mike, does this mean you know that's what the women have planned?" Gil asked.

"I have no idea what they're scheming." Mike replied. "But if I were on the other side... that's what I would do. Remember guys, women are nesters by ancestry and we're the hunters. They want peace restored. Be strong and we'll be back to normal within the next few days, I promise."

As for Herb, he was no match for Mike and clearly annoyed he was deceived.

"Mike, you double crossed me and I won't forget it." Herb said, as the other men crowded out of the grillroom, slapping one another on their backs.

"Perhaps you've learned an important lesson." Mike said. "Never tell someone you're not their friend while you're still playing a game of chess with him."

The board president was basking in victory. He successfully quelled the member's outrage and masterly outmaneuvered, Herb. Yes, he was glowing... for now.

CHAPTER 24
CHECKMATE

THURSDAY MORNING, Jerry and Laura's doorbell rang at seven-thirty. He was sitting on a stool in the kitchen, sipping his coffee and reading the morning paper, while Laura was on the treadmill in the den watching Matt Lauer's interview with a diet guru. Jerry opened the door to find a six-foot-two mass of muscle wearing only a black bowtie and matching bikini, standing on his doorstep. His worse nightmare had just become a reality.

"Hello," the unsuspecting escort said, flashing a dazzling smile under his blue eyes and sandy brown hair. "My name is ***Hot Rod*** and I'm here for Laura."

Jerry didn't say a word or move a muscle. His body seemed paralyzed, including his thoughts, while his eyes remained focused on an impressive stick shift housed in the escort's bikini. Would the volcano erupt, or simply fizzle in a display of admirable self-control?

"Oh, hi…I'm Laura." Jerry heard his wife chirp, as she pushed past her husband and shook the visitor's hand.

"Come in…did you say your name was ***Hot Rod?"***

"Yes Laura," the unsuspecting courtesan responded.

"Wow! That's a sexy name," she said, placing her hand on her cheek as her husband's self-control meter was about to boil over.

Remembering Mike's warning, Jerry tried desperately to keep up a display of bravado, while his beautiful wife, dressed only in revealing leotards, escorted ***Hot Rod***, into the kitchen.

"I'm *at your beckon call* this morning." ***Hot Rod*** announced.

That was Jerry's flash point. Forgetting Mike's appeal to be strong, he walked into his bedroom, opened the closet door and retrieved a twelve-gauge shotgun from its case, placing two shells in the chamber, then leaving for the kitchen like a lion stalking his prey.

"Alright you under-dressed walking piece of meat!" Jerry cried out. "Get out of this house before I blast that hot rod sticking out in your panties... into ***road kill*!"**

The young courtesan immediately placed his hands over his bikini bottoms, grimacing at the thought.

"Jerry, what on earth are you doing?" Laura demanded. "Are you crazy? Put down that gun, right now!"

But, before her husband could respond**, *Hot Rod*** was running for the front door. **"I don't get paid enough for this crap!"** He said, as the door slammed behind him, Jerry's hand flying forward in the same direction. Lowering his shotgun to the floor, Jerry assumed the expression of a puppy found peeing on the floor. He lowered his head while cowering his eyes, then reaching for Laura's hand, leading her to their bedroom.

"You really do love me, don't you Jerry?" She cooed.

"Honey, I've always loved you," the repentant husband said, with a twinkle in his eyes.

"Then promise me, you'll never again do anything to hurt my feelings," she demanded.

"I promise, Laura. Tomorrow, Mike's going to give back everything he took away."

Eyebrows raised, Laura looked confused. "Well...does it mean I have to ask Cathy, if it's okay to let you use my wah wah again?"

About the same time that morning, Sylvia Gibbs opened her front door to find a ***god like* creature** standing, half naked at her front door.

"Hi Sylvia," he said cheerfully. "My name is ***Sure Shot*** and I'm here to serve you for two hours this morning."

Sylvia, one of the rocks of the women's movement, smiled, **then suddenly collapsed** like a tree brought down by a husky lumberjack. When her husband Bob, came downstairs, he found a half-naked man fanning his wife, who was out cold on the floor.

"Who the hell are you?" Bob demanded, picking up an umbrella from the stand, raising it above his head and ready to strike the intruder, surmising they were the victims of a home invasion.

"I'm ***Sure Shot,"*** the tall, well tanned and fair haired young man, meekly answered, taking a step back, his hands in a defensive posture. "I'm here to serve your wife for two hours this morning."

"What in god's name did you do to her?" Bob demanded, shaking the umbrella in a menacing manner.

"Nothing sir," the young courtesan said, his face ashen and retreating back against the foyer wall, staring at the umbrella. "She answered the door and when I introduced myself... **she just collapsed."**

Bob lowered his hand. "Well ***Sure Shot***, I think it best that you leave before she recovers and has a relapse."

"Thank you, sir." The young man was clearly contrite and Bob found he couldn't be angry.

"I'm sorry if I scared her," the boyish hunk said, lowering his eyes.

"**Sure Shot**...Oh, what the hell is your real name, son?"

"Tommy sir," he replied in a high pitch voice, clearing his throat.

"Just go home, Tommy. She'll be fine in a few minutes."

The well intended courtesan, scurried out the door and within a few moments thereafter, Sylvia regained consciousness.

"What happened, Bob?" She gasped.

"You fainted," he told her, cradling her head in his arms. "Don't you remember anything?"

"I remember answering the door and seeing a near naked man standing in the doorway," Sylvia said, her eyes opening wide. "So, I wasn't dreaming. Where did he go? He...said his name was ***Sure Shot*?"**

"I think he's running in the fifth race at Belmont." Bob told her. "Sylvia, aren't we a bit old for these kind of games?"

"You men started this war of words and deeds. Did you expect us to roll over and play dead?" She snapped, raising herself from the floor, pushing her husband's hand to one side.

"No, I don't ever expect that from you, but...***Sure Shot*?"** Her husband quipped.

"Well, it's **TIT FOR TAT?** You had that bimbo, Sophia in our house. Today, it was my turn, and oh, how I loved his name, **Sure Shot."**

"He was only a boy, Sylvia." Bob scowled.

"Not from what I saw he wasn't," she told him. "I need a drink. I struck out with Sophia and lost ***Sure Shot***. It's just not my week."

Shaking his head, Bob was taken by surprise. He never heard his wife reveal her feelings with such sexual overtones.

"Can we call a truce, Sylvia?" He pleaded. "Mike's reinstated the women's member guest and called off his bulldog, Ed Fitzgerald?"

"On one condition," she told him. "Tomorrow night, I want to come home to a husband wearing a bow tie, black bikini and nothing else! Oh,... and I wouldn't mind if you called yourself ***Sure Shot,*** for the night."

"You have a deal Sylvia, as long as I can call you...***Sophia?***" Bob said with a devious smile.

"You're on stud," his wife said with a twinkle in her eye.

The next day, something approaching normalcy returned to Happy Hills. The women declared victory and the men didn't care. They got their honey pots back, which in the end…was all that they wanted.

CHAPTER 25
TRAINING DAY SEVEN

THE NEXT MORNING at the practice range, George greeted Nora and then began a series of stretching drills with her. It was a warm July day and it wasn't long before they were dripping with perspiration.

"That'll do it, Nora." George said.

Nora reached for the towel on her golf bag and patted her face dry.

"Before we start practice, I have a question to ask." George said.

She speculated he was about to get personal and attempt to take their relationship to another level as Cathy, had predicted. It's not that she didn't like George, or think he wasn't a fine figure of a man, especially compared to some of the men she dated, but Nora, desperately wanted to keep the relationship focused on preparing for the match with Bill.

His question definitely took her by surprise and gave her a sense of relief.

"Nora, where are most golf matches won?"

"Whoever has their putter working that day."

"Good, how do we increase our chances of making our putter work on any given day?" George asked.

"I guess practicing," she answered in a cavalier tone.

"It's beyond practice, it's knowledge of the golf course and getting into the designer's head." George said, then explaining that most putting greens are designed higher in the back and lower in the front for drainage purposes. "You always want to putt up a slope rather than down, you have better speed control of the ball." Further explaining, "if the golf ball is on the right side of the hole and on the lower level of the green, the putt will usually turn to the left, and if the ball is on the lower left side, it will usually turn right.

"Ideally, a golfer should always hit the green on the flat side or below the hole." George continued, relating his years of experience in order to narrow the gap between Bill Harper and Nora.

Secretly within, George felt she had little chance against Bill. Aside from the physical gender gap, Bill was flat out a better golfer than Nora. But…if he could prevent her from being embarrassed, he would have accomplished his job. He would keep those thoughts to himself, always encouraging Nora, that on any given day, anyone can be beaten. Why then, did he continue the charade? Cathy knew.

George went on to explain, "Knowing the direction of the grass is vitally important, since it usually follows the sun, the ball having greater speed rolling with the grain and less against the grain. As for the grain direction, it can be determined by the color of the grass. If it's darker, it means you're putting against the grain and if lighter, with the grain. Knowing grain direction will help determine speed control of the ball, being faster in the afternoon than the morning. The early dew slows the speed of the ball, while the afternoon sun dries out the greens, making putts faster."

Nora had played the game long enough for her to think she knew most of the winning techniques, but George's knowledge of the game was encyclopedic. She started towards the golf cart when she heard…

"Not so fast." George told her, then handing her a spiral flip-over pad. "We're going to diagram the direction a ball takes on every green. I want you to keep the pad with you every time you play this course and especially during the match with Bill. Remember, you have to be concerned about the location of the sun and the time of day. They'll determine the speed of your putts."

George and Nora rode the course, diagramming all eighteen putting greens in the pad given to her by the pro, rolling balls from every angle of the green. At the end of the eighteenth hole, they went to the practice green to test her newfound knowledge.

"Good workout today." George said, when Nora concluded her putting session. "Join me for some lunch?"

"Sure, give me a few minutes to clean up and I'll meet you in the dining room."

Ten minutes later, Nora was leaving the locker room when she bumped into Cathy.

"Where are you off to?" Her friend asked her as they embraced.

"I'm having lunch with George."

"Are we getting to the next stage in this relationship?" Cathy asked with a smile.

"Don't be silly, it's just lunch."

"Maybe for you it's just lunch, but not for him sweetheart." Cathy said, poking her finger in her friend's shoulder.

"Oh, you and your imagination." Nora frowned, thinking it was so like Cathy to jump to conclusions, especially when it came to men.

"Changing the subject for the moment, did you hear what happened at the Gibbs and Dicks houses last night?" Cathy asked.

"I don't have time now." Nora told her. "But how about dinner and a movie tonight?"

"Perfect, it's Fred's card night. Call me after lunch. I want to hear all of the juicy details. I'll wager dinner and the movie…George puts a move on you while you're sipping on an ice tea."

"Cathy, give it a break!"

"Afraid I might be right?"

"OK…smarty pants…you're on!" Nora said, returning the friendly poke, then retreating to the dining room to meet George, hoping to prove her friend wrong.

"I hear the turmoil ended last night." George remarked, after the server had taken their order, Nora the house salad and his, tuna on whole wheat.

"Well, it has for now." Nora told him, staring at his sky blue eyes, accentuated by a well defined tan, thinking what an attractive man he was, even though older appearing with his silver hair and rounded shoulders. "News does really travel fast around here. How did you know?" She said, trying to dispel her sultry and naughty thoughts of what it would be like with George… snapping her head in dismissal, her eyes moving side to side.

"Are you OK?" George asked, when Nora placed her hand to her neck, then twisting her head side to side.

Embarrassed he noticed, she blushed. "I must have crimped my neck at the range," she explained. "What were you saying, George?" Nora asked, fleeing the moment.

"Oh, about last night. Cathy scooted by and filled me in on the gossip," he said. "You two are very close, aren't you?"

"We're practically sisters. We grew up together as kids. She's always been there when I've needed her, especially when Nick died. I couldn't have made it without Cathy."

"It had to be a rough time for you," he said. "I know, because I went through it when my wife passed. Having to cope with the loss of someone you love that you figured would be there forever isn't easy. I was sad at first and then angry she left me. There were so many things left unsaid. You wish you could have just five minutes more to say it all," he lamented.

Nora was seeing a different side of George, not the hard nose taskmaster, but a compassionate person who obviously missed his wife. How wrong Cathy was she thought…but was she?

It was amazing how much they had in common. The hour flew by and when she signed for lunch, George remarked, "I guess I owe you. Can I reciprocate with dinner one day next week?" Nora, taking her last sip on her ice tea…gasped.

There it was…and Cathy…was proven to have been right. George had made his move, a bridge she wasn't prepared to cross, taking the relationship to the next level. He was nice all right, but his age and the thought of a relationship based on two dead spouses was a bit too much for her to deal with right at the moment.

"George, I'm flattered you asked, but right now I have so much on my plate and I don't think it wise for the both of us to take this any further right now. I really want to focus on preparing for the match. I do hope you understand?"

"Should I…not ask anymore?" He said, clearly disappointed.

"George, you won't know unless you do, will you?" Nora teased him, making light of the moment, while providing a patch to his dignity. Had it been compassionate to keep the dating option open? Nora didn't know, but she saw from the smile on his face, she had given him hope. And for the time being at least, it was all she could do for him…but what about the future?

CHAPTER 26
THE GIRLS NIGHT OUT

"DON'T YOU GET TIRED of being right?" Nora asked that evening, when she and Cathy were being seated at the restaurant?

The Tiger Dragon wasn't a five star eatery, but it was frequented by local diners as the food was good and there was never a report of missing cats from the neighborhood.

Ornamental lanterns adorned the perimeter of the ceilings and hung just below the red leathered booths on both sides, separated by two rows of centered tables. The servers wore bright yellow and red garb, accented with embroidered tigers and dragons.

"What are you talking about?" Cathy asked, curiously looking at Nora over the rim of her oversized *martini* glass.

"George is what I'm talking about." Nora snapped.

"Oh shut up! He didn't? I just knew it would happen." Cathy giggled, slapping her hands on the table while her feet bounced to the floor in rhythmic beats.

"Stop your gloating, he asked me out to dinner, not to my bedroom."

"Well girl, dinner was only the first stop."

"Cathy!"

"Okay, okay, what did you say to him?" Cathy asked impatiently. "This is like a dentist pulling out a tooth…a piece at a time."

"Well smart aleck, I said no." Nora said playfully. "Then I told him… he should ask you out, because you're a lonely housewife looking for some kinky action."

"You like to see your friend in pain, don't you?" Cathy grinned. "You're just bent out of shape because dinner and the movie is on you. Now girl, let me in on all of the details…or, I'll call George and tell him you're really hot for him." Cathy giggled, sipping on her *martini.*

"And you said I was bad?" Nora snapped, feeling they had taken a step back in time when they were thirteen, Cathy demanding to know if Billy Johnson had kissed Nora in the movies.

* * *

"Nora Owens! You tell me… are we best friends or not?" Cathy demanded.

"Of course we are Cathy."

"Then you have to share with me…that's what best friends do. Did Billy try to kiss you?" Cathy pressed her friend.

"You have to swear not to tell a soul if I tell you?"

"I swear! I swear! Now tell me Nora."

"May you always see bugs in your food if you tell anyone. Cross your heart, fingers and toes, Cathy…and swear again."

"You're ridiculous Nora," her friend's hands pumping up and down in a gesture of frustration.

"Then I'm not telling you!" Nora huffed.

"OK! OK!" Cathy agreed.

"Then repeat after me. "May I always see bugs in my food if I tell anyone."

Cathy reluctantly complied, repeating the pledge, both reverting to their adolescents.

"Well?"

"That's not all he did." Nora said, with a smile, exposing her braces.

"NO WAY, Nora. What else…what else did he try?" Cathy asked with great anticipation.

"He put his arm around me and after he kissed me…his hand went…you know where." Nora said, glancing to her breast.

"Nora Owens, **SHUT UP!"** Cathy gasped. "What did you do?"

"I was so shocked, I dropped my soda cup on his lap. He leaped up from his chair and ran to the bathroom. I was so embarrassed, I left the movie and walked home."

"What a jerk! Did he ever call you again?"

"He did, but I told my mother I didn't want to speak to him."

"What did your mother say when you told her?"

"I never did. I was too embarrassed. Now remember Cathy, you swore not to tell a soul."

"I know, I know." The freckled face Cathy, repeated. But...would she hold to her promise?

* * *

"I told George, I wanted to keep the relationship on a friendship basis, because I wanted to focus on the match."

"How did he handle it?" Cathy asked, sipping her martini.

"I thought...pretty well. Especially when he asked if he should try any more." Nora revealed.

"What did you say to that?" Cathy asked, leaning forward, munching on an olive.

"I said he wouldn't know if he didn't ask."

"You said that to him? Why would you do that? You're encouraging the man." Cathy scowled.

"Because, I saw a different side of George. He's a gentle and caring person."

"Did he fall asleep during lunch?" Cathy asked playfully.

"No, why would you ask a question like that?"

"Because girl, the man is twenty years older than you. When you reach his age...he'll be asking where you put his false teeth and for you to repeat everything you say."

"Cathy, you're as bad as ever." Nora said, laughing. "You still owe me on Billy Johnson. I'm surprised you're still alive after swearing and crossing your heart not to tell anyone."

"Nora, do you see who I see?" Cathy asked, peering to the side of their booth.

"Yes, just ignore him." Nora demanded. "Let's hope he doesn't see us."

"He has to be here the one night we want to enjoy a quiet dinner." Nora grumbled as she held her menu in front of her face.

"I must say, he's sitting with a real looker." Cathy told her.

"Did you say looker, or *hooker*?" Nora snapped.

The conversation was about Bill Harper and a woman seated three booths forward and across to their left, unaware they were the topic of a snippy conversation.

"Anyone who would go out with Bill...has to be desperate." Nora whispered.

"Come on." Cathy said in a cajoling tone. "She doesn't look desperate to me and you can't deny he's a real hulk?"

"Well, he is good looking and does have a rather devilish look about him." Nora reluctantly admitted. "But why does he have to be so damn crusty?"

"He's not so bad in bed, either." Cathy said in a low voice, looking at Nora…impishly.

"Cathy Daley!" Nora whispered. **"You didn't!** When? Where? How?" Nora gasped, tongue tied and shocked by her friends admission.

"If I explain the circumstances, you have to promise not to tell a soul and promise you won't try and get even with me because of Billy Johnson?" Cathy pleaded, gulping the rest of her martini, waving her glass to the waiter indicating she needed a refill.

"Billy Johnson was years ago." Nora protested. "Get on with it!"

Cathy leaned forward, brushed her hair aside and after a deep sigh…was ready to reveal her soul.

"A year ago, Fred and I had a blowout argument," she started. "To this day, I don't remember what the fight was about. Anyway, I stormed out of the house and went to the *Pink Pillow* lounge. I was there for one drink to cool down. I'm sipping my martini when I heard someone say, 'No woman as beautiful as you should be drinking alone.' I was vulnerable and he was so good looking. Three drinks later, we're in the *Shady Lady Motel*. He was good, real good."

"Did it end there?" Nora whispered, not wanting to be overheard.

"Are you nuts? When you decide to eat ice cream you don't take a spoonful…you binge." Cathy gloated.

She knew her friend had a wild streak as a teenager, but the affair with Bill was over the top, even for Nora. What seemed to bother her most, was the fact that Cathy, had never confided in her before about the liaison with Bill.

"Just how long did this ice cream binge last?" Nora asked, with a raised eyebrow.

"Six months," maybe a bit longer.

"Did Fred know?" Nora asked, her elbows on the table and leaning forward.

"No!" Cathy said scornfully. "Men will believe anything you tell them as long as they're getting some occasional honey. They figure they could cheat… but never their wives."

"Who broke it off?" Nora asked, the palm of her hand on her forehead.

"I did." Cathy said shrugging. "I had my fun, but I couldn't continue the risk of hurting Fred in that way. Besides, he wanted me to leave Fred and live with him."

"Get out of town!" Nora puffed, leaning ever more closer to her friend, putting both hands on the top of her head, then glaring at her friend.

"Don't you give me that look. That's exactly what he wanted me to do and I have to tell you…there're days I wish I'd taken him up on the offer."

"Does he stay in touch?"

"For awhile we'd meet now and then and he'd try to convince me to leave Fred. But over time, he saw it wasn't going to happen." Cathy said, reaching for her second martini from the waiter.

"When was the last time you…saw him?" Nora said, not wanting to ask the more personal question.

"Three months ago." Cathy said, taking a large gulp of her drink.

"And you waited all of this time to tell me? Shame on you, Cathy Daley."

Nora felt a profound sense of sadness. She had never dreamed of Cathy, for all her brash talk, of having an affair. But things were starting to add up, as she remembered the many times Cathy, had hinted at trouble between her and Fred in the past year or so.

After lunch, they went shopping, something which usually excited Cathy. But this time, Nora sensed her longtime friend was uneasy.

"What's wrong?" Nora asked, as they browsed through the shoe department at Saks.

"Do you think any less of me because of what I did?" Cathy sheepishly asked her friend.

"I love you." Nora assured her. "You'll always be my freckled-face friend and nothing will ever change that."

"In that case, I do like the bag we saw when we first came in." Cathy said, sniffling.

"It's not your birthday!" Nora snapped

"Didn't I make this the most interesting evening you've had in a long time, just as I promised?" Cathy asked.

Taking a tissue from her bag, Nora patted away her friends tears, then put her arms around her. When they embraced, Cathy squeezed her tight, as though she never wanted to let go.

"I'll tell you woman, you really know how to work a person." Nora said, patting her own eyes. "The bag is yours."

"I love you, Nora." Cathy said. "Let's always be friends and never let anything ever come between us, promise me."

Although assured of the commitment to their friendship, Cathy had a sense, events were taking a course, which might endanger their relationship.

CHAPTER 27
LADIES DAY

LADIES DAY at Happy Hills was an adventure for golfers as well as their caddies. Twenty-four women usually participated and club professional Dave Thompson, anticipated complaints from at least half of them. Their discontent ranged from why they were playing with someone they didn't care for…to a question of a rule infraction committed by another player the previous week. It wasn't long before it started.

"Why is it the men can have breakfast served everyday in the men's grill and we can't even get a roll or bagel at the halfway house?" One woman asked on the sticky Tuesday morning.

"You have to take that up with the board." Dave said. "I have no control over the food served at the club."

"I know you draw out of a hat to make the pairings," another woman said. "But I don't want to play with Maggie Howser. The woman wears so much perfume that you have to wear a gas mask to play with her. Can't you put her with someone else for today?"

"I'm sorry, the pairings are already arranged." Dave told her. "Please bear with it for now and I'll see what I can do next Tuesday."

The complaint pace quickened and when Dave, thought he heard from the last of the lady warriors…

"Why does it seem like I'm always starting on the tenth hole instead of the first?" A portly woman demanded. "You must devise another system to make it more fair."

"I'm sure it just seems that way," the pro responded. "Actually, we rotate the women's starting holes to make it fair, just as we can't have all of the good or marginal golfers in the same groupings."

"That's nonsense," she protested. "I started on the tenth last week and again today."

"I promise to make sure, you start on hole number one next week." Dave told the protesting duffer, one of the poorest golfers in the club.

After a few minutes of quibbling, starter and caddie master Ed Fitzgerald, barked, "Hold it down," as the gathered caddies in the bag room awaited their assignments.

"Tommy, you have the Dicks' group."

"Yes!" The young caddie cried out, pumping his fist and clearly elated, his reason soon to be apparent.

"Why does he get the big boobs lady?" Protested another caddie.

"Because she requested him!" Ed snapped. "And if you were smart, you'd get requested.

When they ask for you, it means they like you. That gets you bigger tips for your pockets. You have the Howser group, Jimmy."

"What! That woman's a traveling perfume store. Please Ed, not me," he pleaded.

"Just...don't get too close," the starter warned.

Fitzgerald continued assigning his caddies to specific pairings of four and then told them to proceed to their group.

"Good morning, ladies." Dave said, feeling battered by complaints. "You have your hole assignments on your carts. I ask that you please fix all divots on the greens and any questions that may arise, do ask your caddy for a ruling. Have a great day of golf and play well."

The carts slowly moved in single formation to their assigned holes and another ladies day was under way. "God bless them all," the club pro whispered, wiping his brow with a towel.

"My god, who bathed in perfume this morning?" Asked one of the women.

"Maggie must be close by," another replied, rubbing her nose.

"What does she do, swim in the stuff?" Still another asked, cringing her face and reaching for a hanky.

"What do you see here?" The stout Maggie asked, taking the putter from her caddie. "Where's the break, left to right or right to left?" She inquired, removing her visor and running her hand through her short salt and pepper hair. The young caddie stood directly behind Maggie, placing himself in harms way and two successive whiffs was more than he could endure.

"Left or right, Jimmy?" She asked once again. When she received no response, Maggie turned to reprimand the young man, only to observe the caddy and her fellow golfers walking towards the next hole, blowing their noses and shaking their heads.

"Ladies, where are you going? You didn't finish the hole."

"You won the hole!" Sheila cried out, with her back turned away.

"Tommy, please give me my five wood." Laura Dicks commanded. Taking it from him, she bent down in such a way, making it apparent to all…she wasn't wearing a bra. As Laura swung her club back and forth, her unfettered breasts were bouncing to her tempo. Sweat poured down the young caddy's forehead, his eyes moving in concert, following the beauty of Laura's bounty. When she finally swung the club, her breasts appeared to be launched along with the ball and leaving her body, causing the young caddie to instinctively reach out to save them, then tripping over a golf bag, falling flat on his face.

"Are you okay, Tommy?" Laura asked, as he staggered to his feet.

"Yes Mrs. Tits!" The startled caddie cried out, then, realizing what he had said…turned a deep scarlet. Laura and her partners giggled, as the embarrassed caddie scampered to the next hole.

It took the women almost five hours to finish their round of golf, but just an hour to injure four caddies, one hit by an errant golf club, another run down by a golf cart, a third overpowered by Maggie's scent and still another, bruised from trying to save Laura's prized boobies.

"What's with you guys?" The caddy master, asked.

"I quit!" A caddie cried out. "There's not enough money you can pay me to work for these maniacs. Take a look at this!" Raising his shirt, he exposed a large welt on his back. "That dame almost kills me and then pays me a lousy fifteen bucks, claiming I made her miss putts by giving bad reads," he sputtered. "I could have laid a string down for her and she'd still miss the hole by ten feet. I'm done. Find yourself another punching bag."

It was traditional for the women to have lunch before beginning the ***CAT CLAW GAME***. No one seems to know exactly when it started, but most of the men felt it originated when the first two women ever stepped on a golf course. It was rumored, most of the women looked forward to the ***CAT CLAW GAME,*** more than they did playing golf. And so…the game began.

"Did you see what Laura was wearing today?" Shelia asked.

"Don't you mean what she wasn't wearing?" Cynthia snipped.

"They have to be store bought? They can't be originals." Lisa jabbed.

"The caddie certainly didn't care!" Cynthia observed. "Seems like they got his jollies ringing. He followed her around all day like a dog in heat."

"Talk about bravery?" Lisa said. "Maggie's caddie had to endure her rancid odor for eighteen holes."

And…while the pre-lunch drinking took hold…so did the gossip.

"Have you girls heard about the affair between one of our young teaching pro's and one not to be named member?" A woman at the table asked, greeted by a chorus of, **'WITH WHO?'**

"You can't leave it there without telling us," another told her, leaning forward and sipping on her cosmopolitan.

"Well," the coy woman began. "My sources tell me, the young man and a member were hot and heavy in the rear parking lot and they weren't discussing how to grip a club." Several of the ladies giggled, gulping on their drinks and pursuing the member's name.

At yet another table, the game participants included Cathy Daley and several other women.

"The greens were as slow as mud today," one woman complained. "Why can't they be consistent? I guarantee…if it were men's day…the greens would be perfect."

"My caddie was so old he couldn't see the hole to give you a proper read," another quipped. "I wasn't sure he was going to finish eighteen holes before dropping dead. And I can say…he wasn't getting mouth-to-mouth from me."

"He's a fixture around here," another sitting at the table told her. "I think he's been here for over forty years."

"He may be a fixture." Cathy remarked. "But someone should talk to the man about his bathing habits, he smelled awful."

"He's not that old, he certainly noticed Laura's boobs bouncing around as she passed by on the sixth hole. Someone ought to tell her about the new invention called a bra?" Still another woman jabbed.

"That girl defines ditzy." Cathy scoffed. "She'd probably respond, saying she read somewhere, that it's healthy to aerate them whenever you can."

"Sharon, you're the golf chairperson." Marion said, reaching for a salmon pate. "Isn't there a dress code about that sort of thing?"

"The board makes the rules around here, you should know that. Ask your husband if he objects to seeing those floaters bouncing around?"

Marion didn't respond, but raised her chin, turning her eyes away at the reprehensible suggestion, then adding her own **CAT CLAW** item.

"I understand Nora, hired a professional to help her in the match against Bill Harper? Does she really think she has a chance to beat him? Seems like a waste of time and money. Why doesn't she just resign from the club so things can get back to normal around here."

"Marion, why don't you button it up." Cathy hissed. "At least Nora, has the integrity to fight for what she considers to be right, not just for her, but for all of us here. Loyalty is a rare commodity. Ask your husband about that too, why don't you? I understand he stabbed his friend, Mike Grace in the back the other night."

"Cathy Daley, you and Nora have been trouble makers for years." Marion snapped, scowling in such a way to completely distort her face. "Maybe if you got a life with your husband and Nora found a man, you'd fit in better."

Marion's comments struck a raw nerve, particularly since Cathy, never thought it appeared that trouble between her and Fred, was apparent to other members...but Blake would pay.

"Listen to me you bleached blonde battle-ax!" Cathy roared, as she rose from her chair. "My relationship with my husband is none of your damn business. But you've opened the door sister! You complain about Laura's breasts and my friend's courage to challenge Bill Harper? What have you ever stood up for in your life? And by the way, while we're talking about standing up, your breasts could use a major overhaul. They look like they've been on life support for years."

"Okay girls, lets settle down." Sharon said.

"Are you going to let her talk to me like that?" Marion demanded.

"I'm afraid you lit the fuse." Sharon told her.

Marion began to stand from her chair, when Cathy, fired the last salvo.

"Oh, don't get up Marion," she said. "There's still some desserts on the table...that you haven't finished!"

Today, the ***CAT CLAW GAME***...was at it's best.

CHAPTER 28
TRAINING DAY TEN

THE TIME TO PREPARE for Nora's match was dwindling with each passing day. She looked her usual, radiant self, dressed in turquoise shorts and matching golf shirt, as she went through her stretching routine, preparing for her practice session with George.

It was a warm August morning, but tempered by a whispering breeze. All in all, it was a good day to practice.

"George, before we start, I'd like to ask you a question about the day of the match."

"What's up Nora?" He asked, not dressed in his usual long pants, but shorts and a collared lavender shirt.

"I want you to caddie for me during the match with Bill. I need you by my side, in case I don't have the right thinking cap on," she said, using a play-on-words. She needed every edge if she was going to have a chance in her match against Bill.

"I don't know if that's a good idea. I don't want you looking over your shoulder before every shot, wondering if I approve of your club or shot selection."

"George, every baby needs a pacifier and you're it for me." Nora countered, placing her hand on his shoulder. "Please, I need you to be there," she said in a low, but effective tone.

Nora was confident he would agree and she also knew why. But she was not, she told herself, using him because he was attracted to her. It wasn't after all, as though she had ***completely*** *dismissed* the idea of accepting him as a suitor.

"Take out your seven iron and hit a few balls for me. We can talk about the day of the match later," although in his heart of hearts, the forlorn pro, knew he couldn't refuse the request.

Nora complied and proceeded to hit balls with her seven-iron until George, having apparently seen enough, told her to stop.

"Okay Nora," he said. "I see you hit that club about a hundred and fifty-yards. Can you fade and draw the ball with the seven?"

"I can fade the ball left to right, but I have trouble drawing it right to left."

"There's always one club a golfer should fall in love with and most pro's agree it should be the seven-iron." George said. "If your tee shot is blocked out by a tree on the left side of the fairway, obstructing your next shot to the green, what do you normally do?"

"I usually chip out to the fairway, why?"

"Most golfers do the same and lose a stroke on that hole. But if you had a shot that went around the tree from right-to-left, chances are you wouldn't lose a stroke. That's what a draw of the ball can do for you. Let me demonstrate with your club."

After George, hit several balls to make his point, he worked Nora hard for the next two hours. So hard in fact, she raised a blister on her hand…which, as soon as George saw it, meant practice was over for the day, telling her, as they took leave of one another, to soak her hand in salt water.

However, Nora had a better idea than soaking her hand in salt water and called Cathy, asking if she wanted to go to the beach, where salt water was plentiful, not to mention sand and sun.

"I don't know if I have a bathing suit that fits." Cathy told her. "It's been a while since I've been in one."

"No excuses, woman." Nora demanded. "Tear a pair of shorts if you have to, but get your butt in high gear because…**WE'RE SHOWING OFF OUR WARES TODAY!"**

Half an hour later, she arrived at Cathy's in her blue Jaguar convertible and they were on their way to the beach.

However, showing off their wares would invite an unusual kind of trouble that neither would welcome.

CHAPTER 29
A DAY AT THE BEACH

IT WAS A LITTLE after noon when the girls spread their blanket on the warm sand. Cathy placed a basket of sandwiches and fruit on one corner of the blanket and her boom box on another, while Nora, put down a jug of ice tea before taking off her shorts and shirt, revealing a yellow two-piece bikini. Watching Nora undress, Cathy wondered how it happened that her friend was still without a Prince Charming.

No slouch in the looks department, Cathy disrobed to a green bikini, revealing a trim, athletic figure. Her short brown hair matched the color of her eyes and although her father was Irish and mother Italian, Cathy's Mediterranean complexion indicated her mothers' genes dominated. She was, Nora noted, as she rubbed lotion on her friend's back, already beautifully tanned.

Once settled, Cathy turned to a station playing the music of her favorite group, the Beach Boys.

"Was this a great idea or not?"

"One of the few good one's you've recently had." Cathy snipped.

"What does that mean?" Nora demanded, raising her head from the blanket, glaring at her friend.

"Oh nothing." Cathy said with a shrug. "Concentrate on your tan."

Nora sat up and hugged her legs. "Tell me," she insisted. "I know you want to."

"This business with Bill, has consumed your life and it's also divided a lot of people at the club. I'm just wondering if it's all worth the trouble." Cathy told her, then resting her head on a folded towel.

Nora felt a pang of guilt. After all, this was her fault, all of it. Maybe she could have been more patient with Bill, she thought. But then…

"Cathy, the guy's a jerk!" Nora snapped. "He started this whole thing by calling me a jackass and then suggested…no, demanded, I be suspended."

"Whatever happened to sticks and stones?" Cathy hissed. "We had that drilled into us when we were kids. It seems to me…it fits the present situation."

Nora's eyes narrowed. **"That's a lot of hooey!** Why are you suddenly sticking up for the guy?"

"All I'm saying…you could have let it slide. Don't you think challenging him to a match was a bit over-the-top?"

"Is this my friend, Cathy Daley talking, or the **Cathy…who slept with the guy?"** Nora snipped, then snapping her towel in place, lying down and unclipping her bra.

But just as Cathy was about to answer, two twelve year old boys appeared and without warning, threw a pail of water over them, Cathy and Nora, jumping to their feet, forgetting their bikini tops were unclipped.

"Wow! They're beautiful!" One of the boys cried out, drawing the attention of others.

"You know, there're right," observed a man who was apparently their father.

"Are these two little devils yours?" Cathy demanded, clasping her arms over her breasts.

"I don't know why you're so upset," he told her. "They're just boys."

"But you're not!" Cathy cried out. "Now take off, or the pepper spray in my beach bag will make the rest of your day very unpleasant."

"Can you believe that guy, condoning what those kids did?" Cathy grumbled, clipping on her bikini top. "What are you smiling about?" Cathy asked, still puffing from the incident.

Several onlookers witnessed the free peep show, some applauding the spectacle as Cathy, vigorously brushed sand from her arms and legs while sneering at the onlookers.

"Well, I was just thinking, maybe you could have let it slide. Don't you think your reaction **was a bit over the top?** After all it was just two young boys playing. Was it worth the trouble?" Nora said, as they settled down on the blanket again, this time with their bras in place.

Cathy, understood what Nora was hinting, but chose not to ignore the issue and give her friend the satisfaction of a non-response.

"It's always worth the trouble to teach men a lesson." Cathy told her. "And the younger the better."

"Then why criticize me for teaching Bill a lesson? That's exactly what I was trying to do in challenging him." Nora asked, reaching for a sandwich from the basket.

"Nora, it's the way you went about it." Cathy said, biting into an orange.

"What do you mean?"

"Was it really necessary to make a scene at the dinner in front of all of the members? If you had to challenge the guy why didn't you simply do it on a personal level, face to face with the man? Didn't you think about the consequences?" Cathy said, discarding her orange in disgust.

"What consequences?" Nora demanded, her tone becoming belligerent, not expecting her best friend to criticize her actions with such fervor.

"Do you really think you have a prayer to beat him? **You lose and you're out of the club! Where does that leave me,** Nora?" Cathy cried out, peering towards the ocean's horizon.

There it was...Cathy was mortified at the thought of Nora, being forced to leave Happy Hills. Her entire social life at the club centered around her relationship with Nora, and while her home life wasn't exactly firing on all cylinders, Cathy would lose an equilibrium maintained at the club.

Nora began to understand her friends sudden reversal of support, never fully realizing the consequences of her actions and how it would affect those closest to her. Perhaps she did handle the entire matter poorly, she thought, questioning if her actions were really worth the trouble?

"Cathy, I'm so sorry. **I never realized how you felt.** I guess my temper just got the best of me and after I pulled the trigger, it was too late to change things. But honey, don't ever think I would abandon you **if by chance**, I'm forced to leave the club."

"It just...wouldn't be the same without you." Cathy said, continuing to stare at the waters edge.

The thought of losing to Bill, was never an acceptable alternative for Nora. She knew it would be an up-hill battle, but her confidence in finding a way to win was the reason she was the women's club champion for so many years. Now...Cathy had opened the door of doubt and it wasn't comfortable. She felt a sudden queasiness in the pit of her stomach, the reality of her actions triggering the thought of the potential consequences. What had she done? She was never more vulnerable. The coming days would determine if Nora, would simply resign from the club and avoiding the embarrassment of a humiliating defeat, or take her medicine and fight to the finish.

Yet, this wasn't her only conflict. Nora had no explanation, as to why her recent dreams of nocturnal passion, included the one person who was her biggest critic, Bill Harper. But this too... would soon be resolved.

CHAPTER 30
LADIES MEMBER GUEST

THE SKY WAS a Caribbean blue and a soft summer breeze gently swayed the pink and yellow banners of *welcome* adorning the grounds of Happy Hills Country Club, as a parade of cars lined the entrance, awaiting to announce their arrival and drop off their golf bags for the annual women's member guest outing.

It was a yearly event in which the wives of members asked a friend to play golf for the day at Happy Hills, a festive occasion giving members an opportunity to showcase their country club.

Breakfast was continental and served in the dining room. Lunch consisted of hamburgers, hotdogs and chicken along with fruit and soft drinks available at three stations on the golf course.

A round of golf usually required three and a half to four hours for a foursome to complete. Because of the large volume of players in a member guest outing, completing the round was closer to six hours, for accomplished golfers, an absolute nightmare.

The cocktail hour was scheduled to begin at six o'clock followed by dinner at seven, both planned on the presumption the tournament would take six hours to complete, allowing the women forty-five minutes to shower and dress for dinner.

The valet parkers accommodated guests, issuing green tickets of redemption and directing them to the locker room, which is where…on this particular day…it all begins.

"Can you believe how small this locker room is!" One of the guests, a bit overdressed for the occasion, scornfully said.

"What do you expect when you're treated like *second class citizens*," said another guest.

At ten-fifteen, the visitors began filing into the dining room for breakfast, keeping an eye out for their host of the day. The food station, which was left of the entrance, was limited to coffee, rolls, bagels and assorted pastries.

"Is this what they're serving for breakfast...at a member guest?" Judy Feinstein, the invitee of Nora, cried out her objection rather vociferously.

"Where's the lox? Where's the omelets? Can you imagine this? What's wrong with this place?" The outspoken Judy, scoffed, slapping the side of her white Capri's, then tugging at her canary yellow golf shirt.

At eighty-two and a champion complainer, Judy's face was gaunt, with rivers of wrinkles and protruding cheekbones, which a generous amount of make-up failed to conceal. She was rather tall at five-eight, slender and slightly hunched. A fair golfer for her age, she wasn't happy unless everyone knew about her displeasures of the moment.

Judy's husband Mel, was an upscale art dealer. Nora's passion, were the works of impressionist painters, Monet and Renoir. One Saturday, she and Nick stopped in Mel's gallery, located in Chelsea, Manhattan. So the friendship began, Mel supplying Nick, with an occasional birthday or anniversary gift for Nora. The couples became close friends and often played golf together at their respective clubs.

When Cathy first met Judy, at a dinner with Nora and her husband, she had thought her as '*Bitchy* and too forward." Nothing had happened subsequently to change her opinion. Judy had the *audacity* to ask Cathy, why she had no children and later over dessert, if the diamonds in her bracelet were real. Cathy excused herself from the table and if looks could kill, Judy's neck would be between her two hands. Nora followed her friend to the bathroom and when she entered, found Cathy grunting aloud, her fists fully clenched.

* * *

"Are you okay?" Nora asked, her stressed out friend.

"Where did you find that flaming maniac? How could you be friends with her!" Cathy raged, as another member entered, glancing at her and Nora, then entered a stall.

"Cathy, she's really not a bad person...once you get to know her."

"Get to know her! I know her for one evening and I'm ready to commit murder."

"Judy's really a kind person, she wouldn't hurt a fly." Nora said in her friend's defense, but understanding how she could offend those who met her for the first time.

"Nora, if you don't put a muzzle on her...well, I won't be responsible for stuffing a potato in her mouth and taping it close!" Cathy threatened with animation. "Asking me if my diamonds were real, what stones on the woman. What's next, wanting to know if my boobs are real?"

They both returned to the table in time for the serving of after dinner cordials.

"So Cathy, is this your first marriage or second?" Judy innocently asked.

Before Cathy could respond, Nora interrupted. "So Mel, I understand you're retiring from the business soon?" Looking at Cathy with pleading eyes, bending her head ever so slightly.

"Retire! Are you kidding?" Judy interrupted. "He'd drive me crazy being home all day. Besides, I'm contemplating plastic surgery and he has to keep selling so he can pay for the procedure."

"Are you having a complete make-over?" Cathy snipped, not letting the opportunity of throwing a dagger slip away.

"No…just a facial…dear." Judy, sensing the question had purpose. "But, I'm not sure if I'll do it. Cathy, you look like you've had a boob job, did it hurt very much?" Judy asked, returning the spear, but unsuspectingly igniting the fuse...a very short fuse.

Cathy slapped both hands on the table and stood from her chair, her complexion matching her red dress. **"Judy, you're the most offensive woman** I've ever met and I'm surprised you're still alive!"

"What? I'm just making conversation. **I'm trying to know you better**, what's wrong with that?"

"Well I don't want to know you any better. You're rude and offensive." Cathy said, then leaving with her husband.

"Nora, what did I say?" Judy asked. "That woman has a problem. She's certainly not very friendly."

"Judy, you can't just ask people personal questions you've just met for the first time. They find it offensive." Nora told her.

"How do you find out about people if you don't ask questions? I don't know what's wrong with your friend." Judy mumbled.

That was Cathy's first encounter with Judy Feinstein, a woman oblivious to her probing questions and salty demeanor. Her mouth could clear a table in record time and agitate the calmest of personalities.

* * *

"Hey Judy, over here!" Nora called to her friend.

"What's with your club here?" Judy asked, embracing her.

"What's wrong?"

"Don't they know how to serve a breakfast? No eggs, no lox, how cheap are they?" Judy persisted, as most of the guests found their host and settled at tables with other members.

"Have a bagel with coffee." Nora suggested. "We'll have a good lunch and dinner."

"What?" Judy muttered, adjusting the gold belt to her Capri's. "Am I the only token Jew here? This club needs a few of us and then they'd see what a real breakfast is like," she complained in one breath and then in another…"By the way dear, I love your outfit," referring to Nora's mint colored golf shirt, complimenting her emerald green shorts, her hair in a pony-tail, accented with a green ribbon tie back.

I love her to death, Nora said to herself, but questioned if Judy, was the right choice for the occasion.

"Judy, you remember Cathy?" Nora asked, her look begging for composure from her friend.

"Weren't you the one needing a laxative when we went to dinner?" Judy asked, referring to their first meeting, Cathy storming out of the restaurant for no other reason than to escape the impetuous woman.

Cathy looked at Nora, her contemptuous expression said it all, **'Why did you invite this woman?"**

"Judy, this is my guest, Jan Phillips." Cathy replied, keeping her cool… for the moment.

"Jan, let me ask you, are you as disappointed as I am at this so called breakfast?" Judy pressed her fellow guest.

Taken by surprise with her question, Jan looked at Cathy, with raised eyebrows. "Judy, I'm not big on breakfast."

"I guess…I'm the only one then. Oh well, so what's your story, Jan?" Judy asked, unflappable as usual.

"My story?"

"Are you married? Have kids? Is it your first time around? What's your story?"

Nora and Cathy both cringed, but before they could change the subject, Jan answered the question.

Clearly, Nora was far more patient than if she had been meeting Judy, for the first time. It occurred to her, once again, to wonder why on earth she had invited the woman and then reminded herself that she had always felt sorry for her, who was understandably enough, friendless.

"Yes, I'm married with three children and no, it's my second marriage."

"Boys, girls?" Judy persisted. "How old? You said children, you don't look that young?"

"I think it's time for us to leave and get to the carts." Nora interjected.

"What's with the looks?" Judy grumbled. "I'm just making conversation."

As Nora, started towards the exit, Cathy pinched her derriere.

"Ouch! What was that for?" She asked, hopping forward.

"You know damn well what it's for," she whispered in her ear. "I can't believe the gall on that woman." Cathy hissed.

"Let's get to our carts and enjoy the day." Nora implored, taking hold of Cathy's hand.

"Good morning." Dave Thompson said, greeting guests and their hosts as he prepared for the start of the event. "As club pro, let me welcome you to our annual member guest outing at Happy Hills. As you can see, the beautiful weather was special ordered for today's event. But, it will be hot, so please drink plenty of fluids to avoid dehydration."

When Dave spoke, people listened, even the men. On this occasion, the women gathered in golf carts around him and hung on every word. No matter what the individual levels of play, they took this occasion seriously.

"Please notice the sheets on your cart as they explain the rules for today's event," the pro continued. "It will be a shotgun start, which means you'll be starting at different holes on the course. Best ball will be the format. All participants will tee off and then choose the best ball for their second shot. Everyone, except the person whose ball you chose, will hit the next shot and so on. Each team must use two drives from each golfer. If they're any issues during play, ask your caddie for a ruling. Now, if they're aren't any questions, please take your carts to the starting hole assigned to your group and have a nice round of golf."

The golf carts moved in unison, resulting in a scene that resembled one featuring bumper cars at a carnival.

"Ladies! Ladies!" The starter cried out, as he attempted to bring order and direction to the massive traffic jam.

Nora, Judy, Cathy and Jan were assigned to the third hole, which was a par three.

"They had to start us at a par three!" Judy complained. "It's the worst kind of hole to start in a tournament. Why couldn't they have started us at a par five? At least there's some room for error."

Nora took her guest by the arm and drew her aside. **"Stop it, Judy!"** She demanded. "Stop it right now before you ruin the day for all of us."

"Stop what? What am I doing?"

"You're being a nudge, that's what." Nora told her. "You haven't stopped complaining since you got here. First it was the breakfast, then asking personal questions to Cathy's guest and now mouthing off on what hole we're starting on."

She had hesitated to be this frank with Judy in the past, but today, perhaps because her nerves were already on the edge over the competition with Bill Harper, she couldn't take it any more.

"But your breakfast was awful and I was just being friendly with Jan." Judy told her. "Is that so terrible?"

Seething, Nora rolled her eyes, as she was fast approaching the end of her patience.

"All right! All right! If you want dull, I'll give you dull." Judy muttered, removing her visor and slapping it on her leg.

"Girls, this is Sid, our caddie for the day." Nora said when they reached the third hole, where an elderly man, wearing the garb of a white shirt and pants was waiting for them. Taking the putters from the four golf bags, he proceeded to walk towards the green.

"Girls, Sid doesn't see or hear too well, so you'll have to speak up when you want his attention." Nora explained.

"Oh, that's just great! They start us on a par three and give us a deaf and blind caddie." Judy muttered, loud enough for all to hear, except of course… Sid.

Nora gave her impervious friend a look that shut her up for the next four holes without incident. But…the eighth hole was Judy's time to let loose.

"Sid, where's the break on this putt?" Judy demanded.

Sensing she could be trouble, he looked her in the eye and firmly replied, 'It's left to right, Mrs. Feinstein."

"You're sure, Sid?"

"Yes, Mrs. Feinstein."

"Well…we'll see." Judy said and proceeded to putt accordingly, only to hit the ball too hard, rolling ten feet past the hole.

"That was a lousy read!" Judy scowled, as the ball missed it's mark.

"You didn't tell me the putt was down hill. How can you play this game if you have a caddie who can't read greens?" Judy said, shaking her head as she walked past Cathy.

"Judy, leave the caddie alone." Cathy intervened. "You missed the putt, not Sid."

"If your guest would speed up her play we'd have more time to read the greens." Judy snapped back, blaming Jan, for slow play.

Nora saw Cathy flush and unless she could think of some way to prevent it, Judy was about to get an earful. But it was too late, Cathy wouldn't let her off the hook.

"You're the rudest individual I've ever met!" Cathy said with distain. "You're making this day an absolute nightmare!"

"What did I say? Jan is playing too slow," the older woman protested. "Can't you see we're a half a hole behind the group in front of us?"

Cathy turned to Nora, her head lowered, as though she were a bull from Pamplona, about to trample the annoyance of the day.

"Nora, if you can't control this nasty woman, Jan and I will leave." Cathy snarled.

"Judy, you promised to keep it buttoned." Nora said.

"Look!" Judy declared, hands on hips. "I don't want to spoil your day... but the fact remains, the breakfast was lousy, we started on a par three, our caddie is blind and can't hear a thing, and your friend is a slow player. What am I saying wrong?"

"Cathy, give me a minute please?" Nora said, taking Judy to the side.

"You're embarrassing me." Nora told her. **"No! Don't say a word!"** Nora demanded, as Judy was about to interrupt. "You're spoiling what's supposed to be a pleasant day and making it very uncomfortable for Cathy and her guest. I love you Judy, you know that, but if comes down to Cathy and Jan, leaving because of you, then you're the one whose going. Now, either you button it up or call it a day."

Nora felt awful tearing into her friend, but Cathy and her guest didn't deserve to have their day spoiled because of Judy.

"I don't know what to say. You know me, I'm a born yenta. I love to talk. I don't want to spoil the day for you guys and if you want me to leave...I'll understand."

"Judy, what I want you to do is to apologize to Cathy and Jan, and then think before you speak for the rest of the day. Can you do that?"

Could she trust Judy's impulsive nature? Nora wasn't sure, but didn't want to be put in the position of having to ask her to leave, or Cathy and Jan, to be uncomfortable for the rest of the day.

"Girls, if I offended you...I apologize. I guess when you get to be my age, you try to spice up your day a little, so you can forget there aren't too many left." Judy said, lowering her head.

Nora took notice, her friend was playing the old lady card, which had worked for her in the past when her mouth had become an issue. Nora was amused to see it work again, Cathy and Jan being the marks this time around. And Judy would not disappoint them, giving an outrageous explanation in which they looked at one another, mouths open and grinning.

"Most people *pass gas* from their derriere's." Judy told them. "Unfortunately, I *pass it* from my mouth," she explained, then careful to avoid confrontations during the balance of play.

The second hole was the last to be played by the girls in the shotgun format. They had played all eighteen and retreated to the locker room to shower and prepare for cocktails and dinner.

Soft piano music greeted members and their guests arriving in the dining room. There was a tempting array of hot and cold hors d' oeuvres that even Judy, couldn't find fault to complain about.

"What's this I hear, about a woman member challenging the men's club champion to a match?" Asked one of the guests, as she bit into a pate filled cracker.

"It's not just any member," her host replied. "She's the women's club champion."

"But I don't get it. Why would she do that? Is she one of those gay rights women?"

"No, no, it's not like that," the member said. "In fact, that's her over there, the tall red-head. Her name...is Nora Cummings."

"She's certainly a beautiful woman," remarked the guest.

"I guess I can tell you Liz," the member said. "It's not like it's a secret." And she went on to tell her guest, a journalist for Long Island's most popular newspaper and the writer of a nationally syndicated gossip column, the background story of the feud between Nora and Bill. She gave explicit details of the running battle between the two, including the way the board of directors had sided with Bill, through constant intimidation, rule changes and curtailing women's golf play at the club. The host member went on to explain, how the ladies member guest program had been cancelled by the board and rescinded after the women had threatened a strike.

Anyone watching Liz Peters, would have realized she was hearing something she knew would make a great story.

On the other side of the room, Judy was showing her captive audience, glassine photos of her grandchildren.

"Why they're beautiful Judy." Cathy said, as she passed them on to her guest. "How old are they?"

"Allison is nineteen." Judy said, her exquisite jewelry noticed against the backdrop of a stylish, one piece black dress, highlighted by a diamond studded, gold linked belt. "Mark's eighteen and Jennifer is seventeen. They're my babies," she told them. "I just adore them. My sons are great fathers. They're both art dealers, like their father. Unfortunately, one lives in Georgia and the other in California."

"Do you get to visit them often?" Jan asked.

Nora was pleased the exchange had relieved some of the tension created earlier by Judy.

"Mel and I get to see two of the three grandchildren in Georgia more frequently than the one in California." Judy told her. "We go to the coast only twice a year, it's a long trip for us."

This was a different Judy, from the to one which they had been exposed to on the golf course, a woman whose eyes glowed as she discussed her children and grandchildren.

Observing the ill-will fade away, Nora was pleased the girls had a chance to see the other side of Judy, the one she knew so well, as they still had a long night of socializing ahead. The cocktail hour was over and the members and their guests moved to their assigned tables.

Volunteers moved from table to table, trying to sell raffle tickets to a fifty-fifty drawing and several other prizes on display along the wall of the dining room. The girls bought several tickets each, placing them in their purse. It was while they were eating their salad, that Judy, noticed a woman glaring at them from the next table.

"What's going on with her?" She asked Nora.

"Her husband's a board member and she struts around here thinking she's special." Nora said with a shrug. "She also represents a small number of women who oppose the match I have with the men's club champion."

"Maybe I'm a member of the wrong club, you girls seem to have more fun here."

"Judy, if you came to this club, I'm afraid half of the members would resign."

"Why? Because I'm Jewish?"

"No, Judy. They'd resign because you're a genuine pain in the ass!"

"See Nora, now I know you really do understand me."

After dinner, the awards ceremony began with lady's chairperson Sharon Kelly, announcing the winners of various categories. The three teams with the lowest scores won crystal bowls with inscriptions indicating the position of finish, the size of the bowls determined by the teams finishing position.

"The team which came in first place, consisted of Nora Cummings, Cathy Daley, Jan Phillips and Judy Feinstein." Sharon announced, her yellow chiffon dress swirling with each movement, as she handed the girls their prizes to the polite applause from the other participants.

"Nora, don't go yet." Sharon said. "The two remaining awards, are for closest to the pin on the par three seventeenth hole and the longest drive. Strangely enough, they seem to be going to the same person, none other than our own, Nora Cummings." Her fellow team members stood and applauded, then, were soon joined by others. Table by table added to the building crescendo, in what began as the opening shot by those who stood behind Nora, in her quest against, Bill Harper. There was thunderous applause, a lot of it, and then, someone called out, **"You can do it Nora,"** a vote of confidence that brought tears to her eyes.

"Speech! Speech!" The audience cried out, until Nora, held up her hands indicating she was surrendering to their appeal.

"Ladies," she began, wiping away the tears. "I'm overwhelmed by your incredible support."

"We love you, Nora." Tammy Grace, wife of the board president, commanded. Once again, the audience rose from their chairs, indicating their appreciation for her efforts to attain parity with the men.

"Are you OK?" Sharon whispered.

"I'm fine." Nora assured her. "Friends, I'd like to share a story with you, I believe appropriate. When I was growing up, my mother was very special and dear to me. She worked in an environment controlled by men and although she was loyal to my father, she would always say to me, 'Maintain your dignity and fight for what you think is right, even if it hurts."

Remembering her mother made her wistful. She wished the woman she had admired and so loved, could be here today to see how her daughter's friends had rallied around her. But, that was not to be. Although a loving mother, Barbara Owens was somewhat detached and a social avant-garde, spending the winter months in Florida with Nora's father. There were no grandchildren attachments and so, she felt the remaining years of their lives should be dedicated to their interest, both avid sailors.

"I love being a member of Happy Hills, and when my husband Nick was alive, he loved it too. Being a dutiful wife, I never thought about the inequities we have to endure at the club. But, when Nick passed, I suddenly felt isolated by the rules, which no one can deny, makes us second-class citizens at Happy Hills. I was Nick's wife and yet, to remain here, I had to be voted in by an all male board of directors."

Nora paused and looked out over the sea of faces, all poised for her promising words. She had, she knew, given these women something to hope for, and she was more than ever, determined to make their dreams come true.

"Now, I find we can only play at certain times on certain days," she went on in a firmer tone. "Unlike the men, we have no grillroom and no access to a decent breakfast before we play. One can say, and it's quite true, that we knew the rules of the game before we joined the club. But as in any good marriage, there are adjustments when inequities exist. Ladies, I'm no hero. You're the heroes for taking a stand and letting the men know we care about how we're treated as women. If I lose..."

"You'll beat him, Nora!" Someone cried out, eliciting a spontaneous ovation.

"If I lose...and I'm under no illusions of it not being a strong possibility," Nora continued, "I'll be sorry to leave the club, but hopefully, it will result in some gains for all of you. I didn't intend to make a speech here and I hope I haven't offended any of you, especially those who oppose my challenge to Bill Harper. I love you all for your support and hope you'll be there when I need it the most. Thank you."

"We'll be there for you, Nora." Several supporters cried out, standing and applauding, many of them reaching out to take her hand, as she made her way back to the table.

"That was incredible." Cathy said as she hugged her friend.

"I'll tell you something." Judy declared. **"This club is where it's happening.** I never saw anything like this in my life. Hey, waiter, bring me over a double martini with lots of olives. I think I'll get drunk, then wake up and ask myself if I've been dreaming."

Liz Peters walked over to Nora's table and introduced herself. "That was some speech," she said. "You certainly had the members eating out of your hand. It sounded more like a nominating speech at a convention and I do intend that as a compliment."

"I'm sorry." Nora replied. "Do I know you?"

"No, but I hope we can get acquainted." Liz told her. "Here's my card. Give me a call when you're free...so we can chat."

After glancing at the card, Nora handed it back to the gossip columnist.

"No thanks Liz, I'm not doing this for publicity."

"Oh, but that's where you're wrong, Nora." Liz Peters assured her. "Publicity is exactly what your going to get, whether you want it or not."

"Then put it this way, I'll choose how far and where I want this to go."

"I can be a big help to your cause and of course, for the other women here." Liz told her.

"Thanks, but no thanks. I don't want to make this a public circus."

"I'm afraid it's too late for that," the columnist said, returning the card to her. "If you change your mind, please, do call."

"So what did you win?" Judy asked.

"A Nike golf bag and a driver." Nora said. "Cathy, weren't you going to buy a new bag? Because if you were, look no more. I just bought one six months ago. Here, take this one." Nora said, handing her the navy blue and white bag.

"Are you sure, Nora?"

"Maybe it'll get you to the practice range more often. It's yours. And Judy, I can't use a another driver, this is for you." Nora said, handing it to her unflappable friend.

"A *Taylor Made Burner*! This is the latest rage. You may want this for yourself."

"I've learned one thing about golfing equipment." Nora said. "If it's not broke… don't fix it. I've just about tried them all. Jan, I'm sorry. I wish I had something to give you."

"Just watching you play today and seeing how you carried yourself up at the podium was enough of a gift." Cathy's guest told her.

Coffee and dessert was now being served. An array of colorful cookies was placed on each table as well as a platter of assorted fruit.

"It's now time for our raffle drawing." Sharon Kelly announced. "I need a volunteer to pick out the tickets from the bin."

Maggie Howser was the first to raise her hand and Sharon could only hope that someone had put a plug in her perfume spray. All of the secondary prizes were called without incident. The members and their guests, anxiously awaited for the final drawing, which was the twenty-five-hundred dollar, fifty-fifty prize. When number four forty-four was drawn, a shout of, **"I won! I won!"** Came from Nora's table…Jan Phillips had the lucky ticket and scurried up to collect her prize, then, retreating hastily from the podium and back to the table.

"I'm fine." Jan said, when asked if she was alright. "Someone must have bathed in perfume, it was a bit much," she continued, then informed by Cathy…it was the *Maggie's* ***Chanel*** that was the culprit.

All had a good laugh and then enjoyed the cookies and fruit on the table. The four women chatted the balance of the evening discussing an array of topics from national politics to movies each saw and liked or disliked.

Nora was particularly pleased that Judy, had behaved herself. And the fact that Jan, had won the fifty-fifty drawing, meant everyone went home a winner. But most of all, Nora was deeply touched by the overwhelming support she had received from so many of the women. It gave her a sense of new energy in her match against Bill. Now, she wasn't fighting just for herself, but for all the women in the club. What Nora wasn't prepared for, is what appeared in Liz Peters' column the next day. Her cause would be catapulted beyond her expectations and would be the talk of Happy Hills.

CHAPTER 31
HAPPY HILLS GOES NATIONAL

"HOLY SMOKES!" Mike Grace bellowed, when he opened the newspaper the next morning as he and Tammy were having breakfast in their kitchen.

"What's the matter?" Tammy asked.

"Here!" Her husband motioned, pointing to the society section. "It's Liz Phillips column, see the headlines**. *'HAPPY HILLS' SIMON LEGREE."***

"Read it out loud." Tammy told him.

"Harriet Beecher Stowe's character, Simon Legree, in her famous novel, *UNCLE TOM'S CABIN***,** has turned out to be a real life character at the prestigious, or should I say, the infamous, Happy Hills Country Club in Huntington Village. It appears club president Mike Grace, is intent on labeling the wives of members as their country club…slaves."

Mike could feel his face grow hot. It was his firm belief that Nora, was behind the story. He was so infuriated, his thoughts rambled on different ways to dispose of her.

"It would be wrong for me to call the women of Happy Hills, club members," he read on, "because technically, they're not. They're *tag-a-long parts* of the equation. Their husbands names are in the club's directory and they're the one's who enjoy the full benefits of the club facilities. If a members spouse dies, **Mr. Simon Legree** and his board of cronies, vote on whether the spouse can remain a member.

Golf tee times are limited to the women of Happy Hills, who dress in a cramped locker room and have no access to breakfast, while their husbands enjoy the comforts of a spacious locker room and enjoy an array of breakfast choices in the men's grill.

But finally, one woman has said, **'ENOUGH IS ENOUGH.'** Nora Cummings, the women's club champion, has taken the barbaric rules of the fifty-year old country club head on, by challenging her male counterpart to a winner take all match. If she wins, the board of directors must pass resolutions equalizing all of the facilities in the club and the board must be represented by an equal number of women. But if this courageous woman loses, which will in all likelihood be the outcome, she must leave the Happy Hills Club.

Nora's challenge, has inspired several women of the club to declare a four day strike, granting no marital favors to their husbands as a protest to **Mr. Legree's,** cancellation of the annual women's member guest outing. Seems like the knuckle-biting husbands of Happy Hills, demanded that **Simon Legree,** immediately reinstate the event in order to bring heavenly bliss back to their homes.

Nora Cummings and the women at Happy Hills should call THE NATIONAL ORGANIZATION OF WOMEN, and have them show the board how women power can be demonstrated. Stay tuned, because this columnist intends to keep you updated on the latest happenings at ***UNHAPPY HILLS***. Oh yes, the match is scheduled for Saturday, August 8th and Sunday, the 9th. This is a must see!"

"That's wonderful, just wonderful!" Tammy exclaimed, when her husband had finished.

"Are you out of your mind woman!" Mike snarled, crumpling the page into a ball and throwing it on the floor. "We've been made the laughing stock of Long Island. That woman has brought the outside world into our club!" Mike shouted. **"Oh, Lord, why didn't you take her instead of Nick?"**

The board president paced the room, mumbling and swearing an oath. He would see to it, that Nora's days at the club would be numbered. He suddenly stopped, placing his hand on his chin, his expression now of an obsessed person who found the answer to a devious plan. Mike knew what he had to do.

CHAPTER 32
THE HILLS ARE RINGING

"SHARON, DID YOU SEE the Liz Peters' article?"

"Maggie, did you read the paper this morning?"

"Denise, did you see the article about Nora, in today's society page?"

The phones were abuzz, shattering the peace on this Sunday morning and Nora, would not be immune to the gossip.

"Nora, it's Cathy. Are you awake?"

"I am now," she said, looking at her clock radio? "Hey, do you realize it's only seven- thirty? If you're not dying, remind me to kill you when I see you." Nora snapped, hanging up the phone. She then punched the pillow into shape and attempted to resume her sleep, when the phone rang again. She picked up the receiver and muttered, "Why don't you make passionate love to Fred and leave me alone."

"Well, I don't know who's Fred, but I'm sure my husband would be upset if I did," said Tammy Grace. "I'm sorry to be calling you so early, but I thought you should be made aware of the Liz Peters article in today's paper."

"Oh, Tammy! I'm so sorry, I thought it was someone else calling. I haven't seen the paper as yet," she told her.

Tammy proceeded to read the article, with the result that Nora, was rendered speechless.

"My concern is that people are going to blame you for going public with this entire issue." Tammy suggested.

Her hand over her mouth, Nora was stunned. Her first emotion was that of anger, feeling she had made it perfectly clear to Liz Peters of not wanting to make her struggle public. Then, she had remembered Liz's response, the issue was already public. Perhaps, she thought, it would indeed help her cause as the reporter suggested. On the other hand, Nora didn't need the added distraction already created by her challenge to Bill. She felt Liz, was unfair in not running the story by her, but, then again...she knew Nora, would decline.

"You've been a supporter and it's been greatly appreciated." Nora said. "But I swear to you Tammy, I didn't give the information in the article to Liz. She approached me last night and wanted to meet me to do an interview, but I turned her down."

"I believe you, but be prepared to receive a lot of flack...because it's going to get nasty."

"Thank you for the heads up, Tammy. I know it's difficult for you in light of Mike...being the board president."

"Mike needs to accept the inevitable." Tammy declared. "He's just not ready to surrender on his watch."

As soon as Nora, concluded her conversation with Tammy, she called Cathy. "Why didn't you tell me about Liz Peters' article?" She demanded.

"I tried to darling, but remember...you hung up on me." Cathy snipped.

"You should have called back!"

"Why were you sleeping anyway? You're usually up at the crack of dawn."

"I was out last night. And don't ask with who...because it's none of you bees' wax."

"I'll bet I know anyway." Cathy hissed. "Did you give in to George? You didn't, did you?"

Nora hesitated, she wanted to keep Cathy hanging, even it were for a brief moment.

"It was just dinner and a movie," she told her, toying with her inquisitive nature.

"Oh girl! Have you gone crazy? **You're playing with fire!"** Cathy screeched.

"Drop it." Nora demanded, stringing Cathy along. "I need to talk to you about this article. Tammy called right after you did. She really thinks the fallout is going to hit the fan and I'm in the direct line of fire."

"I can understand why." Cathy said. "Everyone saw you talking to Liz last night."

"That's the problem." Nora said. "They're going to think I gave her the information for the article."

"What did you say to her?"

"She requested an interview and I told her I didn't want this to be a public issue."

"How did she respond?"

"She said it was already a public issue."

"Well, she had to have spoken to someone from the club, the details are too specific." Cathy snapped.

"But who?" Nora posed, placing her hand to he forehead.

"I think I can find out." Cathy told her. "Liz played in the member guest so it had to be the member who invited her or another person in the foursome."

"Hold on Cathy, I have a program listing the members and their guests. Here it is, let's see...Liz Peters played with...Sylvia Gibbs! The other twosome was, oh yes, it had to have been... Laura Dicks. She and her guest played with Sylvia. It had to be ditzy, Laura." Nora surmised.

"You have to inform Tammy." Cathy told her. "She has to remain an ally."

"But how can we be sure it wasn't Sylvia?" Nora asked. "Give her a couple of drinks too many and she could very well have spilled the beans."

"I hear what you're saying, but giving Tammy a different alternative, will have **her no good husband** thinking about someone other than you."

"Leave this to me." Tammy responded, when Nora called. "I'll make sure Mike, doesn't focus his wrath in one direction."

Nora was grateful for her help, yet wondered why Tammy, would stick her neck out for her? Was she like Nora, silent and passive to the inequities when Nick was alive, now coming out to fight for change? If she was, Nora thought, Tammy, would be a welcomed friend to the cause.

"We have to meet for lunch." Cathy said. "You're certainly making life around here interesting. How about one o'clock at the club?"

"I don't think it's a good idea to meet at the club. We're going to run into a lot of people who'll be asking questions."

"Nonsense girl, that's part of the fun. You may not know it, but you have the board right between a rock and a their *wishful* hard place." Cathy said, now immersing herself in the fray.

"What do you mean I have the board between the...what you said? Gosh you have such a way with words, Cathy?"

"That's why you love me so much. The board's going to be scared out of their wits about this. I'll bet they call you to propose a meeting, asking...no, *begging* you, to come to some sort of understanding just to keep the National Organization of Women from picketing the club. Nora, this is big time news. **The board have their gonads in a vice** and you're the one who can make them become squashed walnuts."

"I'm not looking to have NOW come to the club." Nora insisted.

"You and I know that, but the board doesn't and what they don't know is ammunition for negotiation."

"You're sure about this?" Nora asked, seemingly unconvinced.

"As sure as I can fake an organism, and believe me girl… I can do it with a smile and tell him that was the best one ever. `Oh, oh, Fred, you got the spot! Oh! Oh! Yes! Yes! Yes! Oh God!"

"What do you think, convincing enough?" Cathy giggled.

"You sick, sick puppy, you're absolutely shameful. I'll see you at one." Nora told her, hanging up and shaking her head.

Perhaps Cathy's relationship with Fred, was one big fraud, she thought to herself. Could her past infidelity with Bill, still be a resonating factor in her attitude towards her husband? Or, was Cathy, fighting ***the demon of guilt***, preventing her from the truth, that her marriage was doomed when she entered the Shady Lady Motel with Bill.

Nora showered, washing away her speculation, as she prepared to meet her friend and answer questions on the Liz Peters' article from the curiosity seekers at the club.

Meanwhile, the quiet Sunday morning which Mike and Tammy usually enjoyed, was being pierced by the constant phone calls from board members who were furious about Liz Peters' article, depicting Happy Hills as a biased country club.

Mike had only one ally in Bill Harper and that relationship was melting like an ice cube in the sun. But it was Bill, who suggested the emergency meeting to discuss the current crisis.

Having agreed one o'clock was the most likely time to get the members together, Mike and Bill divided the list and made the calls. Bill was diverting from his normal routine, preferring to be on the golf course this Sunday morning, rather than making calls to members from his home and disrupting potential plans of other members.

The mood was tense and the remarks about their board president never more hostile, as the members waited for him to appear. Meanwhile, in the dining room next door, the other subject of their wrath was preparing to have lunch with Cathy.

When Mike finally arrived, he was fully prepared to hear calls for his resignation, but hoping to stave off the assault with a plan to diffuse the current crisis. The board members came to a hushed silence. They were out for blood and waiting to spring at the first opportunity their prey slipped into their clutches, particularly Herb Blake, who felt he was blindsided by the board president.

"I want to thank everyone for coming to the meeting on a day that's supposed to be one of peace and relaxation with your families." Mike began. "We all know by now why the meeting was called. The Peters' article in today's paper was a jolt. What started out as an effort to maintain certain traditions at Happy Hills, has blown into an unwanted...public firestorm."

"You shouldn't have pushed Nora and the other women of the club so far, Mike." Herb bellowed, intent on drawing first blood from his rival.

"I'm not here to disagree with what should have or could have been done in the past." Mike assured him. "The real issue gentlemen, is what can be done to diffuse the situation so we can get back to business as usual?"

After his statement, Mike realized, he unintentionally provided an opening for his detractors. But the crafty fox, even at the worst of times, always had an ace up his sleeve.

"I think it's fairly obvious to us what the first order of business should be." Herb said. "And that's for you to resign as board president**."**

"Yes sir Mike! You have to resign!" An angry Gil Kelly, seconded the motion.

"Gentlemen!" Mike protested, holding up his hands. "Are we going to submit to the pressures of the media and the women of this club? I want you to think of the consequences of my resignation. The women will smell blood and demand full equality in our club. Your next board president would be seeing half of you in skirts asking why there aren't bagels at the halfway house, or suggest we change the color of the curtains in the dining room? Is that what you want?"

"No Mike." Herb said stiffly, his ambition ready to throw Mike to the wolves. "But perhaps we can get back to normal without surrendering. Your resignation would be a token gesture and a good first step in healing the damage you've caused."

"It's the logical way to go." Fred Daley agreed.

"Why don't we give Mike, a chance to explain his idea on how to make this mess go away?" Bill suggested.

"You're no help, Bill!" Herb told him. "You're as much to blame as Mike. You kept pushing Nora, until she went public and made us the laughing stock of Long Island...no, the entire country."

"Well there's where you're wrong!" Mike said angrily. "There's credible evidence, it wasn't Nora, who fed the information to Liz Peters. I have it on good authority...it was the wife of another board member who leaked the information."

"Is this another attempt to save your skin?" Herb insisted, about to be jolted by Mike's revelation.

"Well Herb, I think you had better sit down, because what I'm about to say will come as a shock to you and the other members." Mike said, with a wryly grin of an attorney about to expose the credibility of a hostile witness.

"When I saw the article, Nora was the first person to blame in my mind.

Then, I did some old fashion detective work. I looked at the member-guest pairings to see who had invited the Peters woman, and discovered…it was *Sylvia Gibbs* and *Laura Dicks*."

"WAIT JUST A MINUTE MIKE!" Bob Gibbs said, standing and pointing a finger at the board president. "You have some nerve accusing my wife…"

"Hold on Bob! Sit down and let me finish what I have to say!" Mike said forcibly, Herb approving the hostility towards the sly president.

"When Tammy called Sylvia and Laura, they claimed they hadn't mentioned a word to Peters. They did mention seeing Nora, talking to the columnist. When Tammy called Nora, she said Peters, requested an interview but she declined. Then Tammy, heard from a number of people, there was someone else who spoke to the reporter, someone who was a bit tipsy and may have been Peters' source."

Mike paused, reaching for a glass of water and took a long satisfying drink before continuing, adding to the suspense hushed room. He slammed the empty glass down…then…

"IT WAS YOUR WIFE, HERB! It was Marion, who spilled the beans to Peters."

"That's a damn lie!" Herb said, standing, then kicking his chair with such force that it hurled backwards, rolling end over end. "This is another attempt to deflect your own incompetence, Mike. For you to stoop so low is a disgrace to the members of this board."

"Call your wife Herb and ask her!" Mike demanded, holding out his cell phone. "If I'm wrong, I'll apologize to you and the other members and resign on the spot."

Herb stared at the cell phone for what seemed like an eternity, contemplating the challenge. He assumed Mike, wouldn't have made the challenge if it weren't true and Marion, was indeed the offender. Finally, shoulders hunched, he turned and walked out of the boardroom without comment. It couldn't have been clearer, Herb was a man, who knew his days as an effective board member…were over.

Mike however, was aware he wasn't out of the woods just yet. The other board members still needed to be convinced his leadership in this crisis was needed.

"It's upsetting for me to be in the position to hurt a fellow board member," he said in a conciliatory voice. "But…our mission today is to solve a problem."

"Simply discovering, Marion leaked the story to Peters, still doesn't resolve the image of us created by the press." Fred cried out. "We have the responsibility of fixing the current problem and frankly…I don't know how it can be accomplished with you remaining as board president."

"I believe you're right Fred." Mike said. "Resolving the problem should be our first responsibility. But having me resign is not the answer. In my opinion, it would hinder rather than help resolve the issue."

"How do you figure, Mike?" Ralph asked.

"Let me explain. What's the article by Liz Peters inferring? That the women here at Happy Hills are not equal to the men? Well, they're right! Is that what we want at the club. Ralph, let me ask you a question. Do you want women to have equal access to the men's grill? Think about what it would mean. It's an end to off color jokes, cursing out an umpire or just rubbing your crotch when you have an itch."

"Of course not!" Ralph replied, slapping another member on the arm, then sipping his beer.

"And you Gil Kelly." Mike continued. "Do you want equal tee times for women so you can labor behind a couple of their foursomes any day, any time, including the weekends? How does four and a half or five hour rounds instead of our usual three and a half to four sound to you?"

"Not so good. " Gil admitted.

"And you, Fred." Mike continued. "Are you ready to go to the full membership and propose assessing them a few thousand dollars extra per year for five years or more in order to provide equal facilities for the women? Because you know as well as I do, if we did, it would cost us millions?"

"Maybe that's what we need to do to make the problem go away." Fred scoffed.

"Well, I'm here to tell you…if that's your solution, not only will I resign as board president, but I'll resign from the club and I suspect several other resignations will follow." Mike said, puffing out his chest defiantly. "This club was established as a men's club fifty years ago and if you polled the membership, their answer would be the same as mine. Then see, if the remaining members are willing to pay the extra freight caused by reduced membership."

Fred wasn't a supporter of Mike**,** but he had to admit, what he was saying made a lot of sense. The membership WOULD be depleted, if the men found themselves facing the prospect of a gender-neutral club and significant increases in dues and assessments. He could see by the way the members were looking at Mike, they were ready to be persuaded.

"What I'm proposing…is we cut the head of the problem off and like the body of the chicken…the problem will eventually die."

"Give me the axe, Mike!" Fred volunteered. "Just tell me where you want us to send your head?"

Fred's gesture, visibly relieved the tension in the room.

"Very funny, Fred. But do you promise to run after the rest of my body so Tammy, can have an open casket?" Mike joked, the room now being skillfully orchestrated by the sly president.

"Mike, at your current weight, I won't have to run too far." Fred said, enjoying the playful jousting, the other board members, now well positioned for ***El Presidente.***

"Well Fred, you're no light weight yourself!" Mike shot back.

"Tou-che` Mike. Now, how about explaining your chicken dance? The opening act was good, but not enough."

Mike had his audiences' full attention. Fred unsuspectingly, delivered the sheep to the board president.

"The women at the club want peace and quiet as we do," he began. "If we give them some crumbs, they'll soon forget about Liz Peters and things will get back to normal."

"What kind of crumbs are we talking about?" Bill asked, in a skeptical tone.

"I propose we use the olive branch approach." Mike replied. "We ask Nora, the head of our chicken, to meet with the board so we can clear the air. Then, we make some changes to give the appearance they've won something for their efforts. Let's say, we make bagels and rolls available at the halfway house **every** morning, we renovate their locker room and offer more tee times. They'll pick up the crumbs and Happy Hills will be ours again."

"Mike, how do we know this will work? Your other ideas were a disaster. First you squeezed Nora, then the maid service idea bombed and exploded in our faces, and now...you're asking us to trust you again."

The grin on Mike's face, concealed his contempt when pressed by Fred. First Herb, now, another Judas. Mike puffed on his cigar, while his calculating mind worked in overdrive. "I admit to underestimating the situation." Mike told them. "But this time, the entire board will immediately know if my plan works. Once we meet with Nora, you'll have your answer. **If she rejects the olive branch, I'll resign immediately,"** he pledged.

"What about Peters?" Bob asked. "How do you propose to make her go away now that she's got her hands on a story?"

"Bob, if no one else talks, she'll have nothing to write about and will move on."

"What do we do, if the *National Organization of Women* shows up?" Bob persisted.

"I believe if we make our women happy and Nora is on board, NOW won't be welcomed at Happy Hills."

"Mike, I think it would be a good idea, if you grabbed a drink at the bar so we can discuss your proposal." Fred told the board president. "We'll call you when we're ready."

He was being dismissed and Mike, didn't like it one bit. He glared at Fred, as he left the boardroom. It was apparent to him, that Fred, would push the other board members to remove him as president. But the sly fox...had a plan.

Cathy entered the dining room and saw Nora, sitting at a table, staring aimlessly out a window overlooking the golf course. Nora was wearing an emerald green blouse, accented with a strand of white pearls, matching her white Capri's. "Penny for your thoughts?" She said, startling her friend.

"Oh, Cathy, I didn't see you coming."

"How could you?" Chuckling. "You were too busy looking for Bill Harper to come running down the course, pleading to be easy on him."

"Cathy, you're really a sick person, and what's with the teeny-bopper look?" Nora, referring to her friends white blouse, checkered mini-skirt and yellow sneakers.

"You're the sick puppy!" Cathy hissed, slipping onto a seat opposite her friend. **"So you went and did it, didn't you?"**

"Did what?" Nora asked, after they ordered a glass of Chardonnay.

"You know what I'm talking about. Don't play coy with me, Nora Cummings. I know you better then you know yourself." Cathy hissed.

"Oh, are you talking about my dinner...with George?" Nora asked, coy as ever.

"No, your dinner with Brad Pitt. I understand Angelina, got tired of him and threw him out the door and you just happened to be walking by. Of course I'm talking about, George." Cathy scoffed. "Stop playing with me and give me the details."

"It was just a dinner." Nora said, biting off a piece of celery and smiling.

"Sure it was. Tell me about the main course...did you sleep with old George or didn't you?" Cathy barked, as curious as ever and losing patience with her friend.

"What do you mean old George? He's not that old." Nora said, sipping on her wine.

"Son-of-bitch, Nora. **You slept with the old bastard!** And on the first date!"

"You're assuming a lot...and keep your voice down." Nora demanded, blushing, turning to see if others had heard her friends outburst.

"Are you serious? Your complexion is the color of a *jelly apple*! What's the matter? Couldn't you find the old buzzards, *Wee-Wee?"* Cathy jabbed.

"Cathy! That's cruel, and besides...he's bigger than you think!" Nora giggled.

"So you did sleep with him!" Cathy howled.

"Keep your voice down, do you want to announce it to the whole club?"

Sparring with Cathy, was pure enjoyment for Nora, as she delighted in seeing her friend squirm for the lurid details of her assumed liaison with George. She had every intention of savoring the moment.

"How could you?" Cathy insisted. **"It was supposed to be *hands off* lessons."**

"Stop it Cathy! A woman has needs you know."

"So you were horny, I can understand that, but...with George? The man eats *oatmeal* at breakfast," for God sakes.

"He's an appealing man." Nora told her. "You don't have to make a joke out of everything...and by the way, I eat *oatmeal* for breakfast."

"Yes, but you have all of your teeth, now tell me the juicy details. When did he ask you out? What did you say? Scratch that, obviously you said yes... and to more than a date! What movie did you see, or did you eat first? I want it all and don't leave anything out. So...what are you waiting for? Tell me."

The waiter arrived with their second drink, this time a martini. Nora, stirred her finger against one of the three olives, then taking a long sip of her drink, silently tormenting her friend before beginning her tale.

"As you remember, George had asked me out once before and I turned him down. I told him I wanted to focus on the match. When he asked if he should try again, I told him he wouldn't know until he asked. Well, he didn't wait too long to test the waters, so I thought about it and said to myself, why not. He was like a schoolboy when I said yes. He asked me what I said and I repeated, I would go out with him, but...on one condition."

"That he take a *Viagra* before he picked you up?" Cathy interrupted, "Okay, okay, don't look at me like that. I'm sorry, continue."

"Well, George picked me up at the house for a six o'clock movie. We saw *Perfect Strangers* with Susan Sarandon. She lost her husband in 9/11 and after some prodding from friends, she attends a grieving conference where she meets her perfect stranger. It was a real love story, a lot of tissues kind of movie."

"Sounds like it was a pre-lubrication job by an *old fox* who really knows what he's doing." Cathy scoffed.

"Would you please...stop referring to George...as old!"

"Okay, he's a teenager and you couldn't wait to tear his clothes off."

"You know, you're insufferable."

"Yeah, yeah and I love you too. So go on."

"Well, after the movie...we had dinner at *Gino's* and he took me home."

"Is that where you made it with him, in your home? Don't you pay him enough for a room at a hotel?" Cathy scorned, leaning forward, her expression perplexed at the thought.

"No Cathy, he took me home, kissed me on the cheek and said...`Good night."

"What happened to the woman who had needs and just told me, he's bigger than I might think?" Cathy asked, her arms extended, palms up and with an animated expression.

"Oh, do you mean..."Yes! Yes! You've got the spot George, don't stop! Oh, George, that was the best one yet?" Nora, mimicking her friend, then biting down on an olive with a raised eyebrow and grin, indicating her satisfaction in knowing she had gotten the best of Cathy.

"Why you...no...good...dirty dog!" Cathy yelped, eyes peering. "How could you do that to me, breaking my shoes like that?"

"**TIT FOR TAT!"** Nora told her. "If you can't take it, don't dish it out. Did you really think I would sleep with him on a first date?"

"Why not, you harlot? It's 2007 not 1907. Oh, I could just strangle you, Nora Cummings."

"Yes! Yes! Yes! You got the spot honey." Nora continuing the playful teasing of her friend.

"Alright, you've killed me already, save the other five bullets in the chamber."

"I'm savoring this Cathy. It's not too often I get a chance to turn the tables on you." Nora gleamed.

"Just when I thought I had an advantage over you...I lose it." Cathy said, ruefully. "Well, our glasses aren't empty, so you might as well tell me the rest of it."

"There's nothing to tell. It was a pleasant evening. He asked if he could call again and I told him, `Honey, with a manhood like yours, how could a girl refuse." Nora continuing to enjoy her ruse, as Cathy peered at her, twitching her head in distain.

"Go ahead, have your fun. But remember, payback is a bitch...and it'll happen when you least expect it."

As they were leaving the dining room, someone called out to Nora, from the men's grill.

"I wonder what he wants?" Nora said in a low voice, as he came toward them in his beige pants and black golf shirt, collar turned up.

"Beware of the devil bearing gifts." Cathy warned.

"Hello." Mike greeted the two women with a contrived smile. "Nora, can I have a word with you in private?"

Cathy raised her eyebrows, but to Nora's considerable relief, left without comment.

"Let's sit at one of the tables in the dining room." Mike suggested. "It will give us more privacy. As they started towards the dining room, the board president reached for Nora's arm.

"Please, excuse me for just a moment. I want to inform my secretary we'll be sitting over there in the corner, just in case I'm needed."

Nora smiled and proceeded to the table, her curiosity in overdrive.

When her Nick was alive, he warned her, and not in pleasant terms, never to trust the crafty president. What did he want? Was this a chance meeting or did Mike, have a specific agenda? She was guarded and for good reason.

"Nora, I need your help." Mike began, when he retuned, ***ten minutes later***. "Let me ask you a question dear. Before all of this nonsense with Bill, were you happy being a member of the club?"

"Why do you ask?" Nora cautiously replied. The question, so unexpected, she was taken aback, but had no intention of letting him know he had caught her off guard.

"When Nick passed away, did you know I was the deciding vote to maintain your membership?"

That too came as a surprise, since she had always thought, Mike and Bill, had voted against her remaining as a member.

"I had no idea Mike." Nora said, maintaining her defensive posture with the crafty president.

"Nora, do you like it here?"

"I do, but as you know, I'd like to see some positive changes made at the club."

"I think you and I can work together to bring about change, making our club a better place for all of the members," he told her. "But, without outside interference. The fact remains, if the club is subjected to unwanted notoriety and outside pressure in an attempt to make Happy Hills gender neutral, I can assure you…the result will be mass resignations."

"Given the attitude of the men, I expect it would." Nora agreed. "What changes did you have in mind?"

"The match with Bill, is the foremost issue and I'm not suggesting to call it off. But what I am advising…is that the terms of the bet be changed."

"What do you mean by a change in the bet?" Nora asked, sitting back in her chair.

"No one wants to see you leave the club." Mike said in a conciliatory tone.

"You may think…Bill does, but he's just a pigheaded fool who sees women in a different light than you and me. I imagine it's why he's still single."

Nora was amused. Mike was suddenly aligning himself with her, bad mouthing his so-called friend. She wondered what was up his sleeve, which made her more guarded with him.

"What I'm proposing…is that the match becomes an annual event at the club. It would take place after the men and women's championship. I truly believe it would attract a good deal of membership interest, sort of a world series golf. What do you think of the idea? You know I value your opinion."

"It's an intriguing idea," she told him. "But what if I beat Bill? We had a bet on making the club gender neutral, with women elected to the board if I won?"

"Let me explain the changes that I'm proposing and I think you'll agree, they'll be real improvements as far as the women are concerned. **First**, we'll construct a lady's grill room so they can have access to the same breakfast and lunch as do the men. **Second**, we'll expand the women's locker room. **Third,** they'll be equal tee times for all golfers. Nora, this is a compromise in which everyone wins, something I've learned as an attorney if you want to achieve progress."

"What about women on the board?" Nora deciding to press her apparent advantage, knowing Mike, wouldn't have proposed such radical changes without first consulting with the other board members. She sensed the board feared the publicity and the possibility of NOW making their presence felt. The proposed changes were monumental and Nora, recognized it would change the complexity of the club in favor of the women. She felt a sense of exhilaration. Her efforts and that of her supporters, would result in a new environment and…**her exoneration.**

"Nora, I could lie to you and say that will happen immediately, but the fact is…I can't sell it to the board right now. Maybe somewhere down the line it will become a reality, but I wouldn't hold my breath on that one. First let the proposed changes take place. I'm sure you'll agree, they're significant."

Nora appreciated the honest answer given by Mike and would have been suspicious if he agreed to all of her agenda. But…did the board president, who swore to rid the club of his antagonist, lull her to a pre-planned position, the consequences of which would place Nora, in an unenviable situation.

Mike had no intension of surrendering to Nora and her supporters. Not while he was board president. The *tete-a-tete* with her had a purpose. She was simply a pawn in his grand scheme to maintain control of the board and put things right at the club.

"How are you going to convince Bill, to go along with the change?" Nora asked, unaware Mike, was playing her like a puppeteer pulling the strings.

"I'm sure you heard, that he's on the hook for bond refunds to those members who choose to leave the club…in the event you do beat him, and I can assure you…many will. The board has already calculated a membership exodus of thirty percent or more if Bill…does lose. Obviously, it will create a financial strain on the remaining membership in dues and assessments. Nora, if we're to save this club, it has to be with compromise for the welfare of the entire membership."

Nora moved forward in her chair and pondered Mike's proposal. She didn't want the club to suffer, yet, the decision to go along with Mike's plan had just been placed on her shoulders and hers alone.

"Can I sleep on this?" Nora asked him. "I want to get some feedback from the other women of the club."

"I'm afraid we don't have the luxury of time," he told her. "The board is in session right now deciding on the fate of the club. They're some rebels in there who can't see the forest through the trees. We have two choices. This thing can be resolved rationally by responsible individuals, or left up to those who have threatened to fight this regardless of the consequences. Nora, I don't want to see the club ruined and I know you don't. I need your help to bring this issue to closure?" Mike said, embracing Nora's hand, his head tilted to the side in a pleading expression, but one of calculating deception.

Nora, gently released her hand from his, but was impressed by Mike's conciliatory approach. But experience had taught her not to blindly trust him, a man with his own agenda. His proposed changes would make club life significantly better for women, but she wondered if he could pull it off with the other board members. If the changes were made, who would fault her to agree on a compromise for the betterment of the club? She found herself wishing Cathy were here, to help her make a decision.

"Well, Nora?" Mike pressed. "Can I count on your support?"

"Is the board willing to put the improvements you're proposing in writing?"

"I can guarantee that. But you'll have to assure the board if Liz Peters, NOW, or if any other organization contacts you volunteering their services, or requesting an interview, you'll decline."

"I can live with that. But the horse is kind of out of the barn. I can't stop Liz Peters from writing what she wants, or keep NOW or the public from attending the match."

"But if the dynamics of the match change, interest will wane, that's the important thing." Mike assured her.

She wasn't afraid to make decisions affecting her personal life, but, this would have an impact on *all-of-the-women* in the club. There would be criticism if she agreed or disagreed with the proposal, but, which one…would rally the most support?

"Okay Mike. I'll go along," she said. "But if you or the board fail to keep any of the changes, all bets are off."

"Good!" Mike said, not bothering to hide his relief. "We'll keep our promises and to show good faith, I want you to do something never done before. Go into the boardroom with me so they can hear what you and I have accomplished."

Nora was reticent to do what he was asking, yet, her skepticism was overshadowed in wanting to see Bill's face when Mike, announced the agreement. It would also validate her decision by seeing first hand the board's reaction to the proposal.

"Nora, I'm going to ask you to wait in the lobby so I can prime the board's pump before I call you in." Mike said, then entering the board room.

"We're not finished yet!" Fred scowled, his face contorted with distain.

"I'm here because I think I can be of help in determining your decision," he told them.

"I'm afraid you're out of order." Fred said, angrily pointing his finger. "We won't be strong armed by you!" Snarled the determined adversary.

The other members supported Fred's firm handling of the intrusion, many shaking their heads, mumbling their distain for Mike.

"What if I told you, I have Nora Cummings sitting in the lobby, ready to give her full cooperation in making all of our problems disappear?" Mike snapped.

"I'd say you've had a few too many." Fred told him, drawing laughter from the others in the room.

"I'm dead serious, Fred!" Mike barked.

"What did you do Mike, drug her?" Bill asked with sarcasm, his support of the president waning.

"You of all people should listen to what I have to say." Mike demanded. "Because I just got you off the hook to reimburse those members who decide to leave, if by chance, you should lose to Nora. Oh!...I do think I have your attention now, haven't I?" He added, as Bill, sat up straighter in his chair.

"Whether I'm your president or not, this club will still face the music with Liz Peters, NOW and any other person or organization who wants to make us the laughing stock of Long Island with their headlines," the puppeteer went on. "We now have the opportunity to make this all go away with little effort. Do you want to hear how?"

"We're listening." Bill replied. "Go ahead."

"Hey, that's not so bad." Gil said, when Mike, explained what he had promised to Nora.

"Have you calculated the cost of those physical improvements?" Fred said with sarcasm.

"Have you calculated the costs if we don't?" Mike shot back.

"Fred, the proposal makes a lot of sense to me." Bob said, after which everyone agreed except Fred, who clearly saw himself as Mike's remaining opponent.

"Before he barged...in here, we agreed to remove him as board president for the betterment of our club. And now, you've changed your mind? Don't you guys realize he'd do anything to save his bacon?" Fred said, clearly still disgruntled.

"Give it a break, Fred!" Ralph demanded. "The man just saved our club from imploding. If that's a scheme...then I'm all for the man and the plan."

"Okay Mike." Fred said, not bothering to hide the fact he was skeptical. "Bring Nora in...so the board can hear it from her."

"Not so fast!" Mike bellowed. "I have some terms I want to get on the table."

"I knew it!" Fred muttered. "Here it comes, guys."

"Fred, will you button it up for a minute." Bill told him. "Let's hear what he has to say. Go ahead, Mike."

"First, we cannot renege on our promises, which will have to be in writing. **Second,** no more talk of removing me from office until my term expires and I want that in writing. The most important provision concerns you, Bill. **You have to zipper it up** with Nora, until this crisis is over. You'll get your sweet revenge by kicking her butt in the match, agreed?" He asked, looking directly at Bill and then the other board members...with his palms up.

"She's such a cocky pain in the ass." Bill grumbled. "She deserves anything I can dish out.

"Buster, I just saved you a lot of dough." Mike reminded him. "I don't like the bitch either, but if this will save our club...then so be it. Agreed, Bill?"

"Agreed." Bill said, reluctantly acquiescing.

"Alright then. Now, I want everyone to applaud with gusto. I want that bimbo to hear we're all in agreement. Let's go, applaud. Louder! Now let me hear you say, 'Good job, Mike."

They followed the puppeteers command with enthusiasm, all except one.

"Now let me get her in here so we can put this thing behind us." Mike told them, going to the door.

It was a long day, as Nora's eyes struggled to stay open. She imagined a warm bath soothing her body while sipping on a glass of wine. She peeked at her watch, just then, she heard…

"Nora dear, thank you for being so forbearing." Mike said with a trusting smile. "The pump is primed and ready to go."

"I heard," she said. "It sounded like a political convention in there." And smiling, she followed him into the boardroom, her eyes making contact… with Bill Harper.

Nora's position towards Bill, was still somewhat confusing, not able to understand the conflict between the two by day and yet…the un-explicable passion she shared with him in her nightly dreams. Her answer…would be forthcoming.

CHAPTER 33
TWO OF A KIND

AN HOUR LATER, all of the board members had left the meeting. But Mike, asked Bill, to remain behind. He reviewed the plan with him, one which would cleverly negate all of the promises he assured Nora and approved by the board members.

"Are you sure about this?" Bill asked, pushing back his chair and stretching his legs. "If it doesn't work, it'll blow up in our faces."

"One of the advantages of being a criminal attorney is you meet some very savvy people who find themselves in awkward situations." Mike told him. "The guy who gave me the idea, tried it in a similar situation as the one we're in with Nora. Believe me, timing and secrecy are the keys."

"How are you going to handle this with the other board members?" Bill asked.

"With the exception of Fred, they'll be delighted to know our club achieved a status quo, that everything will remain the same and we'll be back to normal."

"What if Fred, doesn't play ball?"

"Let me handle, Fred. I have something on his wife that will keep him in line."

"Want to share it with me?" Bill said frowning, as it occurred to him if Mike, was thinking in terms of blackmail, his fling with Cathy, might be exposed. "Does this have anything to do with me?"

"Don't fret about this. "Mike told him. "It probably won't come down to using the information unless Fred, decides to be stupid. Do you remember what you told me about Herb's wife, Marion?"

"You mean the rumor she had a one night stand with one of the young caddies some years ago and another member more recently?" Bill asked.

"Rumor?" Mike said with a grin. "Tammy didn't get the information from Marion, I did. All I needed was to threaten to expose her escapade to her husband. She had a choice of being a loudmouth in Herb's eyes, or a cheat, she chose the former."

"She's protecting someone else." Bill told him. "She certainly couldn't have named me. I'm not that desperate and besides...she's uglier than sin."

"Not directly, but who cares if she used you to flatter herself. It gave me the information I needed."

"You know Mike, you're a *perverted dog.*" Bill said, with a touch of admiration in his voice.

"This *perverted dog* always likes to have an ace up his sleeve. All of this planning will go down the tubes if you happen to lose to the bitch."

"It can't happen, not unless I break a leg during the match." Bill said in a sarcastic tone.

"Sweet Jesus." Mike said, rubbing his hands together. "I can't wait to see Nora's face when she loses the match and the agreement on the same day. You just know she's going to spread the word that she forced our hand and we conceded to making the improvements for the women."

"What if she goes to Peters or NOW, after she realizes...she was duped?"

"She'll be the laughing stock of the club when she pulls out the so-called agreement and sees nothing but blank papers." Mike told Bill, with a wide grin. "As far as her going to Peters and NOW, they'll consider it sour grapes from the loser of the match."

"I didn't think about that, but it does makes sense." Bill admitted. "But can we hold her off that long? The match isn't for another week."

"I'll just tell her we're still in the process of getting bids from the jobbers and we should have the agreement before the match, but we won't give it to her until an hour beforehand." Mike said.

"That's cutting it kind of close, don't you think?"

"Bill, it's a three-page document. It'll take her less than five minutes to read it."

"What if she insists on making copies?"

"Do I sense some doubt about this?"

"You're the attorney." Bill told him. "I hope this doesn't came back to bite us."

The plan was froth with danger. Bill was now questioning Mike's judgment as well as his own, perhaps clouded in order to save face before the members. The price could be too high and not just monetarily.

"Stop worrying," he told Bill. "I'll tell her the copy machine is down and give her the original to hold until the match is over. But she must promise not to show it to anyone, so we can make the announcement together after the match to show good fellowship. After you kick her butt and she asks where the announcement will take place, I'll simply say, `What announcement?` I'd love to have a picture of the expression on her face when she pulls out the so-called agreement and sees just three blank pieces of paper. We could hang a shot like that on a wall, so any future women with aspirations of turning our club into a gender-neutral freak show will think twice about it."

The grinning president chomped down on his cigar, Bill, peering at him, still questioning the soundness of his plan and the possible legal ramifications which would affect him far more than Mike.

"You should have been in politics, Mike." Bill told him in an unflattering tone. Although he had his doubts, Bill continued his support for the club president, but was prepared to go his separate way in the event Mike, went too far...his plan unique, but more likened to a CIA cloak and dagger approach.

Outwardly, Bill continued to show his distain of Nora and her attempt to attain parity for women at the club, but privately, he admired her guile and feisty personality. She was a conquest not yet conquered, her beauty as alluring as no other at Happy Hills. He masked his lustful feelings for Nora, through carefully choreographed opportunities, but in truth...he wanted her.

CHAPTER 34
BREAKFAST AT CATHY'S

IT WAS A RAINY Monday morning and practice with George was cancelled, giving Nora, another day for the blister on her hand to mend. She was reading the morning paper and sipping coffee when the telephone rang.

"What did the weasel want?" Cathy snapped.

"Invite me to breakfast and I'll fill you in on the juicy details."

"You're invited, now get your skinny ass over here, I'm hungry."

"Do you need anything?"

"Are you still talking? Leave." Cathy snipped.

"Alright, I'm coming."

"You're still talking."

"Do you need anything!" Nora insisted.

"Still talking?" Cathy said, abruptly hanging up.

Nora just shook her head, sensing her friend was in a fowl mood. Perhaps she had an argument with Fred, she thought, as she closed the door to her home, stopping at the bakery before arriving at Cathy's.

"What are you smiling about so early in the morning? Hurry in and get out of the rain." Cathy said, still dressed in her robe.

"I see you got all spruced up for me." Nora said dryly, suspecting something was amiss.

"If you're not comfortable, I do have a spare robe?" Cathy snipped.

"Aren't we in a good mood this morning?"

"Don't start with me, Nora. My so called friend is making me miserable this morning. I don't know who the ass-hole was labeling it as a friend, but if I ever find him...and I say him because no woman would ever call it a friend...I'd hit him with an eight iron right between his petunias! Then...let's see if he calls **them** his friend."

"What a day I picked to have breakfast with my friend. I do mean me, not your"…Nora started, but giggled trying to be uplifting with Cathy.

"Oh please! I don't understand why the guy upstairs didn't turn the tables on men, just once or twice a year? He had a mother, he should understand."

"He knew men couldn't handle the mess. Nick's legs became jelly at the sight of blood. I remember the time I cut my finger chopping lettuce. I asked Nick, to get me a band-aid and peroxide. When he came to the kitchen and saw all of the blood in the sink, he nearly passed out."

"Yeah, but when they're horny, blood or guts, they have convenient blinders." Cathy snapped.

"Help yourself to the coffee," she suggested, as they walked into the kitchen. "Did you bring anything interesting?"

"Bagels and some pastries." Nora told her, pouring herself a cup of coffee and buttering a bagel. Cathy joined her, munching on a cheese danish, sipping her coffee between bites.

"Is Fred home?"

"No, why? Do you want the miserable twerp?" Cathy said, turning her head towards the window.

"What's going on with you two?"

"I asked the man a simple question about the board meeting yesterday and he gives me some crap he can't discuss it with me because of some archaic rule of secrecy." Cathy replied, waving her hand high above her head and raising her eyebrows.

"I told him there's no secrets between a husband and a wife. You know I had to keep a straight face on that one." Cathy suggested.

"Yes, I know. 'Oh, you got the spot.' Yes! Yes! Don't stop!" Nora giggled.

"You're not letting go of that, are you?" Cathy muttered. "Come on, let's go in the family room."

It was a cozy retreat, a fireplace on one wall and French doors opening to the pool on another. Two floral couches surrounded a glass coffee table trimmed in oak.

"So, what went on with Mike, yesterday?" Cathy asked, curling up on the couch with a pillow between her arms.

"You haven't answered my question about you and Fred." Nora reminded her.

"I thought I did?"

"No, that was Cathy, trying to throw Nora, off the subject. Come on, spit it out. I can see something's bothering you." And then, following the direction of Cathy's eyes. **"Oh, no,** not the pool boy. He can't be more than twenty-five." Nora scoffed.

"Hey, I'm only thirty-eight. Who said women can't do the same as men and go for younger blood? Besides, life gets stale. Sex with your husband becomes like eating hamburger every day, there's no change in the menu. Fred's naked, I'm naked and that's it. It's like two squirrels hurrying so they can get back to burying their nuts for the winter. Didn't you ever feel that way with Nick?"

"Of course, every couple experiences low points, but you can always work it out if you care enough to make the effort. Add some variety to the menu. Dress-up like a cheerleader, nurse or just a plain old slut, and when he comes home from work, they'll you'll be, one of his fantasies come true."

"It doesn't sound like much of a come on to me." Cathy said, lowering her chin to the pillow.

"You'll never know unless you try it…will you?"

"What about our fantasies?" Cathy insisted. "Did you get Nick to play the game for you?"

"When he saw I was trying to please him, he wanted to do the same. Sometimes he'd hire a chef to cook a candlelight dinner for us at home."

"Take a look at that body out there." Cathy interrupted. "How can Fred bring that to my bed? I'd hire him as my chef anytime, even if he only cooked *cornflakes*!"

"Cathy, we all get old." Nora said. "But if you love someone, you never see their imperfections."

It was a poignant moment and Nora felt a halo of tears spring to her eyes.

"You miss Nick, don't you? I can still see your pain." Cathy said, regretting she opened old wounds for her friend, remembering the heartbreaking call from Nora.

"We had a great life together, as short as it was." Nora said in a low tone, reaching for a tissue. The painful reminder of Nick's death struck at the core of her essence. She had always kept her memories of him in her heart, locked away in the privacy of her soul. Their love was special, a one time romance she would cherish for eternity.

"Well, I'll give it a try." Cathy said. "But do me a favor? Close the drapes, so I won't have to look at that young *Adonis* out there. Now, I've confessed my sins. Tell me, what the hell did Mike, want with you yesterday?"

Nora gave all of the details to her friend, acknowledging her prediction that Mike, the board, or both, would be desperate to seek a solution with Nora, avoiding the public scrutiny of Liz Peters and NOW. She also expressed her trepidations in making the decision of their proposal to resolve the issue on her own.

"How I wished you were there to help me, because I'm not sure I did the right thing in agreeing to go along with him. And I didn't like the way Bill, smiled at me in the boardroom."

"It seems like you've accomplished everything you wanted without the risk of leaving the club when you lose to Bill." Cathy said casually and in a matter of fact certainty.

"What do you mean when I lose to Bill?" Nora huffed.

"No offense friend, but he's very good."

"In bed, or on the golf course?" Nora snipped, fed up with Cathy, depleting her chances.

"Both, if you want the truth!" Cathy responded, now standing, hands on hips. "And frankly, I'm tired of your insinuations."

"You don't know how to spell the word "truth" much less tell it!" Nora blurted. It wasn't often she and Cathy quarreled, when they did, she always felt miserable afterward. But at times, Cathy went too far.

"Oh, the one who just happened to hit the ball by accident that almost gave Bill, **'a third nut,'** your quote, not mine, or was it because you were trying to prove a point?"

"What point?" Nora snapped. "And by the way, it was your quote, not mine. You're the one whose always interested in my business."

"Whatever!"

"What do you mean, I was trying to prove a point?"

"That you think you're just as good as any man!" Cathy snarled.

"Why…why…you hussy you!" A flustered Nora, blurted out.

"Lesbian!" Cathy, snapped back.

"Lesbian?"

"I couldn't think of anything else," said a snooty, Cathy.

"I'm leaving! You don't need me anymore, not with pretty boy out there to keep you company. I hope he can measure up to Bill Harper."

"At least I have something to compare him to!" Cathy cried out. "Give my regards to **old George**…while you're at it. And open those damn drapes before you go!"

Nora stormed out of the house. She was upset with her friend, particularly with her cavalier approach to her relationship with Fred. At least she had a husband, someone to share her life with. Nora was bitter, not towards Cathy, but fate, that it took Nick from her life. And, that wasn't all of it. She was appalled at the thought, that her friend had an affair with the one man, she privately found challenging and who stimulated her voyeuristic dreams. How would she resolve this conflict?

CHAPTER 35
PRACTICE DAY FIFTEEN

IT WAS A CRISP Tuesday morning when Nora, still smarting from her argument with Cathy, met George, for the day's practice. Neither called the other that evening, which had made for a sleepless night.

"Tough night last night?" Asked the pro, after Nora hit her seven iron poorly for the third time. "Want to talk about it?"

"No, I'd rather not."

"Well, it's affecting your practice," he told her, trying to get her to focus.

"It doesn't make a difference any more." Nora told him. "I've made a deal with the board, win or lose…I get to stay and the women at the club get meaningful concessions."

She had promised Mike, not to reveal the agreement, but Nora, thought George, deserved an explanation for her lackadaisical practice. He wouldn't be the only person she would reveal the agreement to…as Mike, had predicted to Bill.

"Are you telling me now you don't care if you win or lose?" George demanded.

"What I'm saying is…the pressure is off me to win." Nora said, rather impatiently. "I suppose I shouldn't have told you but…"

"When I took you on, I saw a real challenge by a gutsy woman." George interrupted. "Now…all I see is a quitter!"

"George, please." Nora placing her hand on his arm. "I had a terrible fight with my best friend last night. Don't pay attention to what you see or hear from me today. Haven't you had your bad days?"

Nora had taken her bad temperament out on George, who was, she knew, fond of her. Perhaps too fond.

"Please," she implored the suitor.

"Okay," he told her, with a submissive look in his eyes. "But please, no more talk about losing to Harper. I wanted to smack the guy the first time he called me Georgee. Agreed?"

"Agreed." Nora said, gratefully. Her determination to win her match against Bill, was tested. But, George's pep talk was all the spark she needed to remind her, that others were counting on her. She had to give it her all. But would other conflicts arise which would test her resolve to press on?

CHAPTER 36
RECONCILIATION

"FRIENDS MAY BE MAD yesterday, friends may be sad today, but true friends are never mad or sad tomorrow." Nora said, cradling the phone close to her ear. "Sound familiar?"

"Fifth grade in the school yard." Cathy told her. "You pricked my finger and yours and we put them together. It was our first day as blood sisters. We had to swear out loud to always live by that motto."

"Well, today is tomorrow." Nora said. "What do you want to do?"

"You wouldn't believe me if I told you."

"Try me." Nora dared.

"Well, I started thinking about what you said to me yesterday."

"Which part? I said some dumb things yesterday." Nora admitted.

"Ditto. I get a little wacky at that time of the month and besides, you were asking me to give up sweets."

"Give up sweets? What are you…oh, the young hunk."

"Anyway, I've been thinking about what you told me about varying the menu. Where can I buy some of those outfits you were talking about?" Cathy asked to Nora's surprise.

"That's easy." Nora told her, propping herself up on her bed. "We can do it right on line. How about you and I playing nine holes after lunch tomorrow and then we'll come here to pick out the outfits on my computer? I'm meeting George at nine, but I'll be done by twelve. Come on Cathy, it's been a while since we've played. I'll meet you at twelve-thirty in the dining room."

"Okay. And Nora, I really didn't mean to call you a lesbian and George… old. Sometimes my mouth works faster than my brain." Cathy confessed to her friend.

"That's all right." Nora assured her, grinning. "When you called me a lesbian, I asked myself how you knew about the strange way I've been feeling whenever I'm around you?"

"You too?" Cathy said laughing. "I've been getting the same strange feelings. Now, can I ditch Fred, so you and I can move in together? You bimbo...did you really think you'd get me on that one?"

"I'll see you tomorrow, you Jezebel." Nora said, feeling better about her friend.

"Lesbian!" Countered Cathy.

Sometimes, Nora thought, they sounded like a couple of schoolgirls. But of course they weren't. Both had serious concerns to deal with and despite the laughter, she could only hope they could resolve their issues. But...they would get more complicated, more than even she could have imagined.

CHAPTER 37
START SPREADING THE NEWS

WHEN NORA walked into the club's dining room, she saw Cathy, sitting with Sylvia Gibbs and Sharon Kelly.

"The girls are going to join us for lunch and nine holes." Cathy said, as Nora sat down. Although cordial, Nora was disappointed she wouldn't be able to spend the time alone with Cathy. She wanted the opportunity to bond with her friend and perhaps help her resolve some of her issues with Fred.

"We heard the good news." Sylvia said to Nora.

"It's about time we women stood up for our rights." Sharon added.

Turning towards Cathy, Nora peered at her friend. She had asked Cathy, to refrain from telling anyone about the agreement until it was officially announced. Mike's prophecy to Bill, was in motion.

"We women?" Cathy exclaimed, her face flushed, trying to deflect her misstep. "Why Nora, was the one who put it all on the line. If she lost the match to Bill, she would have had to leave the club."

"Don't get touchy Cathy." Sylvia said, her pumpkin colored golf shirt accentuating her tan complexion. "We don't disagree with you, but when your husband is a board member the secrecy is so deafening it can turn a woman to drink. In fact, that's exactly what I need before playing golf with you, Nora."

"Talking about golf." Sharon said. "How's your training with George Harris progressing?"

"He's a good teacher, very patient and focused."

"How old is he?" Sylvia asked. "He looks about sixty-five."

"No, he's not that old." Cathy said, before Nora could respond, still seeking redemption.

"Not that old? This wrinkled bag sitting next to you is sixty-two." Sharon reminded her.

"Well, you know how it goes. When you're in your thirties, like these two spring chickens, old is in your forties." Sylvia said. "When you're in your forties, old is when you pass fifty. The bar keeps going up until the doctor tells you for the first time that you're shrinking. And incidentally, that's when you know it's time to change doctors. Where's the waiter? I still need a drink."

"Well ladies, I don't know about you, but I promised myself I'd take whatever steps necessary to keep *Father Time* at bay." Sharon told them, patting the side of her hair.

"Sharon and I go to the same ***"at bay"*** doctor." Sylvia revealed. "He's not cheap, but he is good."

"Now don't go giving our secrets away." Sharon demanded.

"Listen sweetie, I'm fifty-two and you're sixty-two." Sylvia added, cupping her breasts with both hands, "and...I don't mean up here."

"I see we have a happy group here today," the waiter said, a skinny youth with a bad case of acne. "Ladies, what can I get for you?"

"Sharon, did Gil mention the deal the board made with Nora?" Sylvia asked, after the others had ordered ice tea and she, a scotch sour on the rocks.

"No, he didn't. How about Bob? Did he say anything to you?" Sharon wanted to know.

"After our escapades with ***Sophia*** and ***Sure Shot,*** Bob's been as tight lipped as a monk in a monastery." Sylvia said with a grin.

"We heard about ***Sure Shot*** and how you passed out at the door." Cathy said, smiling.

"Girls, it's no secret I like my occasional cocktail." Sylvia said. "But when I opened the door and saw him standing in the doorway with the biggest six shooter bulging from his beautiful bikini briefs, it was just too much for this girl to handle."

"Sounds like Cathy's pool boy." Nora blurted out without thinking.

"Come on Nora." Sharon said, laughing. "Give us the details."

"Well, what can I say?" Nora shrugged her shoulders, trying to ignore **her *faux pas*** and the fact Cathy, was looking at her as though she wanted to strangle her. "He's young, handsome and a hunk." And then, said to the waiter..."I've changed my mind, better bring me a dry martini?"

"I'll have the same." Cathy demanded, glaring at Nora.

"What the hell, make it three!" Sharon chimed in.

"While you're at it, make mine a double." Sylvia said. "Girls, golf should be very interesting today. Maybe this time, one of us can hit that bastard, Harper."

Lunch was accompanied by more drinks and a vast quantity of gossip, today, a stronger aphrodisiac than the desire to play golf…and later…the women becoming, the gossip of the club.

"Boy, these martinis pack a punch." Sharon announced after her third.

"One more and my soul is open to the first taker." Cathy declared, her hand fanning her face.

"In that case," Sylvia said…then waived to the waiter, summoning him to the table. **"Another round for the table and put it on my tab."**

"Not for me." Nora told Sylvia. "One more of these and I'm a goner!"

"Then I insist you join us. You can't be the only sober person sitting here while we have a true confessions session." Sylvia insisted.

"Don't be a pooper party, Nora. Oops, I mean party…pooper." Cathy said, smiling and holding her hand over her mouth.

"I guess I'm out voted." Nora said reluctantly. "Lot's of olives with mine."

"Sylvia, are you happy with your boob job?" Sharon asked.

"Yes, I am," she declared. "Aren't you with yours?" Sylvia wanted to know.

"I don't know." Sharon replied. "One seems like its…hic, excuse me. As I was saying, I think one sank lower than the other." Then, she suddenly lifted her blouse and undid her bra, popping out both breasts in full view. "Girls… what do you think?"

"Sharon Kelly!" Nora called out. **"Put those away!"**

"Hells bells, Sharon." Cathy said, pausing to sip on her martini. **"Those babies look fine to me."**

A passing member looking at Sharon, hit the oncoming server, also admiring the free peep show. The tray of food flew high in the air, as both men fell to the floor, their heads covered with spaghetti and lettuce.

"They're not cooked…I mean crooked." Sylvia said, completely ignoring the collision.

"Okay, if you say so." Sharon responded, as she tried to clasp her bra together. "I think… I need some help," she pleaded, as she struggled with the clip.

The young server jumped to his feet. **"I'll do it for you!"** He cried out, then tripping over the tray and falling into Sharon, landing face first between her two exposed breasts. The young server's eyes moved up and towards the twin peaks, with a grin from ear-to-ear, thinking he died and went to heaven.

"What? Is this dessert?" Sharon said, looking down at the young server. "We really have to do this…hic, more often, ladies"

"Let me…tuck you up." Sylvia told her.

Club manager, Paul Henry, came over to the table at the request of other members having lunch. "Ladies, lower your voices and please, refrain from any further ***lewd*** behavior."

"Paul...hic...who's **having a *hissy fit*?"** Sharon asked. "We're just having some fun."

"Ladies, I think it might be time to go home," the manager suggested.

"Hey Paul!" Sylvia barked. "How do you know what time we should go home? We still have to play nun...nine holes. Go away!"

"What's this about your...pool boy, Cathy?" Sharon demanded.

"Let's talk about something else." Nora suggested, knowing in her present condition, Cathy, was liable to say more than she should.

"I hope, Nora...kicks that bastard Bill Harper's beautiful ass!" Sylvia said.

"How do you know his ass is beautiful?" Cathy asked.

"Cause I seen it!" Sylvia revealed.

"When did you see his ass?" Cathy winced.

"When he saw mine!" Sylvia said, sipping on her drink. "That man's seen lots of ass's around here over the years."

"Well...he's never seen this one." Nora declared. **"And he never will!"**

But Nora, dull senses and all, was somewhat intrigued with the gossip at hand, providing further fuel to her nightly liaisons with the man she unexplicably was attracted to. Then, when she saw Fred, pass the doorway to the dining room and do a quick turn around, she knew all too well what was about to happen. Cathy's eyes widened as he approached the table.

"Come on girls." Fred said grimly.

What started out as a leisurely lunch and golf, turned into what can best be described as a ***drunken gab fest***, with Bill Harper, as the target, a bull's-eye at which they could throw their imaginary darts. But it was just possible, Nora thought, they had gone too far. Maybe creating an excuse to suspend them all or worse, make Nora, a scapegoat, someone who should be expelled from the club, giving the board an excuse to dismantle the agreement.

CHAPTER 38
DAY OF THE HANGOVER

THE NEXT MORNING, Nora, awoke at nine-thirty with a throbbing headache. She had slept through the time she was to meet with George and was unsuccessful in trying to reach him on his cell. Cathy, turned towards Nora, who was sitting on the edge of the bed holding her head in her hands.

"What time is it?" Cathy wailed. "My head feels like a ticking bomb about to go off."

"I have the same ticking in my head." Nora assured her. "What's making it worse is the thought of having to explain to George, why I blew him off this morning."

There was a knock at the door. "Girls, are you awake in there?" Fred called out.

"Oh my head." Cathy mourned. "Nora, go to the door and ask him to make a pot of coffee. Tell him we'll be out after we shower."

"I heard you Cathy. I'll make the coffee...and lots of it."

"Why can men hear only when they want to?" Cathy muttered.

"It's called selective hearing dear." Fred commanded through the door. "It's a man's thing."

"Do you have something I can wear?" Nora asked.

"How about a pair of sweats and a tee shirt?"

"That works for me. Do you have a spare head I can borrow?"

"If I did, I'd use it myself." Cathy said, wincing in pain.

Her explanation to George, continued to occupy Nora's thoughts, especially after their most recent flap about her diminished intensity to win the match against Bill.

"Welcome to the world ladies." Fred said, when they joined him in the kitchen. "Here, take a couple of swigs of this, it'll help the hangover."

"What is it?" Cathy asked.

"Don't ask, just drink," her husband demanded.

What followed was a contretemps between Cathy and Fred, about whether she would drink his concoction, which she said tasted foul or pop some Excedrin. The tone of their argument indicated to Nora, the relationship was even more difficult between them than Cathy, had indicated.

"It does work." Fred told Nora.

Not wanting to be in the middle of what seemed pointless, Nora retreated to the shower, did pop Excedrin and went back to bed, tossing and turning with each loud repartee` between Cathy and Fred. It wasn't until two in the afternoon the two women joined one another at the pool.

"Did we ever play golf yesterday?" Nora asked, dressed in the borrowed sweats and a tee shirt, sitting in the chaise lounge next to her friend.

"Honey, the only thing I remember is seeing the look on the waiter's face when he landed in Sharon's lap." Cathy said, then adjusting her sunglasses.

"So I wasn't dreaming last night, it did happen?" Nora cringed.

"It certainly did!" Fred said, joining them, dressed in white shorts and a yellow golf shirt. "You girls caused quite a stir yesterday. A couple of members are asking for the house committee to take immediate disciplinary action. The four of you could have your privileges at the club suspended. The fact that three of the wives husbands are board members make the matter worse. If nothing is done, members will claim favoritism was shown."

"How long of a suspension do you figure, Fred?" Nora asked.

"Probably…a few days or a weekend. They're keenly aware of your match with Bill, so I don't think it'll extend beyond that. Although you never know what the cagey fox, Mike…is thinking. He could very well use this as an excuse to call the whole thing off."

"He wouldn't dare." Nora told him. "The one thing I came away with when meeting with him and the board…they're truly afraid of Liz Peters and NOW."

"Don't underestimate him, he's the best survivor and con man I've ever run across." Fred warned.

Nora had always found Fred, insightful, even though she often times, disapproved of the way he treated Cathy. Now, she knew, she should take what he was saying seriously.

"I still have an uneasy feeling about my meeting with him the other day. First, he has me waiting in the dining room **for ten minutes**, explaining he had to tell his secretary where she could reach him." Nora reflected. "Then, as I was leaving the board room, Bill was grinning, like a wolf telling me…**`I'll be eating you soon.`** When I left the meeting, I had the feeling something wasn't right."

"Maybe you're making too much of it." Fred suggested. "Mike could simply have been trying to find out what Harper's vote would be."

"No, my gut tells me it was more than that." Nora told him. "What was said in the meeting that might tie this together?"

"I can't discuss the details of a board meeting, you know that." Fred said, rebuffing her request.

"I'm just asking for brush strokes. I'll complete the picture." Nora said.

"Fred Daley, you were friends with Nick and Nora, long before you were a board member at Happy Hills." Cathy barked. **"Start talking!"**

Peering at his wife, Fred rubbed his scrubby beard, deliberating his response to Nora, while struggling with his oath as a board member and a friendship of a dead husband. He looked at Nora, then put his hands behind his head, leaning back in his chair. A final glance at Cathy, told her she would pay for putting him in this awkward situation.

"Nora, I can tell you this, while Mike was meeting with you, other members of the board were voting to determine if he had to resign as board president. Liz Peters' article and the threat of NOW arriving on the scene was enough to push the board over the edge."

"What was the vote?" Nora pressed.

"Well you know, that was strange. We almost had the bastard. The board voted him out and then he barges in with a guarantee to make it all go away, saying he had you waiting outside the boardroom and were willing to cooperate in making the clubs' problems disappear. The board swallowed the bait hook line and sinker." Fred revealed.

"Now things are starting to make sense." Nora said thoughtfully. "I wondered why he pressured me to make a decision right on the spot. Tell me Fred, did any board member leave during the discussions and before the vote?"

His arms still folded behind his head, he leaned further back on his chair, transfixed on a point beyond Nora and his wife, deep in thought. Suddenly, Fred's chair touched down.

"As a matter of fact...Bill, did leave. He said he had to go to the bathroom. Why do you ask?"

"Don't you see Fred? That's why Mike, excused himself from the dining room, to meet with Bill." Nora said, her eyes peering, deep in thought.

"That was about the same amount of time... Bill was gone." Fred confirmed.

"It couldn't be coincidence, they had to meet with a purpose. The question is...what were they scheming?" Nora posed.

"All of the board members agreed to the provisions and they have to be in writing before the match, I don't get it." Cathy noted.

"Again, maybe you're making too much of it and he simply wanted to influence Bill's vote."

"No, he knew Bill's vote was in the bag." Nora said. "He had to be plotting something. Bill was too cocky when I was leaving the meeting. I don't know what it is or how we're going to find out, but I *don't* have a good feeling about this whole situation."

CHAPTER 39
THE DIRTY SACRIFICE

THE NEXT DAY, Nora was home trying to determine if her senses were overactive or the appearance of a plot between Mike Grace and Bill Harper was a reality. After showering she dressed in a hurry, anxious to call Cathy, asking if she could come over later that afternoon.

"Fred and I are going to dinner, he's trying to mend fences." Cathy yawned.

"When do you think you'll be home?" Nora asked, feeling guilty about the intrusion but the Grace-Harper issue was all encompassing and robbed her of a night's sleep.

"About nine."

"Can you come then?" Nora asked, pursing her lips and clenching her teeth.

"No problem, I'll tell Fred you're not feeling well. By the way, we never went on line to buy those outfits," she reminded her.

"What outfits?" Nora said, engrossed in her own self-thoughts.

"You know, cheerleaders, nurses, does that jog your memory?" Cathy whispered.

"If you remember, we never did get to play the nine holes of golf either... because a certain friend of mine invited two lushes to lunch with us."

"But, you have to admit, it was worth watching them. They're real characters?"

"IT WAS FUN, I confess, even though I felt like I'd been hit by a Mack truck the next morning. But there's something important I want to discuss with you. After we talk, we'll go on line and see what strikes your fancy."

Nora didn't want to put her best friend in an awkward situation, but under the circumstances, with her back up against the wall, she didn't know what else to do. And if Cathy objected to what she was going to propose, she wouldn't push her, even though convinced, Mike and Bill were setting her up.

To complicate matters, George, hadn't returned the three messages Nora, had left on his cell phone. The match was around the corner and without George, by her side, she understood all too well, her chances of winning would be substantially diminished. With this in mind, she decided to take a ride to his country club and explain why she missed practice, which must have struck him as particularly unusual, since he told her the day before, he would have to discontinue coaching her unless she put her nose to the grindstone.

It was a pleasant Saturday morning and a perfect day for a ride in a convertible. The sun was shining and a warm breeze pressed against Nora's face while her hair flew wildly in the wind. She passed a group of girls, who appeared to be of high school age running in shorts and tank tops, then recalling how it had been when she and Cathy, were the same age. In particular, the day of Cathy's rebellion about being on the track team…

* * *

"Come on Cathy, just run!" Nora remembered telling her. "Talking uses up oxygen."

"My body was very happy with plain old breathing." Cathy complained. "It's pissed off at me because I'm making it harder to get the same thing."

"This is good exercise for your body. It clears out your lungs."

"Sorry Nora, but my body is disagreeing. It was very happy with the contents of its lungs. Why did you have to pick cross-country running anyway? We could have tried out for the hundred-yard dash. You run three hundred feet and it's over. We've already run five miles. Let's see, that's more than twenty-six thousand feet. Why do I always listen to you anyway?" Cathy snipped.

"Because you don't run fast!" Nora barked, breathing heavy and trying to maintain a pace comfortable for Cathy. "Your mother could beat you in the hundred."

"So you're doing this to keep me company?" Cathy gasped.

"Yes, and I wish you'd show some appreciation."

"Well, if I'd known we were running for my benefit, I would have done this a long time ago." Cathy said, dropping on the grass. **"My body and I have decided we don't want your company. We quit!"**

"You can't just quit like that." Nora huffed, still running in place.

"Oh yes I can. I'm getting threats from this body saying if I don't stop this torture, it's going to plant my breakfast all over this park." Cathy threatened, her arms and legs spread apart.

Nora smiled as she remembered how she had collapsed next to her friend. "You know you're crazy don't you? What's coach going to say?"

"He won't care. He's always yelling at us any way. `Gibbons, Owens,' Cathy mimicking the coach's craggy voice. 'If you want to stay on this team… you have to put out."

Nora rolled over and grabbed Cathy around the shoulders, both laughing and poking at one another, the girls being girls, giggling silly and affectionately flipping leaves at each other.

"You're so bad Cathy Gibbons. Come on, let's get some ice cream."

"Now you're talking! My body's smiling already." Cathy said, leaping to her feet with a smile that seemed to light up the world.

* * *

The memories brought a smile to Nora, reflecting how wacky, Cathy had always been. They were good times and they shared a special bond as young teenagers, a friendship Nora, cherished. And that of course…was why she'd do anything for Cathy, but wondered, if she would be willing to do what Nora, would ask of her?

An anxious driver's horn startled Nora, her past thoughts vanishing quickly as she turned onto the road leading to George's club. The assistant pro told her, George was giving a lesson. She headed for the practice range where he was standing alone, wiping perspiration from his brow, his lesson apparently over. As she approached him, he threw the white towel in her direction.

"That's what you did, sister!" George scowled, his normally soft tone, now elevated. "You threw the towel in and made a fool of me."

"You're wrong!" Nora protested. "Do you always jump to conclusions? What happened to the little boy you showed me at dinner?"

"That was personal!" George snarled**. "The training is business and the two don't mix."**

"Oh, didn't you mix the two when you asked me to dinner? Why didn't you bother to find out why I failed to make our practice?" Nora demanded. **"Or didn't you care?** Perhaps I'd been in an accident, or there'd been an emergency. If you had any confidence in me at all, you would have known something important had to keep me from at least calling you. I did leave you three messages…that went unanswered?"

"Of course I was worried," he told her earnestly. "Haven't you seen**…**

that I care a great deal about you? I haven't had these feelings since Joan died. It's difficult to smell your perfume without wanting to hold you in my arms. There...now you have it. So, what the hell happened to you?" George demanded

Nora was taken aback. Yes, **SHE WAS** aware of his feelings, but wasn't prepared to deal with them right at this moment, her focus centered on Mike Grace and Harper.

When Nora, explained about the luncheon and the fact she had... *inadvertently,* gotten looped with her friends, she could see he was amused. When she finished apologizing, he agreed to resume their practice on Monday. It was then, just as she was about to leave, he asked if she were free for dinner. Much as Nora, would have liked to make up for the bother she had caused him, she explained meeting with Cathy, to discuss the situation with Mike and Bill.

George's expression was one of obvious disappointment. Nora kissed him on the cheek and left, only later rethinking, perhaps the kiss might not have been a good idea, considering the way he obviously felt about her. She didn't want to bruise his feelings, but considered him an interesting ***gap filler***, when comparing him to other suitors. Sure, he was significantly older than the other men she dated, but it was their history and common interest that was the allure. But, was she using George, in her determination to beat Bill Harper?

When the doorbell rang at nine-thirty, Nora greeted her friend, both scurrying to the den.

"I know I'm late." Cathy said apologetically. "Fred got into an argument with one of waiters."

"Did he buy off on me not feeling well?" Nora asked, anxious to discuss her plan with Cathy.

"I told him the truth." Cathy said, shrugging off her jacket, then dropping onto the couch and spreading her legs. "I told him we were going to surf the net looking at sites that offer sexy costumes. When he heard that...he told me to take my time. **OK, now tell me why I'm really here?"** Cathy asked with a raised eyebrow.

Nora, didn't know where to start. She was, she knew, about to ask her friend to do something that could open old wounds and result in destroying an already fragile marriage, not to mention, it could jeopardize any possibility of her personal interest in Bill.

"Cathy, I'm stuck in fast drying cement and I don't know what to do." Nora started.

"Is the Grace and Harper thing still bothering you?"

"Those guys are planning something to embarrass me. I can feel it...

but I just don't know what it is or when it's going to happen." Nora snapped, reaching for Cathy's hand.

"So...you want me to find out...from Bill?" Cathy said flatly. "Nora, why the surprised look? I can read you like a book. Besides, I don't have a problem with the idea. In fact, it'll be fun."

"Aren't you concerned about Fred?" Nora asked with a quizzical look.

"I'm not going to do anything that warrants a confession, if that's what you mean." Cathy said, clearly offended.

"I just thought..."

"What Nora? That your friend ***the slut,*** was going to compromise herself in order to get the information? You don't have to worry about that, I know how to handle the fox without being eaten. Besides, I want you to owe me for the rest of your life." Cathy snipped.

It was...a very Cathy like comment, Nora thought. But she also knew, her friend might very well hold her to it. She was most relieved, when Cathy didn't take offense to the idea. Yet, she felt a twinge of guilt. And...what if Cathy, indeed rekindled her feelings for Bill? She was vulnerable, her marriage seemingly frayed beyond repair. Could she compete with her best friend for a man in whom she mistrusted, yet, somehow intrigued her?

CHAPTER 40
THE SPIDER AND THE FLY

IT WAS EIGHT in the morning when Cathy, drove to the bagel store. The church bells were ringing, chiming eight times as she prepared to make the phone call for her friend.

"Hello, Bill?"

"Who's this?" He answered, awakened by the call.

"Cathy, Cathy Daley," she said, clenching her teeth. This was, she realized, going to be more difficult than she had thought. "Am I calling too early?"

"No, Cathy. How've you been? This is an unexpected...but a pleasant surprise."

"I'm good, Bill. I know Sundays are supposed to be peaceful and uneventful, but you know how impulsive and carefree I am." Cathy said, shaking her head side to side and wincing.

"That's what I always admired about you," he told her. "We would have made a great team, ***sweet cakes***."

Cathy had forgotten, it had been his nickname for her and hearing it again brought a smile to her face, reminding her of the first time he had called her...**sweet cakes**.

* * *

"Don't forget, a double scoop of strawberry, dipped in chocolate sprinkles," she told Bill.

"I got it," he said, walking across the street, looking back and winking at her.

Within minutes, Bill returned with a cone in each hand. And then suddenly, seeing Herb and Marion Blake walking down the street, Cathy ducked under the dashboard, curling into a contorted ball.

"Are they gone?" Cathy gasped, Bill, grinning from ear-to-ear. "It's not funny you know. If they saw us, it would be all over town by tomorrow."

"Relax." Bill told her.

But, before he could warn Cathy, that her ice cream had fallen off of the cone and onto her seat, she had already sat down, after the Blake's had passed.

"Oh God! How am I going to explain this one," she screeched.

"Honey, it just proves what I already know." Bill assured her.

"Yes! That you're a klutz with ice cream." Cathy bemoaned.

"No, Cathy, that you have the sweetest cheeks in town." Bill said, grinning. "In fact...I hereby dub thee...**sweet cakes**." Bill said, waving his arm while bending like a knight of the realm.

"Just make sure it's in private." Cathy demanded, as they both had a good laugh...her smile waning as she began the task of cleaning the strawberry ice cream from her derriere.

* * *

Cathy continued, proceeding to ***spin her web,*** the past a feint but pleasant memory.

"Can we meet for a drink tomorrow night about eight?"

"Sure Cathy, what's this about?"

"I can't talk over the phone," she told him. "Where can we go and be sure we won't be seen?"

"How about our old haunt, ***The Shady Lady*?"**

"I'll bring the martini's." Cathy said. "It'll be like old times."

"Looking forward to it...**sweet cakes**."

As soon as she returned home, Cathy called Nora, telling her the first part of the mission had been accomplished. They arranged to meet at the club for lunch and play golf afterwards.

"So, what's your plan for tonight?" Nora asked, as they drove to their ball off the first tee box.

"I don't have a damn clue." Cathy said. "I thought you might have an idea I could use?"

"Go hit your ball." Nora said, as they approached it in the fairway, Cathy's drive substantially shorter than her friends. Her second shot sailed right of the fairway.

"Your mothers nose!" She called out in disgust, slamming her club to the ground.

"Leave my mothers nose out of this." Nora said playfully.

"Hey! I just had an idea." Cathy said. "I know what I'm going to do with Bill."

It took a bit of coaxing by Nora, but Cathy, finally explained in detail what she had in mind.

"No way, Cathy!" Nora cried out when she had finished. "You can't do that to me."

"I'm not doing anything to you. I suppose you have a better idea... ***Princess*!"**

"What's with the ***Princess*** bit?" Nora snipped.

"I'm talking about you going to the dance, dressed to kill in your red *Valentino* dress, dripping with diamonds, all part of your plan to win Bill over, and you ending up challenging him to a golf match." Cathy hissed.

"Well, if I remember correctly...**you didn't tell me you'd slept with the man!"** Nora snapped, then hitting her ball, landing it five feet from the hole.

"If you could do that on every hole we wouldn't need a plan." Cathy huffed.

"What's with the attitude?"

"I'm sorry, Nora. I'm a bit nervous about this whole thing. I guess I'm feeling a bit guilty about, Fred."

"Cathy, I don't want to do anything to affect our friendship or your relationship with your husband. If you want to call the whole thing off... well... I'm OK with that." Nora said with sincerity.

"I'm okay. I did have feelings for Bill, at one time. I kind of feel...that I'm betraying both a friend and a husband. I'll get over it."

Later, when Nora drove her friend home, Cathy reminded her she was going to tell Fred, the two of them were going to the movies.

"So don't answer the phone if the caller ID says it's coming from my house." Cathy added.

It was eight-thirty when Cathy, kissed her husband and told him not to wait up. Then driving to the motel, she parked beside Bill's Bentley and just as she used to do, read the note he had tucked under his windshield wiper, giving her the number of the room.

Not to arouse suspicions, Cathy dressed in the sort of outfit she would ordinarily have worn for a night out with her best friend. On this warm summer night, she wore denim shorts, a white silk blouse and tennis sneakers. Pausing outside the door, she took a deep breath, then, undid an extra button on her blouse before she knocked. The door opened...and there was Bill, standing in the doorway and looking pretty sexy himself. He too, was dressed casual…in beige slacks and an open blue shirt, exposing his chest. This was supposed to be a fishing expedition, but, when Cathy saw him in the doorway, it brought back vivid memories.

"You look and smell as good as ever." Bill said, as he kissed her on the cheek.

"You've kept yourself in good shape too." Cathy told him, admiringly.

"I work hard at it…so I can attract pretty little girls like you into my *web*," he said, pulling her back into his arms.

"Not so fast!" Cathy said, pushing him away. "This ***black widow*** needs a drink."

It amused her to reverse the metaphor, as it did Bill, grinning like a fox anticipating a fine meal, the playful repartee' making his anticipated conquest much more exciting. He busied himself, glancing back at Cathy, while pouring *martini's* in their glasses.

"So Cathy, why are we here? What's so important that you had to meet me on such short notice? I have a hunch there's more on the agenda than playful sex."

Cathy hedged with small talk until she had a second drink and he a third. It was an advantage to know Bill, well enough to be certain, that after a third drink he often didn't know how to stop.

"Enough with the small talk, Cathy. Why are we here?" Bill demanded, his speech slightly uneven.

"Well, I have some good news for you. **I've convinced Nora…**to withdraw from the match."

Bill was genuinely surprised at Cathy's announcement. Sipping on his *fourth martini*, he peered over his glass, rubbing his finger around it's perimeter. Then said…

"Why would she?" He asked, his speech…noticeably impeded.

"Because I told her, you were too good and you'd kick her butt around the entire golf course." Cathy said, slurring her speech for effect.

"You're right, I would have. But we have insurance…just in case." Bill revealed.

"**You bought an insurance policy?"** Cathy asked, assuming the same innocent look she used with Fred, when she wanted him to blurt out information. This was going to be easier than she had anticipated, thanks to the fact that Bill, was never able to hold his liquor very well.

"No, no," he scoffed. "I said we have insurance, but I can't tell you about that. It's a secret."

"It doesn't matter," she taunted him. "I'm sure that whatever it is…can't be very interesting."

"OK, OK. Sit down, here next to me." Bill said patting the bed, gulping down his drink, then pouring another. **"We're using** invisible ink to fool her."

Bill spilled the beans about Mike's plan and Cathy was all ears. She had what she wanted. The only thing left was to make her retreat, without Bill realizing...**he'd been had**.

"My goodness, you fellows are clever." Cathy said, holding up her glass. "Let's drink to your success." As he drank his *sixth martini*, she emptied her fourth on the rug behind the couch. And as she had hoped, Bill's last drink had put him over the top. Before leaving, Cathy covered him with a blanket. When he woke up, as she knew he would do in a couple of hours, he would at least know that she still had a tender spot for him in her heart. But as she went out the door, she paused long enough to throw a kiss to her *former lover* and say, **"Mission accomplished."**

CHAPTER 41
ANOTHER HANGOVER

IT WAS A WARM AND STICKY Tuesday, when Nora left for practice with George. The prior day was her first since her misunderstanding with him and he worked her very hard, she expected no less from him today. Still, it was going to be difficult to concentrate, given the fact that Cathy, had been so cagey on the phone, telling Nora, she had the information she wanted, but with Fred lurking around, she couldn't talk.

When Nora approached her locker, she saw an envelope wedged in the door. It was a letter from the golf committee, informing her she had been suspended one weekend for her behavior in the dining room on Friday afternoon. It was a token discipline and less than she'd anticipated.

The fact three of the disciplined members were wives of board members, accounted for the golf committee's decision, since it would satisfy most of the club members who were waiting for some action against the four violators, while at the same time keeping Nora, in her match against Bill.

George worked her hard and she was exhausted by the time she got home. But not too tired to respond immediately to the message Cathy, had left on her voice mail, summoning Nora, to come to her house as soon as possible.

When Nora arrived, Cathy greeted her…holding an ice pack on her head.

"Come in," she said, moving the pack to her left temple. "Let's go in the kitchen and please don't talk loud."

"What happened to you?"

"Just take out the Excedrin and give me three." Cathy pleaded.

"By the way, the club suspended us for this coming weekend." Nora said as she opened the bottle of pain reliever.

"I'd like to put the entire board in a closet with your friend, Judy Feinstein and a *canary.*" Cathy groaned.

"Why a *canary*?" Nora asked with a bewildered look.

"The old time coal miners brought a canary down the shafts with them. If the canary died they knew there was a gas leak. I want those bastards to see that death is around the corner when Judy walks in the room."

"Cathy, you worry me at times. Now get down to business and tell me what happened last night?"

"Those snakes have really stooped to the bottom of the barrel," she told her, reaching for the bottled water and then swallowing the *Excedrin.* **"Nora...they're out to get you**. You know the agreement you, Mike and the board approved a few days ago? Well, it's going to disappear before your very eyes."

"What are you talking about?"

As Cathy, completed the tale of deception planned by Mike and Bill, the phone rang. It was Bill.

"Hello Bill." Cathy said, putting a finger to her lips, indicating Nora, to remain quiet.

"I'm just calling to see how you are?" He asked. "It sure didn't turn out the way I expected. I remember talking to you and then...nothing. What happened?"

"We were chit chatting about old times when I excused myself to visit the little girls room. When I came back, you were out cold." Cathy said.

"Wow, I don't remember a thing. I suppose I owe you an apology, Cathy."

"Well, I must say Bill, I was somewhat disappointed on how the evening ended." Cathy said...smirking, while she held her hand over the receiver, Nora, giggling and Cathy waving for her to keep quiet.

"What can I say, perhaps I can make up for it another time?"

"We'll see, Bill."

"By the way Cathy, do you remember what we talked about last night?"

"After talking about old times...I haven't a clue," she said, winking at Nora.

"Everything went blank after the third martini. I don't even remember how I got home."

"I thought we were talking about Nora?" Bill asked and still fishing "Do you remember, Cathy?"

"The only thing I remember about her was you saying how you were going to kick her ass in the match," she told him.

Nora raised her eyebrows. Sometimes Cathy's frankness appalled her. But she told herself now, that was Cathy. She'd never change and she had done her a great favor that wouldn't be forgotten.

"I do remember you said you wanted to talk to me about something." Bill said. "What was it?"

"Well, I've been thinking about old times lately and wanted to see you one more time. **I needed the itch off my back, or start scratching again."** Cathy said, trying to control herself, placing her hand over the receiver, then placing it between her legs and bending over with muffled laughter, Nora, shaking her head in utter disbelief.

"And what did you decide?" Bill asked.

"It's hard to come to any decision given what happened last night. I think it best if we put this on the back burner until we have clearer heads. But thank you Bill, for not taking advantage of me." Cathy told him, letting him keep his pride.

Cathy pursed her lips and smirked. Nora, seeing her as the cat, who had just eaten the canary and licking it's paws in the aftermath. Someone had been taken advantage of and although Bill wasn't quite sure...**it was him.**

He hung up the phone, his eyes still on the receiver. **Something wasn't right**. He measured Cathy's words in his head, mulling through what he perceived as camouflage, trying to peel back his memory of last night's conversation. Rubbing the back of his neck, he glanced at the book on the table. It was Craig Barnes' **A Nation Deceived.**

With his eyes fixated, he suddenly thought to himself...**she wouldn't!** But...**what if she did?**

CHAPTER 42
THE CARD ROOM

"DID YOU SEE those Yankees last night?" Gil Kelly asked. "Were they pathetic or what?"

"Right on, Gil. They remind me of my wife." Pete Thomas told him. "All talk and no action."

"Poor Pete, **not getting any nuggie lately?"** Gil said, rubbing his friends head.

"Hey, you should talk! At least my wife knows enough to keep her six shooters in the holsters." Pete bellowed

"With those raisins, your wife doesn't need a holster!" Gil shot back, the room erupting in laughter.

"Very funny, Gil. I'll let Diane know, that her friend's husband thinks her ten thousand dollar boobs are too small." Pete threatened.

"Will you guys stop talking about boobs and play cards!" Jerry demanded.

"Look who talking, the man whose wife has the **biggest friggin forty-fives** in the club. If my wife was built like Laura, I'd have **BRINKS** guarding her day and night." Bob said in envy.

"Hey Bob, I hear your maid for the day, Sophia, was really stacked." George said.

"**Momma Mia!** Was she ever," he replied, cupping his breasts with his hands. "Even Sylvia was impressed."

"Did you ever find out where she works?" George asked.

"What do you think?" Bob replied, winking to the guys at the table.

"Way to go!" You devil you," greeted the boastful claim.

Meanwhile, in the far corner of the dining room, which served as a make shift card room…

"Alright girls, the game is bridge and the stakes are the same as last week." Sylvia declared. "The losing team gets Maggie Howser as a house guest for a week."

"We should put her in a rules committee meeting for an hour." Sharon said. "The only thing they'd suspend is breathing."

"Speaking about the rules committee, did you get your letter, Sylvia?" Sharon asked.

"Yes and I hope you were as amused as I was."

"What's to smile about?" Sharon said sarcastically. "We're being suspended for a weekend of golf."

"That's nothing dear. When I saw the notice…all I could think of was the way that waiter looked up at you with his bulging eyes. I expect he thought he died and was in titty heaven." Sylvia howled, sparking laughter amongst the group.

"That wasn't very ladylike behavior, particularly from the chairlady of women's golf. I certainly wouldn't have exposed myself like that." Marion said, tilting her chin.

"We can understand why." Sharon snapped. **"With those drooping draperies…**I wouldn't expose myself either."

"Easy girls. Marion, you had to be there to appreciate the moment." Sylvia told her. "We'd all had a few drinks and when Sharon's ten thousand dollar beauties popped out, they were a sight to behold."

Sylvia tried to deflect Sharon's remarks, hoping Marion would let it go… but…

"Sharon Kelly, how could you say a thing like that to me?" Marion demanded, putting her cards face down on the table. "Our husbands serve on the board to make this club a respectable place to be a member."

"Our husbands serve on the board for their own pleasure." Tammy Grace hissed, weighing in on the fray. "They're deceitful and manipulative men who want to keep us in our place. I only wish I'd been there to see it for myself."

"I think this might be a good time to order drinks." Sylvia said, winking at Sharon. "Ramon, over here," she summoned the server. "We'll have four fuzzy navels…and pronto!"

"What's a fuzzy navel?" Marion asked. "I'm really not a drinker."

"Don't fret." Sylvia told her. "It's like drinking a Shirley Temple."

"Okay ladies, the game is bridge…"

"Maybe the Yankees ought to fire Joe Torre to bring a different look to the club?" Gil reflected, as he dealt the next hand, puffing on his cigar. "They need better spirit. Right now they look like they're just going through the motions," he said with a frown.

"You don't fire a manager because the players don't put out." Jerry told him. **"It's like me firing Laura**, when she went through that no sex business."

"Hey Jerry, **if you ever do fire** Laura, let us know so we can draw straws for her." Pete said, biting down on a cigar and nodding his head to the other card players.

"I'm in on that drawing!" Bob replied, as did others.

"Thanks, guys!" Jerry said. "It's nice to know his friends are looking to ***buff*** **his wife**."

"Take it as a compliment." Bob advised him, sipping on his beer. "You don't hear any of us talking the same about our raving beauties."

"Yeah Jerry." Pete agreed. **"Laura's got it all."**

"Got what Pete?" Jerry demanded, moving forward in his chair.

"A pretty face?" Pete said tentatively, a remark greeted with a round of laughter, as Jerry, sat back in his chair, grinning and munching on his cigar.

"Pete, you chicken shit!" Gil said. "Why don't you just tell the man the truth? You're hot for his wife and you'd like to *buff* her."

"Is that what you want to do Pete, ***buff*** **my wife?"** Jerry snarled.

"No! No! That's not what I mean." Pete said, clearly intimidated.

"So what are you saying...**my wife's not good enough** for you to *buff?"* Jerry scowled.

"No Jerry, I think she'd be **a *great buff.*** I mean...."

"So you ***DO*** want to *buff* my wife." Jerry interrupted the tongue twisted Pete, leaning so acrimoniously across the table, Pete rose from his chair and made a swift retreat, placing a chair between Jerry and himself. **"Let me at him, I'm going to kill him!"** Jerry continued in a playful but threatening gesture.

"These fuzzy navels are delightful!" Marion said happily, emptying her third glass.

None of the four women were feeling any pain, but Marion, unaccustomed to drinking, was clearly wasted... much to the others' delight.

"How big are your husbands' *wienie's?"* Marion blurted out to everyone's surprise. "I want to know how big they are...**cause my Herb's...** hic...*is very tiny.* Actually, it's about this size," she added...holding two fingers...three inches apart.

The other three women smiled, then indicated their husbands measurements, each glancing at the other's response to Marion's audacious question.

"See! I thought...hic, he had a tiny *wienie.*" Marion said sarcastically, then asking a question she and the others would soon regret.

"Sharon...will you show me your *ten thousand dollar* boobs."

"Sure!" Sharon said cheerfully, **popping them out,** just as Ramon, arrived with their next round of drinks.

"Madre' Mio!" He shouted, then making the sign of the cross. "Come here, Mr. Paul, **the ladies...they have out their *tomatillos'* again!"**

But before the club manager arrived, Marion had exposed her *tomatillos'* as well and it wasn't a pretty sight.

"Mrs. Blake! Please dress yourself immediately!" The club manager demanded, red faced with embarrassment. **"And you too!** Mrs. Kelly."

The manager sent Ramon to the men's card room to summon Herb Blake and Gil Kelly to the dining room.

The girls, with the exception of Marion, of course, had accomplished what they intended, to get the prim and proper Marion...wasted! But, it would not be without consequences.

"The wives go loco!" Ramon pleaded. "They leave out their ***tomatillos'*** for everyone to see. Hurry! Pronto misters."

"Ah no, not again?" Sharon's husband cried out, as he led Herb Blake and others in a race to the dining room, where Marion, was slumped in her chair and out cold, her ***tomatillos'*** still exposed and being stuffed back into her blouse by the other women. It was Herb Blake, would later say, one of the lowest points in his life. As far as he was concerned, someone would have to pay, and...big time.

CHAPTER 43
SECOND THOUGHTS

MEANWHILE, Bill was having second thoughts about Mike's plan of deception. In good part, he wasn't sure what he might have said to Cathy, while in his drunken stupor. If he had inadvertently revealed the plan, he and Mike, could face serious consequences.

With that in mind, he made arrangements to meet his fellow conspirator at Gino's for lunch. The two men took a booth in the rear of the restaurant and ordered before getting down to business.

"Well, what's so important that we had to meet away from the club?" Mike asked.

Bill anticipated that Mike, wasn't going to like what he was about to tell him. But, he was never one to avoid directness when turning down a proposed deal. In addition, Mike would need his support if he wanted to remain president of the board.

"Mike, you've been a successful attorney and I'm a comfortable retiree. Would you agree, at this stage of our lives, we should avoid endangering our status?"

"I can't disagree with that." Mike told him. "Bill, what's this leading up to?"

"This plan of yours, Mike..."

"You mean ours, don't you, Bill?" Mike said, not mincing words.

"Okay, this plan of ours. It only makes what I have to say more meaningful. I want you to know...**I'm no longer** in favor of moving forward with the idea."

Mike was clearly taken by surprise, his expression flushed, his eyes widening under his bushy eyebrows.

"You can't back out on me now!" He said, angrily snapping his napkin and placing it on his lap.

"Listen Mike, we've let our emotions dictate our actions rather than our brains." Bill told him. "We're two smart businessmen. I've thought about the consequences if we get caught and I'm not willing to take the chance."

"How are we going to get caught?" Mike insisted**.** "Only you and I know about the plan."

"Consider the consequences if we do." Bill said. "We can go to jail my friend...because we'll both be committing fraud. Listen to me, you're the attorney and should be warning me to not to do this."

"There's more to this than meets the eye!" Mike said suspiciously. "I said only you and I know of the plan and you lowered your eyes. Am I making a correct assumption?" Mike demanded, peering at Bill, observing his body language for affirmation to his question. But, Bill's silence was damning.

"I thought so, Bill**.** Who else knows?"

"I'm pretty sure...Cathy Daley does."

"How in hell would she know?" Mike growled.

Though realizing it was his own stupidity which had threatened the outcome of Mike's plan, Bill was resolved not to be part of it, nor be intimidated by his conspirators rants.

"We were out drinking and I think it was discussed." Bill admitted. "But don't go off half cocked. I can't be sure. I know Cathy, but she's as hard to read as a French menu. When I asked her what we talked about the next day, she tried to give me a *con job*. It convinced me she knows and if she does, you can be sure she told Nora."

"You stupid son-of-a-bitch!" Mike shouted, slamming his fists on the table, bringing unwanted attention to their booth and prompting the manager to request they lower their voices. "How on earth did you ever succeed in business with that thing between your legs doing your thinking."

"Let's not get personal!" Bill demanded, leaning forward in his seat. "Even if Cathy, doesn't know, I'm still not interested in moving forward with the plan. We'd be deceiving the board as well as Nora, both of whom could file criminal charges against us. It's not worth the risk."

"That woman has to be taught a lesson!" Mike demanded, once again slamming his fist on the table, aware his outburst would attract attention, but not concerned with whom he offended.

"You don't have to deceive anyone with illegal planning." Bill tried to reassure him. "I'm GOING TO beat her. All you have to decide is if you and the board want to change your minds regarding the agreement. You may have to do some fancy footwork, but after I do beat her, she's gone from the club.

The other women will be happy to get back to the way things were. They'll be more agreeable than ever."

But it was too little too late as far as Mike was concerned. **"Have lunch on me...you jackass!"** He said with rancor, dropping a twenty dollar bill on the table, brushing past the manager, approaching to protest their loud outbursts.

"I'll get that bastard for doing this to me." Mike swore, slamming his car door and pounding the steering wheel with both hands, his rage out of control.

He lost his biggest supporter in Bill and admitted, he was seemingly at the end of his rope. What he couldn't anticipate, was a sudden reversal of fortunes...the sly fox seen as a savior of Happy Hills rather than a disgraced board president.

CHAPTER 44
BAD GIRLS BAD GIRLS

THE NEXT AFTERNOON, four women were summoned by phone to appear before the disciplinary committee.

"Ladies, I think you know why you're here today." Ralph began. "Your behavior in the club dining room yesterday was shocking and completely unacceptable to the standards of this club, and I dare say, any other respectable country club. What's more astonishing is the fact that all of your husbands serve as board of directors whose responsibility is to protect the rights of members and ensure the bylaws of this club are followed. Your little peep show in the dining room embarrassed quite a few people and they insist you be severally admonished for your behavior."

"It wasn't my fault!" Marion cried out tearfully. "I told them I couldn't drink, but they insisted I have those horrible *navels.*"

"It's *fuzzy navels,* Marion." Sylvia said.

"YOU SHUT UP SYLVIA! It was you who forced me to drink after I told you I shouldn't." Then, turning her back on the panel of men and pointing towards Sylvia, she declared**..."She's the one who should be punished, not me."**

"What do you have to say for yourself?" Herb demanded.

"Your wife ***ISN'T*** an under-aged teenager." Sylvia hissed. "She was a willing stripper who volunteered to show herself off, and...that wasn't very much."

"SHARON EXPOSED HERSELF FIRST!" Marion wailed.

"What's your excuse, Sharon? That kind of behavior is reprehensible." Herb scoffed.

"Are you sure you want to know?" Sharon replied with a raised eyebrow.

"I insist." Herb said, ignoring his wife Marion, shaking her head frantically.

"Well, you see." Sharon began with a *wily* grin. **"Your wife, wanted to know** the size of our husband's *wienies,* because...," she paused, turning to her fellow conspirators with a devilish look, then stoically turned to Herb and said..."**she felt you had** a very...very...small one. And when we indicated our husbands manhood, your wife said and I quote, **'See, I thought hic... he had a *tiny wienie.*"**

Marion put her hands over her face, bowing her head while the other committee members and women tried to control their snickering.

Herb was aghast, glaring at his wife and if looks could kill, Marion... would be a goner.

"What does my small...uh, my...have to do with you exposing yourself?" Herb demanded.

"Marion wanted to know what ten thousand dollars had bought for me." Sharon said. "So, I showed her, that's when she exposed herself. She wanted to know if a little plastic surgery could help her too." Sharon said with a *poker face.*

"I don't think you should pursue this any further." Ralph intervened.

Herb was too vengeful to be stopped, his agenda steep in payback.

"Tammy, as the wife of the board president, don't you feel any sense of shame? How could you allow such a breach of etiquette to happen in your presence?"

"Yes, I'm ashamed of myself...as you should be for ***backstabbing*** a friend, and for Ralph, who says he'd ***wear a dress*** if Bill loses to Nora." Tammy scoffed. "As for Fred, he's the next Brutus standing in line."

"This not a political forum, Tammy**!"** Fred protested, leaping from his chair.

"Oh come off it!" She told him. "Of course it's political. Both you and Herb, have ambitions to be president of the club and instead of running against Mike, when his term ends, like real men, you tried to undermine him every chance you've had. Now, you're taking the opportunity to insult his wife? How dare you! How dare you both, you poor excuses for men."

"Way to go Tammy!" Sylvia squealed.

"That a girl, Tammy. Give them hell!" Sharon cried out, pointing to the seated board members.

"The fact remains, all of you displayed behavior unacceptable to this committee." Ralph told them. "Other members will be watching and want to know if a board members wife will be treated differently from any other member who behaved in the same manner. As for you, Sylvia and Sharon, this is your second offense within the past two weeks."

"How long have you been a *cross dresser*, Ralph?" Tammy asked, shocking the entire room.

"What in the hell are you talking about!"

"I know all the dirty little secrets...on all of you guys." Tammy, boldly stated. "And if you continue this little ruse, so will the other members of the club. My husband may not be a saint, but he did share his knowledge about some of the ***extra curricular activities*** of his fellow board members. Marion, did you know that your indignant husband and Ralph, are members of a cross-dressers club, which means, just in case you're not acquainted with the term, **they like to dress in women's clothes."**

"What?" Marion shrieked, looking first at her husband's accuser and then glaring at him.

"Yes, it's true, Marion. Every Tuesday night, your husband and our friend Ralph, go to a club of fellow cross-dressers to show off their femininity."

Marion stared fiercely at her husband. "Going to play cards with the boys, you said. Every Tuesday was supposed to be your card night and instead, you're off somewhere **dressing like a woman!"**

"Don't fret, Marion. Maybe Sharon's surgeon will give you both a deal on a ***boob* job."** Tammy snipped.

"Oh yes, and you Fred Daly. Does Cathy, know about you and the summer waitress from Poland?" Tammy asked. "Mike said you were trying to improve her english in exchange for a personal geography lesson, a very personal geography lesson."

"That's a damn lie!"

"Oh, is it? Then why was she suddenly shipped back to Poland? Did she forget her doll set? From what I hear she was barely eighteen...and Mike, helped you stay out of jail. What a shame, you would have made a good bitch for one of the inmates." Tammy sneered.

What the outraged committee members didn't know, was that the ***bad girls*** of Happy Hills had mapped out their plan of attack before the meeting. All had agreed, Tammy would sit silent until the right moment and then let loose. Her knowledge of dirty secrets would be their **ace-in-the-hole** and it worked.

Oh, and Marion, she suspected her husband of some extra curricular activity on Tuesday nights, justifying her own escapades, with a not to be named caddie and not to be named board member, but never dreamed of Herb's outlandish fetish to dress in women's clothing.

"Ladies, we ask that the four of you step out for a few minutes so we can discuss the appropriate action to be taken by this committee." Ralph told them.

Sharon and Sylvia, each took one of Tammy's hand, squeezing gently in a sign of victory, leaving the board room snickering.

"Let's face it guys, we're between a rock and a hard place." Ralph declared when the door closed behind them.

Weeks before, Ralph had an unfortunate encounter with Mike, as he was going into a restaurant frequented by transvestites. He had been wearing his favorite outfit, a blue linen dress, which set off his double string of pearls beautifully. Matching earrings and his golden brown wig, completed his appearance. Mike had looked at him as though he was about to have a stroke, which may indeed have been the case, and asked him what he was doing wearing lipstick and dressed like a woman, to which a rattled Ralph had replied, **'That it was harmless fun.'**

"What the hells wrong with you?" Mike demanded. "Did you play with Shirley Temple dolls when you were a kid instead of tin soldiers?"

Ralph had pleaded with him not to say anything, explaining his wife thought he was playing cards. Mike, although clearly disgusted, had promised not to say anything.

"Herb, I thought he wouldn't say anything." Ralph said in a cowering tone.

"Well, you thought wrong. It also explains why the son-of-a-bitch never seemed to be bothered when I challenged him. He knew he had me dead to right." Herb scowled.

"Boys, I hate to break up this talk fest, but we do have a problem on our hands. What do we do? We're all in the same boat. We can't just let them off the hook and hear it from the other members." Fred warned.

After deliberating for all of three minutes...

"I think we have no choice but to give them the same slap on the wrist we did with Nora, Sharon and Cathy. Make sense to you guys?"

"Agreed Herb." Fred and Ralph said in unison.

"Call them back in so we can get the hell out of here." Herb muttered.

The women came into the boardroom and sat quietly, as they listened to Herb, inform them, that their golfing privileges would be suspended for a weekend.

Things were looking up in all directions. Marion was now a grateful friend, who wanted the girls to know that the next time they had a fuzzy navel drinking party, she'd love to be included.

After thanking the members of the committee for having made a fair and prudent judgment, they started to leave. At the door however, Sylvia, turned around and addressed the men, who had also risen. **"Oh boys! Your slip is showing,"** she said, with a grin. Two of the committee members instinctively looked down.

"Gotcha!" Sylvia gloated, blowing the gun powder from her finger.

CHAPTER 45
ANOTHER DAY WITH GEORGE

"WE ONLY HAVE a few days of practice left before the match." George said to Nora. "I'd like to spend the balance of our time on your approach to the green and your short game. Do some stretching and then take your fifty-six degree wedge and move the ball from thirty yards working it up to seventy-five."

Nora complied with his instructions, stretching for ten minutes and then warming up with her wedge. George watched her intently, looking for possible flaws in her technique. He made occasional comments about her not allowing enough time between shots, as well as asking her to visualize a precise distance when hitting her club rather than just swinging at golf balls.

Nora took notice of the heightened look in George's eyes on every swing of her club and hoped her technique was the only thing he was admiring.

"She's quite a specimen, isn't she?" Mike Grace said, joining in admiration. "It's always a pleasure to watch beauty in motion."

"Are you here to practice or just observing?" George asked.

"As a matter of fact, I'd like to have a word with Nora for a moment… if I may?"

"Mike, we're in the middle of a practice and I'd rather not interrupt her routine. Can't this wait until later?"

"No, it can't George…and considering you're being accommodated at our club, it would seem the same courtesy should be afforded to my request." Mike snapped.

"What's going on?" Nora said, patting the perspiration from her face with a towel.

"Nora, can I have a word with you in private?" Mike asked.

"Can't it wait?"

"I wouldn't interrupt if it weren't of extreme importance." Mike insisted.

"Alright." Nora said reluctantly. "I suppose I can spare a few minutes. Let's sit on the bench over there."

"Seems George, doesn't like me very much." Mike said, walking to a bench with Nora.

"Surely you didn't interrupt my practice to talk about how he feels about you?" Nora said, frowning and wondering what the *cagey fox* was up to now.

"No, I didn't. What I came to talk about was the little scam you and your friend Cathy, pulled with Bill." Mike sneered.

"I don't know what you're talking about." Nora snapped, then starting to get up. "I don't have time for this nonsense."

"Sit down, young lady!" Mike said, then grabbing Nora's arm. "I'm not finished talking to you. I'm particularly concerned about your complicity in destroying the marriage of your friend, Cathy."

"Take your hand off of her!" George barked, standing almost nose to nose from Mike, with clenched fists. "Are you all right, Nora?"

Mike released his grip, Nora pulling her hand away and rubbing her wrist. "I was just indicating where her friend Cathy, hurt herself the other day," he stammered.

"George, I'll be alright." Nora said, with a reassuring glance.

"Just remember *buddy boy,* keep your paws to yourself," said a determined George, poking his finger in Mike's chest, then walking back to the bags.

"Isn't love just wonderful, Nora?" Mike observed. "You can see he has special feelings for you."

"Get to the point, what did you mean when you said I could destroy Cathy's marriage?" Nora demanded.

The veins in Mike's neck thickened as he peered at Nora, his face flushed with contempt.

"Let's put all of our cards on the table, shall we?" He said. "No lies, no pretending. Your harlot friend Cathy, got Bill drunk and the dumb jackass told her about our plan. Well, it's water under the bridge. **I don't like you** Nora and do you know why?" Mike scoffed.

"You're on a roll, don't stop now." Nora snipped.

"When Nick was alive, you blended in at Happy Hills, like the other women of the club. You were classy and refined."

"You mean…I knew my place?" Nora hissed, her expression showing contempt at his suggestion of submission.

"Yes Nora, you did. But since Nick's passing you've been nothing but a troublemaker, behaving like a spoiled adolescent looking for attention. The other women of the club know it's their husbands who are the members, not them. But you don't seem to understand that." Mike jeered.

"We can't get breakfast, coffee or a bagel in the morning. Our golf times are substantially limited and we don't have a place to lounge, play cards or just watch a ball game. Is that asking too much?" Nora lashed out.

"It took more than a hundred years to free the slaves." Mike said in a flippant tone.

"Perhaps that's the problem? The women of the club must never make waves or they'll be ostracized and characterized as troublemakers. What you're saying makes no sense to me. Are we done here?" Nora demanded.

"Not quite." Mike told her. "Let me put it this way. If you don't play ball with me, your friend Cathy, will be told about her husband's escapades with a certain Polish waitress, who had to be shipped back to her country in order to avoid a scandal. I imagine Cathy, wouldn't be inclined to continue a relationship with an unfaithful husband...Am I right?" Mike asked, to the shock of Nora.

She was disappointed in hearing that Fred, had been unfaithful, but she did her best not to show it. After all, it might be one of Mike's tricks to keep her in line.

"By the look on your face, I guess I got your attention." Mike sneered.

"How do I know you're telling me the truth?"

"Ask Sylvia Gibbs, Sharon Kelly or Marion Blake. They'll confirm it for you."

"How would they know?" Nora asked, nervously moving her position on the bench.

"Because my wife told them and the three members of the disciplinary committee, which included, Fred. Tammy threatened if they didn't go light on their punishment, the dirt under all their fingernails would be closely inspected."

"So what are you saying to me Mike? What do you want?"

"I want you to back off on your demands for change."

"Don't you think it's a bit too late for that? Most of the women have heard about the agreement."

"Only from you, Nora. When you cut off the head of the snake and the hissing stops, the danger passes. Oh, I'll make some bagels and donuts available for the women, but they'll be no grill room constructed and tee times will stay as currently scheduled." Mike snarled.

"Is that all?" Nora hissed.

"The price of saving a friends marriage doesn't come that cheap," the steely eyed president scoffed..."And...under no circumstances will you win the match with Bill."

The asking price to protect Cathy, from her husbands indiscretions was high and Nora, wondered if it was worth trying to save, after all, what she perceived...was a marriage already doomed.

"But I can't do that Mike," she said. "You ought to know that."

"Personally, I think he'll kick your ass, but if the unthinkable were to happen... ***you're not to win!*** If you don't cooperate, I'm prepared to call your friend and let her in on our little secret." Mike threatened.

Her emotions shattered, this despicable man was asking her to do something against the very fabric of her being. She suddenly felt nauseous, but she had to respond.

"Of all the dirty tricks. You're really something, Mike. Is there anything you wouldn't stoop to? How do you live with yourself?"

"Well thank you Nora. I do believe you finally understand that **I'll stop at nothing** to keep this club from becoming *gender neutral*. When you lose... and you will lose, I'll expect to receive your resignation from the club." Mike demanded.

"How will you keep the other women from telling Cathy, about Fred?"

"My wife made them swear, that everything which transpired before the disciplinary committee would stay in that room.

I believe the ball is in your court, Nora. Have we cobbled together an agreement?"

Nora buried her face in her hands. She kept asking herself the same question over and over again. If Fred, could do this to Cathy, was their marriage really worth saving, particularly since she hasn't exactly been *Mother Theresa* herself? But Cathy, was like a sister, a lifelong companion. If she told her about Fred, their friendship might surely be a casualty and that would be devastating to Nora. What should she do? She hated Mike for putting her in this position. But, was he or her stubbornness the culprit? It had all started when she struck Bill, with her ball. If she had simply apologized, perhaps all of this turmoil and backroom drama would never have happened.

"Don't fret, Nora." Mike told her. "It's best for all concerned. You save a marriage and I save the club, and...you get the hell out of Happy Hills."

Raising her head, Nora stared at him...expressionless. Whatever else happened, she wouldn't let him see how much she was suffering.

"My friendship with Cathy, is more important to me than a game golf." Nora told him. "You won't have to worry about me," she sadly relented.

"Nora, no one is to know about our agreement," the sly fox warned her. "And I mean absolutely no one."

"Mike, you've won." Nora told him. "There's no need to worry about my keeping silent about this." Then, she abruptly left the bench, the sly fox... close behind.

"What's wrong, Nora?" George asked. "You look upset."

"Someone we both know has died." Mike said glibly. "Isn't that so, Nora?"

She wanted to tell George, what had really happened, but knew she had no right to draw him into this personal affair. When he asked if he could get her a drink of water, she thanked him.

When Nora and George were alone again, Mike having strode off triumphantly, he asked her once again what was wrong. But, Nora shut down…never hearing him, as she watched the board president slowly disappear in the distance.

"I don't believe what that bastard said," was the next thing she heard. "No one died, did they? He had another bone to pick with you. Tell me about it Nora, perhaps I can help. You know I'd do anything for you." George pleaded.

In the end, she maintained her silence. But because she felt guilty at deceiving him, Nora agreed to meet him poolside the next day. It would, she thought, relax them both. But deep inside, she knew nothing could keep her from fretting about Mike's next surprise.

CHAPTER 46
SEX AND THE COMPUTER

NORA WAS PATIENT with her friend, all the time wondering if this band-aid approach was the fix for a wounded marriage. Mike's revelation of Fred's infidelity had come as a complete surprise to her and now she couldn't help speculating if it was in retaliation for his wife's indiscretions? Did he know of Cathy's short-lived flings with Bill and the pool boy? What if Nick, had done the same to her, she wondered? Would she be as vengeful as Fred, or simply leave the marriage?

"This isn't really helping me at all." Cathy said, after a half hour of scanning the web for possible costumes. "It's like trying to buy a dress on line."

"I need to touch and feel before I buy. You know that sex shop in town?" Cathy asked.

"Oh no you don't, Cathy Daley! You're not getting me into that place."

"Come on Nora, this is 2007. Who cares who sees us? We'll wear sunglasses." Cathy said, poking her friend playfully.

It was, Nora thought, one of Cathy's most outrageous ideas. Still, she'd made some important sacrifices for her already, not the least...the one Mike, had exacted from her. She might as well make another. They both left on what would be an adventure neither could anticipate.

"Come on, Nora! Let's go in." Cathy urged her friend, who was hiding in a kerchief and dark sunglasses. The shop, which was in an unimposing building was tucked away behind a Kmart.

"How about you going in and I'll stand lookout?" Nora pleaded.

"Stand lookout! I'm not going to rob the place, you tinsel brain. Now let's go."

They might as well have been bank robbers, Nora thought, as they edged their way into ***Sex Toys Unlimited***, where shelf after shelf was filled with a variety of outrageous items.

"Oh...my...God! Would you look at the size of that thing!" Cathy cried out. "It's as big as a zucchini!"

"Quiet down!" Nora told her, glancing around...observing if anyone had heard Cathy's outburst.

When the clerk asked if they needed assistance, Cathy explained what she was looking for. He led them to an area of the store, where separated by drawn curtains, he showed them a rack of exotic outfits.

"Just bring out what you want to buy," he said. "If you need help, I'm just a curtain away."

Cathy was like a kid in a candy store, trying on several outfits while Nora, stood guard at the curtain, leaving little room between her kerchief and sunglasses.

"How do you like the cowgirls outfit?" Cathy asked, twirling around on her toes in a whirl of red, white and blue leather fringe.

"It's certainly patriotic." Nora told her. "It's great Cathy, can we go now?"

"What's your hurry? Remember, this was your idea, Nora Cummings." Cathy smirked.

"Not to come here!" She reminded her in a scowled whisper. "We were supposed to find something on line."

"What a nervous Nelly you are." Cathy snapped. "Let's see what we can find out front. I'm taking these five outfits, but I might want a few other things as well. If I'm going to do this, I might as well do it right."

"You have a cowgirl, nurse, nun, maid and a gypsy outfit. What more would you need?" Nora asked, nervously impatient.

"Oh, I don't know...**maybe a whip to beat you** with if you don't stop being so damn skittish!" Cathy yelped. "I don't want to miss anything which might be interesting, so please, please, don't spoil my fun."

"See what I mean, now look at this." Cathy said, holding a rubber penis. She clicked it on, the toy twisting in a circular motion.

"Now this...I have to buy," she said with a devilish smile. "You should get one for yourself, Nora."

"I think I'll pass," she said dryly, asking herself if she was now responsible for Cathy's seemingly obsession with *Sex Toys Unlimited*. She wasn't having a very good day and couldn't wait to take a long hot bath as well as getting a good night sleep.

"I have one of those and they're really great," someone said, Nora and Cathy turning to find Laura Dicks, standing behind them.

"What are you doing here?" Cathy cried out, Nora turning away... totally mortified.

"I come here all the time." Laura said, shrugging. "Jerry and I use a lot of these things. The movies they have are really good, too. I recommend you see *DOGGIES ARE NOT THE ONLY ONES*. It's about..."

"That's all right Laura!" Nora interrupted. "We were just leaving."

"Oh! It's you, Nora. I didn't recognize you in the kerchief and sunglasses. Do you come here often?" Laura asked and not about to be put off so easily.

"No! no! She brought me here." Nora said accusingly, pointing to Cathy, who turned ever so slowly towards her friend, her mouth agape...with a peering stare.

"Sylvia told me about this place, she's a regular, so is Doris. Oh, speaking of Sylvia, here she comes now." Laura said, waving to catch her attention.

"Cathy, I could wring your neck." Nora muttered under her breath and pinching her friends arm. "This is becoming a ***HAPPY HILLS SEX KLATCH!*** You insane woman. Why did I listen to you?"

"Hi girls!" Sylvia said cheerfully. "I see we have **new members** of the *Sex Toys Unlimited Club*. I have the toy you're holding, Cathy. It's devastating girl. You can just send the husbands on their way once you have one of those babies."

"I have a great idea!" Laura said. "Why don't we finish shopping and come back to my house for sandwiches and drinks."

"I don't think so Laura." Nora said, adjusting her sunglasses. "I'm a bit *bushed*. But thank you anyway."

"That's not a good thing to say around here." Laura said, giggling innocently. Nora, Cathy and Sylvia looked perplexed.

"A bit *bushed*? In need of a *haircut*? Don't you get it?" Laura cried out, before bending over in a fit of giggles.

"And you want to have drinks at her house?" Nora whispered to Cathy.

"We'd be happy to come!" Cathy replied, poking Nora in her derriere, her friend bouncing one step forward

"No! No! No! Cathy." Nora barked, pulling down on her skirt. "And stop poking me!"

"Nora, ditch the kerchief and sunglasses." Sylvia told her. "The jig is up, we know who you are. Unless you're expecting Father Maloney to pop in?"

"Nora, we have nothing going." Cathy said. "Let's stop for awhile and have some girl fun?"

"Yes, Nora!" Laura squealed. "Don't be a party pooper."

"I have to wash my hair." Nora claimed. "I have ironing to do. Besides, I'm supposed to meet George at the pool this afternoon."

"Nora, call the ***old buzzard*** and tell him you have a headache."

"Would you stop calling him old!"

"Well honey, after seeing the things in here…you might want to start calling him **pee wee."**

"Your insufferable Cathy!" Slapping her friend's shoulder.

"Screw the hair and the hell with the ironing." Sylvia told her. "We have some drinking and girl talking to do sister."

It was a twenty minute drive from *Sex Toys Unlimited* to Laura's house and with every mile, Nora was more and more certain she shouldn't have agreed to come along. These women seemed to be out of control. And perhaps it was reason enough, because as usual, she wanted to protect Cathy, if only from herself. Nora made the call to George, feeling guilty in canceling, but promising to make it another day.

"Make yourselves at home." Laura said. "I'll fix some sandwiches. Sylvia, you know where the liquor cabinet is. Why don't you make a batch of those *fuzzy belly buttons* and have the girls sit in the den?"

"You mean *fuzzy navels*?" Sylvia replied, grinning.

"Don't you think it's a bit early to start drinking?" Nora said. It was becoming a familiar scene lately, that certain members were not social drinkers, but perhaps with a more serious problem, one they hadn't recognized, or worse, didn't want to.

"It's never too early when you're thirsty." Sylvia declared. "Besides, we have the makings of a great party. It's a beautiful Monday afternoon and our husbands are out playing with their little white balls or playing cards."

"Who's playing with their balls?" Laura asked, peeking around the countertop, separating the kitchen from the family room. It was clear from the way Cathy, Nora and Sylvia looked at one another, they were steering themselves to a *ditzy* afternoon with their equally *ditzy* hostess. Laura often reminded Nora, of the naïve character played by Marilyn Monroe in ***Some Like It Hot,*** simple but genuine, a woman whose mind always seemed to be out in left field somewhere.

Laura's ranch style home was nestled on a three quarter-acre parcel and surrounded by tall white pines, supplying ample privacy. The four thousand square foot interior was quite fashionably decorated and apparent, it had a professional hand in it's design. The featured room was a rather oversized step-down den, three quarters of which was surrounded with lush leather couches with a large rectangular table in the center. The bar above, consisted of a mirrored wall with shelves, housing glasses and a variety of fine liquors. Four swivel stools, covered in a leopard skin design, provided an exotic backdrop.

By noon, the women retreated to the patio, sitting at a round table, a blue umbrella in the middle protecting them from the glares of the sun. They were sipping their drinks and munching on finger sandwiches made by their hostess, their eyes fixated at the reflecting waters of the pool.

"Drink up girls." Sylvia told them. **"I have some really good gossip** to tell you about. Did you hear we got Marion, bombed out of her mind the other day?"

"No way Sylvia!" Nora replied. This bit of gossip made her grin. the women who'd been her nemesis, *miss prim and proper*, wasted. "Oh, the day was not a total loss," she thought.

"That's not the best of it." Sylvia giggled. "Remember what Sharon, did in the dining room when we got bombed?"

"Get out of town!" Cathy shouted. "No, don't tell me...Marion...did a Sharon Kelly?"

"Girls, it was a sight to behold. Blake was fully skunked. She asked Sharon, to show her ten thousand dollar boob job and what does Sharon do?"

"You got to be kidding!" Cathy said. "She dropped them again?"

"Well, why shouldn't she?" Laura said, wide-eyed. "Marion asked her to."

The women looked at one another, then...at Laura.

"Mind boggling." Sylvia said, shaking her head. "Just mind boggling." Sylvia continued. "So, after Sharon, plops out her boobies...Marion...does the same, asking Sharon, if she thought anything could be done for her. It was a riot girls. Talk about pancakes."

"Why would Marion...have pancakes under her bra?" Laura asked. "I don't get it?"

"No more fuzzy belly-buttons for you Laura." Sylvia quipped.

"Paul Henry was going ballistic trying to get Marion, to holster up." Sylvia went on, trying to maintain her composure. "But she just looked at him and said," 'Do...do...you like these, Paul?' Sylvia burst into laughter and the other women followed.

"The next day,"...Sylvia continued, patting her eyes with a tissue, "the four of us were called before the disciplinary committee. We didn't know what to expect of course, but we knew it wasn't going to be good news. Then Tammy, came up with an idea. She said, if it seemed like the committee members were coming on too strong, she would take over and boy did she ever." Sylvia said, sipping on her *fuzzy navel.*

"Who was on the committee?" Nora inquired.

"Ralph, Herb and Fred."

"Tammy sat back quietly during the hearing until Ralph, got on his high horse."

"They had a horse in the room?" Laura asked.

"It's only a figure of speech, Laura. God you have a lot of space between those ears." Sylvia jabbed.

"Thanks Sylvia, I'm glad someone noticed. I use Q-Tips every morning… just to make sure."

"Make sure of what?" The perplexed Sylvia huffed.

"Why…to make sure that I have what you said, clean spaces between my ears." Laura said, smiling and placing both hands on her knees.

"Cathy, pass that pitcher of fuzzy navels over here." Sylvia demanded, shaking her head, as she refilled her glass and took a long gulp. "You're a pistol, Laura Dicks."

"Why thank you Sylvia, it's good to have friends who appreciate you."

"Yes…as I was saying, Tammy gave it to everyone of them." Sylvia went on. "They were all squirming in their chairs. It was hilarious to watch, you had to be there to appreciate it."

"What did she say to them?" Cathy wanted to know.

"We aren't supposed to repeat anything about what went on." Sylvia told her. "But let's just say…two of the men…like women's clothes."

"I don't blame them." Laura said. "I like women's clothes too."

"Yes dear, we know. Sylvia, did Tammy bring up the Polish waitress to Fred?" Cathy asked, ignoring Laura.

"What!" Nora yelped, spilling her drink. She couldn't believe what she just heard. Mike had just about broken her this morning, threatening to expose Fred's indiscretion to her friend and yet, Cathy knew. Nora was relieved, that she was no longer under the thumb of Mike Grace, but curious why Cathy, never told her.

"What?" Cathy said, turning to her friend. "You didn't know that Fred, had an affair with a Polish waitress?" The other women remaining silent.

"Cathy, that's the best news I've heard today!" Nora said. Just how good, Cathy might never know. But the fact was, Nora now had the ammunition she needed to bury the club president. But on the way home, she had a change of heart. After all, Cathy had a right to know what transpired between her and Mike.

"Listen," Nora said, as she backed the car out of Laura's driveway. "I didn't want to say anything in front of Sylvia. She relays the news faster than CNM, but there's something you should know." As Nora, went on to tell her, what Mike's visit to the practice range had been about, Cathy sat very still, her hands clenched in her lap, staring out the window. Only when Nora, stopped for a red light, did she notice the tears streaming down her friend's cheeks.

"I have an idea." Nora said, leaning over to hug Cathy. "I think I know how we can teach those two men a lesson they'll never forget."

CHAPTER 47
A DAY AT THE POOL

IT WAS A BLISTERING Tuesday morning in August. The match between Nora and Bill was four days away and as usual, George had worked Nora, exceptionally hard in preparation for her upcoming battle. The plan was the same for tomorrow and Thursday, while Friday was to be a day of strategy, reviewing possible situations which might occur during the match on Saturday.

After her practice session with George, Nora showered at the pool locker room. She changed into a *red bikini* and tied her hair back in a ponytail with a red double hanging ribbon. After rubbing her fair skin with a generous amount of suntan lotion, she placed a towel around her shoulders and walked to a table shaded by a green umbrella in the middle of the pool area, attracting attention as usual, from several of the men who marveled at her striking appearance.

The swimming pool at Happy Hills was Olympic sized and could comfortably accommodate several bathers. The heat of the day attracted a number of members and their children who surrounded the perimeter of the pool, some sitting at one of several tables and others in the water, enjoying relief from the sultry heat.

Placing her straw beach bag on the chair next to her, Nora took out her iPod, turning it to her favorite song. Ten minutes later, several heads turned as Cathy, strolled towards Nora, wearing a yellow bikini, her hair also tied back in a ponytail with a yellow ribbon.

"I can't believe this heat." Cathy said, as she plopped her yellow beach bag on the chair next to Nora. "You must have been dying at practice?"

"It wasn't pleasant." Nora admitted. "But I only have five days left counting today, before the match."

"Did you order anything to drink yet?"

"No, I haven't seen the pool boy. Speaking of pool boys, doesn't yours come to the house today?" Nora asked, with a raised eyebrow.

"See what kind of friend you have?" Cathy crowed. "Yes he does, but I'm with you, instead of seeing that gorgeous hunk. Oh, there's the pool boy over there, let's see if I can get his attention. I'm really thirsty and one hungry lady."

She waved her hand towards the server who was placing a food order on a poolside table. He turned his head and when he noticed it was Cathy, his eyes widened and his face cringed. He lost balance of the dish he was lowering, the entire contents falling on the lap of the member he was serving. He attempted to remedy the embarrassment by brushing the food from the members lap, while looking in the direction of Cathy. The server's arm, inadvertently moved from the members lap to under her sun skirt. The member grabbed her beach bag with her left hand and like a fighter throwing a roundhouse punch, hit the young server squarely on his shoulder, knocking him into the pool. He swam to the other end and away from the member's table. He wasn't seen for the rest of the afternoon.

"Was that the kid from the mall?" Cathy asked.

"I think so." Nora replied. "You've got the poor kid, spooked. Are you sure when you let go of him…you left everything in place?"

When another server arrived to take their lunch order, Cathy asked for a tuna on rye and Nora, a veggie burger, both ordered ice teas.

"Okay, let's talk about Mike Grace." Cathy said, settling back comfortably on the chaise.

"Can't it wait until we finish lunch?" Nora asked, grimacing. "I don't want to spoil my appetite."

"No, it can't wait. I expected you to call me last night."

"I was busy." Nora murmured, with a far away look in her eyes, staring at the blue water glistening from the sunlight.

"With who? Oh, tell me it wasn't with George again?" Cathy snipped. "Come on Nora, what's happening? I leave you for a few hours and you go out with a guy ready to apply for AARP?"

"George makes me feel safe." Nora told her. "He's gentle and there's history between us."

"Yes, about twenty years of history." Cathy groaned. "Think of it this way, when you were born he was twenty. You want safe? Buy a German Shepherd. He'll always wag his tail when he sees you and you won't have to play bingo with his senior citizens friends when you're fifty."

"Cathy, that's cruel. George is a vibrant person."

"So is a vibrator, until the batteries run out." Cathy giggled.

"Well, he makes my toes curl. What do you think of that?" Nora said, with an edge in her tone.

"You want curly toes,' play with one of those toys I bought. It just keeps on ticking and doesn't need a respirator to resuscitate a worn out worm." Cathy snapped.

"Cathy, let's **leave George alone** for now and get to the Mike and Bill situation."

"Nora, I'd stick it to those bastards. They've tried every dirty trick to embarrass you. We have to think of something that's out of sight. Something which will bury them both." Cathy sneered.

Then, a lazy smile came over Cathy's face, as she glared out over the glittering water. Nora, knew her well enough to imagine, that she was visualizing scenarios of Mike and Bill's demise, perhaps tying them together, preparatory to pushing them out the door of a cargo plane.

"I know that smirk Cathy Daley, what are you thinking?"

"Oh, nothing serious…just wondering."

"I think I have a solution to the problem." Nora told her.

"Well, what did you come up with short of murdering them both?"

When explained to Cathy, what she thought would be the most exacting punishment administered to Mike and Bill, Cathy roared with laughter.

"Well, you aren't going to kill them, which in my opinion is a pity. But you'll succeed in running them both out of town. I like it! I like it!" Cathy snickered.

After finishing their lunch, Nora turned towards her friend, leaning on her elbow. "What's going on with you and Fred?"

"Nora, I honestly don't know. There's got to be a reason why he and I have been unfaithful and all the sex toys in the world won't help us come up with the answer. Somewhere along the thirteen years we've been married, we've drifted and I can't pinpoint to any one thing responsible, it just happened."

"Have you tried counseling?"

"Nora, this will kill you. We go to some guy who's supposed to help us. The shrink asks if this was our first marriage and we said yes. I asked if he was married and he said he was. Then I ask if it was his first marriage and he said, 'No… it's my fourth.' Fred and I both cracked up. Here's a guy who couldn't make it with three wives and he's going to give us advice. Needless to say, we paid him and left."

"Did you try seeing someone else?"

"Why? What's he going to say? We have to rekindle the flame? We know the issues. Both of us like to unwrap new presents. The old one's not a surprise any more. Don't you remember when you and Nick, first started dating? Your heart pounded every time he touched you. I call it the ***"forbidden fruit***

***syndrome*"** Why do you think Eve…took that first bite? Now, the fruit is available all of the time, it's not as naughty as it used to be."

"Marriage isn't **a *one box surprise.*"** Nora told her. "It requires work, hard work. You need to create naughty when the menu's getting stale, not just surrender to the first new piece of fruit available."

"Nora, that's all well and good, but the divorce rate in this country **IS** fifty-percent, mostly because people want a change. The one thing the Arabs did right was the idea of the *harem*."

"But, that's for men who have multiple wives." Nora told her.

"But, if it were expanded to women, just imagine opening a new surprise seven days of the week." Cathy said giggling "The divorce rate would disappear and think of the fun. My God! It would be better than shopping for a new pair of shoes."

"REALITY CHECK, earth to Cathy. We live in America and to my recollection, I don't remember of ever reading about a place in our country allowing multiple husbands."

"Nora Cummings…don't you dare spoil my fantasy. Why do you think I was so happy after going to our toy store?" Cathy snapped, then reaching for her ice tea.

"Think about the fifty-percent that do make it…the half-full glass?"

"Yes, yes, Nora. I just happen to like a different drink once in a while."

Nora considered abandoning the idea of trying to save her friend's marriage. Maybe it was for the best after all. Perhaps in the end, if they found someone new, Cathy and Fred could find the magic she had…with Nick.

When she said her goodbye's to Cathy, she walked to the parking lot and was dismayed to discover that one of the tires on her car was flat.

"Can I be of help?" Someone said. When she turned, she saw…Bill.

"What nerve," she hissed. "How can you speak to me after what you and Mike were planning?"

The man scheming to defraud her, now asking to come to her aid? How ironic, she thought. Nora, could only see a fox in waiting, while Bill, lowered his eyes, not capable of denying his past transgressions.

"Please listen to me for a moment," gesturing to put his hand on her arm, Nora taking a step back.

Bill withdrew his hand and raised both palms out. "I admit…Mike and I share in wanting to keep the club from being gender neutral, but what we don't agree on…is how to keep it that way."

"Why should I believe anything you say? You've both lied every opportunity you've had."

"Listen Nora, I understand your reluctance. I'd feel the same if the positions were reversed. As a gesture of good faith, please, let me change the tire for you, and then...let's talk at Gino's. I won't take more than fifteen minutes of your time, I promise."

There was, Nora told herself, no reason she should listen to him, or trust him, except he sounded so genuine. Besides, it would be a fair exchange in return for him changing the tire. On the other hand, why should they go to a restaurant, when he could surely tell her anything he had to say, right here?

"I want us to be comfortable." he said, as though he had read her thoughts. "Let's do this in a civilized way, with no more lies, or deception. All right...?"

"I see we share our like for the same drink." Bill said, in an obvious attempt to loosen the tension of the moment.

It was a long day for Nora. She was tired and irritable and not particularly in the mood for idle conversation. She regretted being there, thinking she should have let him change the tire and left.

"Bill, I'm tired and want to get home, please get to the point?" Nora demanded, placing her hand on her forehead.

"Fair enough, Nora. Look, we've had our differences and I'm not going to sit here and pretend we like each other. But I do want you to know...I couldn't go along with Mike and his scheme to defraud you. I told him he was going too far and in fact, what he wanted to do, bordered on a criminal act."

"**Why are you telling me, Bill?"** Nora asked suspiciously. "Is there something else the two of you cooked up?"

"I don't blame you for being skeptical, I just want our match to be on the up and up. Whatever issues you have with Mike, is now between the two of you. Be careful with him Nora, he'll try anything to win this ***tug-of-war*** with you. I'm sorry it's gotten this far. Maybe some day...look, good luck this weekend." Bill said, lowering his head.

This was a different side of the man she'd encountered in the past. There was a sincerity that would be hard to disguise, even for him, she thought to herself. Perhaps, it should be explored further?

Bill slid across the booth to leave, when Nora, placed her hand on his.

"Thank you, Bill."

"Nora, the explanation was long overdue."

Their eyes met, the same way as in her nightly dreams. Bill's charm and good looks were undeniable, and now, humility. Perhaps, she should...?

"Could you deal with a woman buying you dinner?" Nora asked, not believing she just invited out the *nemesis* who initiated, what was turning out to be a crisis affecting her, the club and Cathy.

"You...buy me dinner? Why?" Asked the stunned, Harper.

"Say...it's for changing the flat on my car." Nora said, with a sensuous smile.

Bill hesitated, but not for long. Grinning boyishly, he accepted her invitation, with the proviso he take responsibility for the wine.

The dinner was delicious. Nora had the *veal scaloppini* and Bill, the *rigatoni Bolognese.* He ordered a bottle of *Silver Oak,* which they consumed with their meal. Surprisingly enough, it seemed as though they had known each other for years. They found their dialogue interesting and sometimes funny. Even more astonishing, at least to Nora, they seemed to have so much in common. After coffee and dessert, they walked from the restaurant to their cars.

"This is the best time I've had in a long while." Bill said, kissing the back of Nora's hand in a courtly manner, sending chills down her spine. Perhaps, just perhaps she thought, she had misjudged the man.

"Nora, I'd like to see you again. Something tells me inside, perhaps faith has brought us together. It may sound crazy, but tonight, over a simple dinner, you've made me feel like a school boy with his first crush."

It was only with an effort, she reminded herself, that they were rivals, and her continued membership in the club depended on defeating him in the next few days.

"Bill…I really don't…"

"Nora, please, don't answer now." Bill said, sensing he may be asking too much too soon. "Can we at least agree that you'll think about it?"

"Yes, Bill," she answered, bringing a wide grin to his face, then kissing her jubilantly on her cheek, afterwards departing for his car. Nora, remained motionless as Bill drove off, placing her hand to her face, flushed with girlish excitement.

When she retuned home, Nora's nightly ritual included sipping on a cup of aromatic green tea while reading herself to sleep. She had just slipped under the covers and picked up her book, when the telephone rang.

"I hope I didn't wake you?" Bill said. "I just wanted to know if you made it home okay."

They talked for another twenty minutes, their conversation ranging from the books they liked to read to his interest in sailing. When they finally said good night, Nora went back to sipping her tea and reading. But it was difficult to keep her mind on the words. Finally, still thinking of Bill and the wonderful evening they shared, she slipped into sleep…dreaming she was in his arms.

But then, the dream turned into a nightmare. Cathy was standing in the bedroom doorway, aiming a gun straight at them, demanding to know…how Nora, could betray her. Awaking with a start, Nora sat upright in bed, her breathing heavy, perspiration oozing down the sides of her temples. Was it wrong to be attracted to Bill? Would she be punished for it in the end?

When the phone rang at eight the next morning, it was Cathy, wanting to know if Nora, could meet her for lunch after practice.

"I can't today," she told her. "I have some chores to do and maybe a meeting to attend. Let me call you this afternoon and if for some reason I get done early, we'll get together. Oh damn, I forgot, I'm getting my nails done at two-thirty."

"Why didn't you call me last night?" Cathy asked.

"I was caught up with things and it was too late." Nora hedged, not wanting to lie outright.

This was, she realized, going to be more difficult than even she could have imagined.

"With George?" Cathy asked.

"No, someone else."

"Well…tell me girl! What's the mystery? Who did you mix your spit with?"

"You're so gross! I have to go, the doorbells ringing. I'll call you later," she said, hurrying her friend off the phone.

While driving to the club, Nora's thoughts were about her dinner with Bill, the evening before. Then, there was the magical kiss, only to be shattered by the bizarre dream the same night. She didn't know if it would be prudent to tell Cathy, about the unexpected turn of events. She only knew, she was intrigued by the other side of the man whom she previously despised, at the same time understanding, she must proceed with caution. She couldn't bear the thought, somewhere along the way, she might lose a lifetime friend or be deceived by Bill, because she lowered her guard.

But, Nora was about to embark in something she never thought herself capable of which would mire her in more intrigue and controversy.

CHAPTER 48
A WOMAN'S WRATH

WHEN NORA CALLED Liz Peters and asked her to lunch, the reporter accepted immediately, seeming particularly interested when Nora, told her there had been several important developments in regard to the match with Bill, on Saturday.

They agreed to met in Gino's at noon, Nora arriving first and requesting a table in the far corner for privacy, Liz joining her a few minutes later. Stylish as usual, the columnist wore a white linen dress held tightly by a gold linked belt. A wide brimmed hat matched the color of her dress and was trimmed with gold lace.

"It's so nice to see you." Liz said, taking a seat opposite Nora. "I didn't think we'd be talking again. You seemed pretty emphatic about not going public, why the change of heart?"

"A person can be pushed so far Liz, before realizing they have to push back or continued to be bullied." Nora told her. "I'm sure you're occasionally subjected to jerks who see a skirt as a weakness."

"I do Nora and as you said, I push back until they back off. Who's the bully we're talking about? The guy you're playing against? What's his name?"

Nora hesitated. Should Bill, be given a free pass based on his recent change of heart, or was it a ploy on her emotions for some other sinister plan with Mike? She had to decide, and quickly.

"Did I ask the wrong question?"

Nora let her heart decide, hoping the gamble would turn out to be the correct roll of the dice.

"No, no, Liz, it's not my opponent."

"Well that's good... because whatever you said, would have come off as sour grapes."

Opening her white and gold *Chanel* pocketbook, Liz retrieved a small tape recorder and asked if she objected to being on record, Nora indicating it wasn't a problem.

"This is all about Mike Grace, the board president of Happy Hills," she explained. "He's the bully, Liz."

Almost two hours passed before they were finished with the interview, Nora's revelation riveting and explosive. Liz thanked her and when they started to leave, who should they run into... the bully himself. She had no option but to introduce Liz, and in so doing, let the cat out of the bag.

"Why do I get the feeling you've broken your word to me?" Mike said, when Liz departed.

"It's over Mike." Nora told him. "The gloves are off and you're probably finished as president of the board and it's no ones fault but your own. You've pulled your last dirty trick, you shouldn't have taken it as far as you did."

Mike wanted to reach out and strangle the last breath from Nora. The veins from his neck were protruded and his eyes peering. He was clearly upset, that Nora, relented to Liz Peters.

"So, you're not only willing to turn your back on your best friend, but to embarrass the club members as well," he snarled. "I might have known you'd pull something like this."

"I'll take my chances with the members." Nora told him. "And as far as Cathy is concerned...she already knows about the Polish waitress. Your bullets are all blanks now."

"We'll see about that!" Mike bellowed. **"You picked a fight with the wrong person,** you... you...Jezebel!" Shouting loud enough for other patrons to turn and look in their direction.

Nora, could only hope, that in the end, the truth would not only prevail, but serve to cement her friendships, particularly with Cathy. At the same time, she realized that **Mike, might be right** and she had just made a terrible mistake.

CHAPTER 49
HOLY COW! HOLY COW!

NORA WAS PLACING clothes in the washing machine when the doorbell rang. Looking through the peep hole, she saw it was Cathy.

"I'm exhausted," her friend said, plopping herself down on the couch. "Do you have anything cold to drink?"

"Hi Nora, how are you? How did your day go? Good to see you." Nora said dryly, thinking not for the first time, Cathy, could do with an etiquette course. On the other hand, if she did, she would lose some of the impetuousness which made her so loveable.

"What's up Nora, how are yah? How's yah day going? Good to see yah. Now...can I have a damn drink?" Cathy said, mocking her friend.

"Okay, okay, but you first. Why are you so tired?"

"N..O..R..A, first a cold drink, or...I go on a no talking strike. Now, a diet Coke would be good." Cathy said, with pursed lips.

"Diet coke it is. Is that all, your Majesty? Perhaps you'd rather have champagne and strawberries?"

"Stop teasing me!"

"Only if you tell me what's wrong with you?" Nora insisted, then tickling her friend into submission.

"I will! I swear I will!" Cathy pleaded, as she giggled to the point of tears.

"You're a wicked woman, Nora Cummings! You know how ticklish I am." Cathy said, the crescendo of her laughter diminished, her expression now serious. "I think **Fred and I are getting a divorce."**

"What!" A startled Nora replied. "Couldn't you guys hash it out?"

"We tried to talk it out, but then, both of us said some pretty ugly things.

His affair with the Polish server wasn't the only shot. He knew about the pool boy and suspected there were others. Anyway, it wasn't civil."

"Does he know about Bill?" Nora asked, her question, somewhat self-serving.

The news was shocking. She had hoped, asking Cathy to extract information from Bill, wasn't the cause of her rift with Fred. Now she thought, would not be the time to reveal her dinner with Bill, or her awful dream.

"He didn't until I told him."

"Why did you do that?" Nora asked. "It must have been devastating for him?"

"You know how I get when my temper flares. The jerk said, I should have married you... because I spend more time with you then him. Are you available?" Cathy's laugh, half- hearted.

"How did you leave off?"

"I was so pissed at him, I just stormed out of the house and came here. It's over. I know it's over. We flung too much mud at one another."

Nora embraced her friend, stroking her hair as she had done so often when they were girls. No longer able to contain her emotions, Cathy, burst into tears, her bravado abandoned.

"Why do I always seem to be in your arms when I'm crying?" Cathy asked, wiping her eyes. "Maybe Fred's right...we ought to get married." Cathy, playfully added. **"Have you ever been with a woman?"**

Nora, patted Cathy's eyes, relieved in seeing a faint smile on her friend.

"If I had...do you think I'd tell you."

"Why not? I'm your best friend."

"Because ***Mrs. Paul Revere,*** I would read about it in Liz Peters' column the next morning."

"Are you saying, I can't keep a secret?" Cathy said, jerking her head from Nora's shoulder

"Just like Jell-O."

"What does that mean!" Cathy barked.

"If you touch it...it jiggles, and if you wait long enough...it melts."

"When did I ever tell a secret on you?" Cathy demanded.

"Billy Johnson in the movie sound familiar?"

"I told your mother because it was funny. He tried to make a move and you almost drowned him with his drink." Cathy said with a fain smile.

"Yes, and she told Mrs. Johnson...who told Billy's sister...who told the entire school!" Nora snapped.

"That's the only time. I shouldn't be chastised for one mistake."

"Okay, how about you telling Fred, I was seeing George?" Nora reminded her.

"That was supposed to be a secret?"

"Girlfriends aren't supposed to discuss what they talk about with other people."

"Let's get off the subject. What did you do today that prevented you from having lunch with a famous person?" Cathy smarted.

"What famous person?" Nora asked, somewhat confused.

"Mrs. Paul Revere, that's what you called me…didn't you?"

Nora smiled at the playful antics of her friend and as long as Cathy was laughing, her thoughts were off her struggles with Fred.

"I met with Liz Peters."

"Shut up! You didn't! You're not going to?" Cathy gasped.

"I have and it will be in tomorrow's paper."

"Sweet Jesus…you crazy bastard! You actually did it?" Cathy said, giggling and shaking her head.

"I had no choice. When Mike tried to blackmail me using you as a pawn, he crossed over the line. When you said you knew about Fred and the Polish waitress, it gave me the opportunity to get the jerk."

"Did you nail, Bill?"

Nora hesitated with her response. She looked at Cathy, her expression indicating something was wrong. Was her friend ready for the truth? Was she, she thought to herself. No lies, no half-truths, no pretenses, it was time to be open…to a point.

"What is it, Nora?"

"I didn't mention Bill to Peters," if that's what you mean." Nora said and then went on to explain the series of events which took place with him yesterday, adding, she knew it might be a gamble, but her gut told her he was being sincere.

"Wow! You just blew me away." Cathy exclaimed. **"Did you sleep with him?"**

"No Cathy, it was just a casual dinner. But I must confess, I saw a different side of him."

"Nora, promise me…you won't go out with him again!" Cathy demanded. "I don't want to be in competition with my best friend."

"Are you saying…you're thinking of resuming the relationship?"

"If Fred and I do split up, I'll be a single thirty-eight year old who puts the likes of Bill, high on my *to do* list."

Once again, Nora was in a dicey situation. She was curious about Bill and wanted to explore the possibility of seeing him after their match. He certainly made it clear he had more than a casual interest in her the last time they talked. But Cathy, was important to her, important enough to find it difficult to refuse her anything? Just then, the phone rang…and it was him. Nora put her finger to her lips.

"Hello Bill," she said, giving Cathy, a warning look.

"What can I do for you?" She asked coolly, acting out a part for her friends benefit.

"I wanted to call to say what a wonderful time I had yesterday," he told her. "I'd like to see you again, Nora."

She was more than curious why he called and was glad he did. But, her feelings had to be muted…for the sake of a friendship.

"Bill, I'm really flattered." Nora told him. "But it's not going to be possible."

"Why not? If I'm not mistaken…we made a connection both of us would never have dreamed possible. Look, I won't take no for an answer. I'll meet you at Gino's seven o'clock." And with that he hung up, leaving Nora, with the chore of having to pretend he was still on the line.

"I'm sorry," she said. "The dinner was great, but I prefer to end it at that. Too many barriers exist and I don't see any reason to see each other again." The pretense was convincing.

Nora hung up the phone, her heart dancing with expectation. Bill, wanted to raise the stakes in their relationship and yet, she had promised not to stand in Cathy's way. Clearly, her biggest hurdle was to decide whether or not she would meet him in a couple of hours. It was a dangerous game, played with *chips of friendship* that she couldn't afford to lose.

"Well! What did he say?" Cathy snapped.

"You heard what I told him. You're more important to me than dating the man whose butt I'm going to kick this Saturday. Let's not talk about him, OK? I didn't tell you the whole story about my meeting with Liz Peters. When we were leaving Gino's, who do you think we bumped into?"

"Not Mike and Bill?"

"You're half right. It was Mike, and he had the nerve to ask why I was meeting with Liz. When I told him, he went ballistic and said, ***`It's not over.`*** The man is really sick."

Cathy listened to her friend, but couldn't dismiss her concerns about Fred, and now, Bill's interest in her best friend. Then, there was always Mike Grace…lurking in the shadows. She had always admired Nora's tenacity and loyalty, but what would she do, if Nora, was forced to leave the club. Fred was loyal to Nora, out of memory to Nick, but would he now blame her for his failed marriage and rally against her, in support of Mike?

"I've seen his type before." Nora said, continuing her rant. "He's pure Neanderthal. You have to kill him to beat him, metaphorically speaking. When he reads tomorrow's paper, it might just do the trick. Liz is going to ask NOW, to come to the match on Saturday. They're going to press Mike, for a meeting with the board to ensure the agreement is honored."

Although Cathy heard Nora, spin her tale… she still believed…all of the trouble could have been avoided, with a simple apology by her friend.

"Wow Nora, there's going to be some fireworks tomorrow. Hey, it's five-thirty already. How about you and I grabbing some dinner at Gino's?"

Admittedly hungry, Nora didn't want a confrontation with Bill and Cathy, surely to develop if they went to Gino's.

"I'm really bushed, Cathy. Can I take a rain check?" Nora said, with a slight yawn, hoping to discourage her friend's persistence.

"You have to eat. So I won't take no for an answer."

"You're impossible. Okay, but not Gino's. I just had lunch there today. How about something light at the diner?" Nora suggested.

"The diner! That place has *races* every night."

"What *races*?" Nora asked quizzically.

"The *races* between the *la cucaracha's.*"

"*La cucaracha's*? Oh my God! *Roaches*? Are you serious?"

"Didn't you read about it in the paper. The board of health closed them down for a week until they cleared the problem. Seems like the raisins in a customer's oatmeal were moving." Cathy hissed.

"How gross!"

"Does Gino's sound better to you now?"

"No, but *Friday's* does. Okay?" Nora countered.

"It you want *Friday's*, then that's where we'll go. Let me go home and clean up. Do you want to drive?"

"Why don't we walk? It's a beautiful day and the restaurant's only twenty minutes away."

"Do you see boots on these feet?" Cathy asked. "I'm not *Nancy Sinatra*. I'll drive if you don't want to?"

Nora was always suspect of her friend's driving skills, now, with all that's going on with Cathy, there was no way she was going to let her drive.

"I don't trust you driving. Something tells me I'm going to be the sober one tonight. I'll pick you up at six-forty-five?"

"Six-forty-five? Not six thirty or seven…but six-forty-five? Nora, **you really need some serious bedtime."** Cathy scoffed. "I'll see you later."

As soon as her impetuous friend departed, Nora called Bill.

"Bill, it's impossible for me to meet you at Gino's."

"Why? Are you…seeing someone?"

"It's not that," she told him.

"Talk to me, Nora. I hope we've gotten over the trust factor?"

Getting Cathy involved could complicate things with Bill. Nora had to decide, should she just step aside for her, or tell him the truth, keeping the door open.

"Bill…it's Cathy."

"What does she have to do with us?" He asked, somewhat perplexed.

"She knows about our dinner last night and freaked out." Nora told him, her hand over her mouth.

"Cathy and I don't have an understanding." Bill said, clearly puzzled.

"But you do have history with her. It's a woman thing. There's no rhyme or reason to it."

"Listen to me Nora, because I'm serious about this. It's been a long time since I've been at ease with a woman. I hoped you felt the same?"

"Oh, I did Bill. I truly did, and I do want to see you again, but I can't hurt Cathy. She's very fragile right now and it's just not a good time. I hope you can understand?"

"What do we do Nora? I feel as though there's an arrow stuck in my heart."

"Let's wait until this thing on Sunday is over." Nora told him, never dreaming this man could be…well, so lyrical.

"There's a lot of dust that has to settle. Liz Peter's column tomorrow is going to raise quite a storm. I couldn't allow Mike, to run roughshod over me."

"I find that fire within you…so very exciting. I always did, even when we were on opposite sides of an issue. I've always respected you for it. The very thought makes my heart beat faster. I'm not exaggerating, Nora. I want to be quite clear about my feelings for you."

She wanted to respond, telling him she felt the same, but for the time being, she wanted him to refocus on her concerns with Mike.

"Bill, as far as Mike is concerned, he's finished. And if Liz Peters, writes what I think she will, she'll put the nails in his coffin."

"Mike is on his own, Nora. He's a run-a-way freight train, on the way to self-destruction. Please, don't let him or the past be a barrier from us getting to know one another?"

"Bill, I'd like that…good luck next week?" Nora said, then smiling after hanging up.

When Nora, arrived at Cathy's house, Fred was coming out the door carrying a suitcase, passing her without a word.

Cathy met her at the door, her cheeks, rivers of tears. "He got an apartment downtown," she said. "He's moving out."

Nora, comforted her as best as she could, offering to stay the night. The next morning, Cathy seemed better until she read the morning paper.

"Oh, sweet Jesus!" She cried out. "**I don't believe it.** Listen to this, Nora.

` Board president Mike Grace, of the Happy Hills Country Club in Huntington Village, can be compared to a dictator of a third word nation, where the women are held in low esteem and in some countries, lower than the family dog. **But be assured readers, the marines are on their way!** The National Organization of Women has pledged their support to the women of Happy Hills. Representatives will be in attendance when women's club champion Nora Cummings, takes on the men's club champion Bill Harper, this Saturday and Sunday. ***WATCH OUT*** Mike Grace, you're riding a slippery slope if you think you can fast talk the women of NOW."

"I'll sue that bitch!" Mike bellowed, reading the same article, his face a dangerous shade of scarlet. "Where does she get off calling me a dictator? This is Nora's fault. She couldn't go along with the rest of the good little soldiers in the club. She had to make Happy Hills the laughing stock of the Island."

"Good little soldiers?" Tammy said, lowering another section of the paper. "Is that what you think of the women in our club?"

"I was just speaking metaphorically! Jesus, Tammy."

He glanced at his wife, then peered at her, shaking his head in disgust.

"Have you ever considered, perhaps, just perhaps…there might be some truth to this article?" Tammy asked him.

"Not, you too!" He cried out. "Have you joined the movement?"

"Mike, I'm your wife, and as your wife I'm going to give you some advice. You had better be humble over the next few days…because if you're not, we may be looking to join another club in the very near future and the choice won't be ours."

A call from Fred, refrained Tammy, from saying all she had meant to say.

"Have you seen the Peters' column this morning?" Fred asked, his tone sharp and angry.

"Yes, I have and its all Nora's doing. Her fingerprints are all over the article."

"Well, if you had handled her differently we wouldn't be in this mess. Jesus Mike, **NOW** is coming here!"

"Listen, don't you point a finger at me. I bailed your ass out with that Polish waitress and I expect a little bit of loyalty from you."

"Go to hell, Mike!" Fred said, breaking the connection.

"Why that son-of-a-bitch, he hung up on me!"

"WAY TO BE HUMBLE, EL PRESIDENTE." Tammy snipped.

"Don't start with me!" Mike barked. "I don't want to hear any wise cracks from you," slamming the door on his way out, mumbling he was going to the club.

"Once there, his secretary handed him twenty-four messages. He sat on his leather back chair behind his desk and reviewed each one, most of which were communications from board members, club members, and most disturbing...from Louise Hopkins, President of the National Organization of Women. But curiously enough, one message was from Harvey Blackwell of CNM. Mike pressed his hands against his forehead and tried to think. In a commanding voice, he told his secretary to call all board members, notifying them of an emergency meeting at one o'clock this afternoon, after which, he called Louise Hopkins of NOW and said in his most charming way, he had received her message.

"We're very interested to talking to the members of your board to discuss the inequities which currently exist at Happy Hills," she told him in a clipped voice.

"Let me make myself very clear on this Ms. Louise, **your organization has no jurisdiction over a *private club*** and the last time I looked at our charter, it was a *private club.*" Mike said, deciding to flex some muscle.

"Do you really want to resist our efforts and that of the ACLU?" Hopkins asked.

"Louise, I'm an attorney." Mike reminded her. "NOW and the ACLU don't frighten me. You can't come to our club unless you're invited. If your representatives set foot on our property **I'll have them arrested** for unlawful trespass."

"Let me give you a history lesson." Hopkins replied. "Our organization was established in 1966 and during the early years, our first president Betty Freidman, ran across many men like you. Be assured Mr. Grace, we've seen it all and have devised alternatives to invitations."

"Alternatives?" Mike responded. "I don't know what the hell your talking about."

"Then let me spell it out for you. Joyce Freidman, who heads the ACLU and the daughter of Betty Freidman, plan to join our organization in picketing Happy Hills every day for the remainder of the year. You can surmise, what that will bring about. Corporate use of your facilities will decline, resulting in a sharp decrease in club revenue. Also, no doubt, some members will quit out of annoyance. Do I have to go further**? Am I getting through to you?"**

"I'll sue both your organizations." Mike threatened.

"You can't win!" She told him. "And do you know why? Just as Reagan said to Gorbachev, *'Because we'll outspend you!'* "Remember, we're a national organization with headquarters in Washington, D.C. and two-hundred fifty thousand strong. Will your membership finance your folly? I think not." Louise Hopkins said, looking in her compact mirror and adjusting her lipstick.

Mike was facing the biggest challenge of his tenure as president of the board. He knew Hopkins was right, the club wouldn't support him in a toe-to-toe battle with two national organizations. Not only would he lose his position on the board, but it was entirely possible, he might be forced to resign from the club. On the other hand, if he cooperated, he could very well be perceived as an innovator in bringing a gender-neutral policy to Happy Hills.

"Perhaps I've been a bit hasty, Louise. I have a proposal for you to consider, one that should work for both of us. But before I explain, would you please be specific what your organization is seeking to accomplish at Happy Hills?"

"We understand, that the board has an agreement with Nora Cummings, which expands the facilities for women, but non-inclusion as board members. We want the women of Happy Hills, to have the right to participate in elections when board vacancies occur, and a guarantee, the board make-up will consist of no less than twenty-five percent female members."

"What else?" Mike quipped.

"The agreement passed by the board with Nora, is in writing and honored, a copy of which is given to NOW for our files."

"What else?" Mike asked with a snarl.

"Nothing, but we do expect to be announced as **invited guests,** when we attend the match on Saturday and Sunday. It will be good for all sides concerned."

Mike was retreating. Louise Hopkins knew she had made her point with him and her voice indicated victory when demanding the invitation.

"Just so there's no misunderstanding. You want the agreement with Nora, in writing and honored, women included in board elections and an open invitation to the match?"

"That's about it Mike."

"Well then, here's *my quid pro quo.* I want the credit for bringing NOW and the ACLU to Happy Hills. It will show the community at large that we have a common interest, which is, to further the rights of women…in **ALL** country clubs. Furthermore, I'd like both organizations to issue a statement, that the Liz Peters' article, did not necessarily represent the opinions of your membership." Mike demanded, leaning back in his chair.

"You should have been in politics Mr. Grace, you're a very clever fellow."

"I've heard that before. Do we have a deal?" Mike pressed.

"I'll say yes, if you agree to one other item which I failed to mention. Harvey Blackwell, of CNM, wants to cover the match on Saturday and Sunday." Louise informed the stunned president.

"What the hell does CNM want with a country club golf match?" Mike queried.

"This match is no longer private." Louise told him. "It has attracted national attention and CNM has more than enough sponsors interested to cover the cost. Look at it this way, it will put you and your club on the map."

Mike told her he would get back to her after talking to the board this afternoon. She cordially parted, but first reminding him, not to delay the process while noting...the possible consequences.

The beleaguered president sat at his desk pondering his strategy. The truth was, he decided, that the CNM coverage need not be a disaster to him if he could turn it to an advantage. With this in mind, he called Harvey Blackwell, the CNM producer.

"What can I do for you, Harvey?" The board president asked.

"Mike, every once in a while, a story comes out of nowhere like a rogue wave, creating enormous viewer interest." Blackwell told him. "The executives here at CNM, feel the match between the male and female champion of your club this weekend, will attract not only viewers who habitually watch golf, but people, who wouldn't miss the opportunity to view a **reality match** with such extraordinary controversy. Our polls show, the recent newspaper articles on Happy Hills, has attracted national attention. The audience is limitless, we could...even go international."

"There must be big advertising dollars involved." Mike said. **"What's in it for us?"**

"Mike, CNM is willing to guarantee Happy Hills...eight million dollars for exclusive rights and an additional five million in an incentive clause tied to viewer participation." Harvey told him.

"This could be bigger than a Notre Dame-Michigan football game. I can have contracts in your hands by tomorrow. We only have today and tomorrow to prepare our viewers, sponsors and crew."

Mike was delirious. He could hardly control his emotions. The offer was a gift from the Gods. Calm down, he told himself, aware Blackwell was waiting for his response.

"Are you prepared, to give me a *preliminary letter of intent* right now?" Mike asked.

"I can fax it to you in half-an-hour over my signature." Blackwell assured him.

"I'll review it Harvey and if it acceptable, fax it back to you over my signature."

Mike went to the bathroom. He locked the door behind him and pantomimed an Irish Jig, while clapping his hands. **"You son-of-a-bitch! You did it!"** The fox had an 0-2 count against him and hit the next pitch out of the park for the winning home run.

Mike was ecstatic, but anxious at the same time. When the fax hadn't arrived by noon, he began to wonder, if CNM had a change of heart. The board meeting was only ten minutes away. He asked his secretary if she received a fax from Harvey Blackwell?

"No Mike, I didn't see one come through," the assistant confirmed.

"Barbara, have you been at your desk the entire time?" Mike snapped, now convinced, the CNM offer had been rescinded.

"Oh, I did go to the ladies room for a brief time," the secretary said. Mike searched for an answer. Perhaps someone used the fax machine and mistakenly placed the agreement from CNM with their papers.

"Did anyone use the fax machine?" Mike pressed the secretary, and when she responded no, he slammed his fists on the desk. As he peered at the floor, he noticed a corner piece of paper under the desk. He picked it up, it's back facing front. He turned the paper to the other side…**and there it was**…the agreement he had been waiting for. He looked menacingly at his secretary, instructing her to make ten copies.

"The next time I tell you…I'm waiting for an important fax, don't you dare leave the room. I don't care if you have to pee in your pants! Do you understand me!" He growled, then calmly walked into the board room, trying to regain his composure and hide his eagerness to reveal his greatest triumph.

"YOU DID IT THIS TIME, MIKE!" Ralph greeted him. "We're the laughing stock of the Island because of your poor judgment."

"You're not getting out of this one, you bastard!" Screamed Fred Daley.

"Mike, this time you went too far!" Gil agreed, while Herb simply said, **'WE WANT YOU OUT."**

"Gentlemen, I'm going to pass out something for all of you to read. Here, everyone take a copy." Mike told them calmly.

Dead silence ensued, as each board member scanned the single page memorandum. "Is this another one of your clever tricks?" Herb muttered.

"Actually, it's a genuine offer by CNM to cover the Harper, Cummings match." Mike said. "I believe you all understand the number **EIGHT MILLION UP FRONT** and the **FIVE MILLION INCENTIVE CLAUSE?"**

"How did you ever pull this off?" Herb demanded.

"Never underestimate the will to win, my friend." Mike said, then lighting up a victory cigar.

The room suddenly exploded. He proved to be the resilient survivor, the champion Chameleon, did it again.

"You sly fox! You did it! **THIRTEEN MILLION SMACKEROOS!** Thirteen million!" Jerry Dicks screamed out.

"YOU'RE THE REAL DEAL!" Gil roared.

To a man, the board members rushed to shake Mike's hand. Even Herb and Fred had to concede, he had magically turned the *"dead man's hand"* of *aces and eights* into a winning royal flush. Bill, was the last to offer his congratulations.

"What can I say? The master has done it again. The club wins and so do you." Bill muttered.

"I've done my part. Now, all you have to do is to beat the bitch. She's been nothing but a thorn in the side of our club. Yes, the club makes a lot of money and both of us will be on national television, but...you're all forgetting one thing. Our club will never be the same. Women will serve on the board and you know what that means. Before you know it...they'll have decorators in here recommending new curtains, rugs and whatever they fancy at the time." Mike warned.

"Well, with all this money coming into our coffers from CNM, there's no reason for members to be concerned about retrieving their bond money." Herb reminded him.

"It's just...not going to be the same." Mike shrugged.

"Who's to say Mike, maybe change is what we need?" Bill said.

"You know, that sounds like a man who's more interested in Nora's *"honey pot"* than beating her in a golf match."

"What the hell are you talking about!"

"I've heard about you and her. I have my sources. I wouldn't let that pistol between your legs do the thinking for you this weekend. We can still salvage some pride when you beat her." Mike warned.

"Watch your mouth...and walk softly my friend. Don't you ever threaten me. You may pull that *El Presidente* bullshit with others, but you don't want to lock horns with me, buster!" Bill said, bouncing a finger off of Mike's chest.

"Take it easy, Bill! I was just emphasizing the importance of beating, Nora. Our club's pride is at stake here, as well as your own. I don't care who you bang or how often, but consider that thousands, maybe millions will be watching this match. How will you hold up your head if you're beaten by a woman on national television!" Mike bellowed.

Bill, understood the implications of the match, but Mike, had touched a raw nerve, reaching Bill's competitive soul, questioning his natural instinct to be at his best when needed. And Mike, showed no respect for the woman he was now pursuing. What he didn't know, was that the board president had an ***ace up his sleeve,*** ensuring Bill...gave a maximum effort.

The news of CNM coverage spread throughout the club like a brushfire in July. Nora and Cathy, were having lunch in the dining room when Laura, hurried over to ask excitedly, if they had heard the news.

"Nora's going to be on CNM!"

"Have you been drinking those *fuzzy navels* again?" Cathy asked.

"No! No! It's all over the club. Mike just announced it to the members of the board. CNM is going to pay Happy Hills thirteen million dollars to broadcast the two day match." Laura assured them.

"It won't happen if Mike's involved." Nora said, wrinkling her nose, indicating her distain for the man.

"That's where you're wrong Nora." Mike declared, joining the conversation.

"Well, well, look what just crawled into the dining room." Cathy hissed.

"I'm not here to pick a fight ladies." He told them. "Can we talk in private, Nora?"

"They're my friends," she snapped. "Whatever you have to say can be said without them leaving."

"Very well." Mike said stiffly. "What you heard from Laura, is true. We have a great opportunity to work together in making the upcoming match one of historic proportions."

"Mike, I wouldn't work with you if the Pope asked me." Nora scoffed.

"You talk to the Pope?" Laura asked, with child like innocence.

"Oh Jesus!" Cathy said, putting her hand on her forehead.

"I'm sorry you feel that way, Nora." Mike continued. "I thought we could put the past behind us now that you've achieved what you wanted?"

"What I want is for you to go away." Nora demanded. "You probably feel like a real hero bringing in CNM with its pot of gold. But, when the dust clears and this club becomes gender neutral, the women of Happy Hills will have a voice in determining policy. And who do you think your pals are going to blame when that happens?"

"Mike, you're really pathetic." Cathy lashed out, having nothing but contempt for the man who threatened to reveal a private matter in her life.

"There's an old expression which I believe has significant meaning in your case." Mike said, ignoring the interruption. ***`Watch out what you wish for...because it just might come true.`*** The men at Happy Hills will have more power over you gals than ever when this is over, because when there's big money involved...it's the men who control it. Who controls the money, controls the rules."

"You can do a turkey strut now, but the day will come when everyone will see you for the phony you've always been. Now please leave, so we can finish our lunch." Nora said, dismissing Mike and feeling pleased with herself.

"Now there goes one sorry, son-of-bitch." Cathy said, as Mike marched away, munching on his cigar.

"Poor Tammy, how does she manage to live with him?" Although she was sorry for her, nothing could make her feel the least bit of sympathy for her *lout* of a husband. He tried to destroy her, conducting his own personal *vendetta,* but Nora, was going to vindicate herself if it was the last thing she did.

CHAPTER 50
FINAL PREPARATION

THE LAST DAY of preparation before the big match was a hot and sticky Friday. The buzz from Mike's announcement was still the topic of the day, particularly since the CNM trucks were already rumbling in the main entrance of Happy Hills.

George, had planned a review session with Nora, to discuss a *hole-by-hole strategy* and possible trouble spots she might encounter. They would ride the course in a golf cart, charting each hole in a spiral notebook and then review their findings.

"Tomorrow and Sunday will be different from members following you in a club championship. They'll be television cameras at every hole, picking up everything you do, every expression on your face. And remember, they'll be millions of viewers watching."

"Thanks George. I feel much better after that description." Nora scoffed.

"If you're not prepared…I assure you, the crowds and cameras will be unnerving, not just for you, but also for Harper. The only question is…who'll be able to handle it better. That's where preparation comes in and it's all going to be mental," he warned her.

He was right, she thought to herself. This would not be like any of the club championships she had played. How does she prepare for the crowds, she wondered. Nora, marveled at how professional golfers maintained their composure under the constant scrutiny. Now, it was she who would be scrutinized.

"It's going to be about focus." George told her. "At the end of the day, you should be mentally exhausted rather than physically tired. Tiger Woods ability to concentrate is what separates him from the rest of the field. You have to disregard everything going on around you and focus on the ball and **where you want it to go.**"

"This is starting to get scary, George."

"Listen Nora, ***total focus*** is what you'll need **throughout** the match. That could be your edge with Bill. You can do this, I know you can. And remember, you'll have the better of the two caddies by your side at all times," he said, trying to inspire his protégé as they approached the first tee.

The first hole was almost three hundred yards in length from the lady's tees and the shortest of the par fours. The fairway was straight and generous with few undulations. Large pine trees lined the right side of the fairway. The cart path was located on the left, where an errant tee shot could find itself out-of-bounds. Crescent shape sand traps protected the front and sides of the green.

"The first hole will be the toughest." George told her.

"It's supposed to be the easiest hole on the course," she frowned.

"Not with hundreds of people lined along the hole and a few million people watching on television. Your knees will be shaking and your hands will be squeezing the club. I want you to take two deep breaths before every shot, including putts. It will drain the pent up nerves from your body. I want your tee shot in the fairway on the first hole. I'm not concerned with distance, but I am with a good start."

George's insight was exactly why she needed him. He was, if she had any chance of winning, her advantage over her opponent.

"Remember, most greens are designed by golf architects to be higher in the back than the front for the purpose of drainage. So if the flag is in the middle of the green, you want to land your ball in front of the flag in order to have an uphill putt, rather than putting downhill. If you land the ball to the right of the flag, the putt will more than likely break to the left. If the ball is left of the flag, the putt will break to the right."

"We already went over that in an earlier practice." Nora reminded him. But he was so absorbed in coaching...he didn't seem to hear her. Nora wondered, if he wasn't more nervous than she was.

"On this first hole, you don't want to be short and land in the traps." George said. "I'd rather see you a bit long on the green and then two putt the hole for a par. Pars will be the name of the game this weekend. Let's go to the second hole."

Nora took copious notes while the pro detailed the strategy of the next seventeen holes. Afterwards, they went to the putting green and spent another hour practicing putts within ten feet, being George's contention, the tournament was going to be won or lost on the putting greens. When they decided on lunch, they found the dining room bustling with club members and CNM personnel. There were no available tables, but the club manager had one brought out for them and as they were being seated, several members called out encouragement.

"Hey, there's Nora!" Cried out a member. **"You rock Nora!"** Another bellowed. Person after person stood from their chair to applaud, not to do so would have been a betrayal to their lady champion. The noise was deafening. Nora was so overwhelmed that her hands were trembling.

"How would you like to try and make a three foot putt now?" George told her.

After ordering lunch, a man dressed in a blue blazer and red tie approached them and introduced himself as Harvey Blackwell, from CNM.

"I'd like to discuss tomorrow's agenda if you have a moment," he said, only to be interrupted by another round of applause.

Nora appealed for quiet. The support was overwhelming and meant a great deal to her, for she had hoped, she wouldn't be branded a trouble maker by the women of the club and the members gave her their answer. She stood to address her supporters, wearing a flowered pink golf shirt and pink shorts, her hair in a pony tail with two cascading pink ribbons.

"Tomorrow and Sunday, you'll have an opportunity to witness a match between the male and female champions of your country club. But more importantly, whatever the outcome, you can be proud that wonderful organizations have come to Happy Hills, to witness a transformation from a non-inclusive club...to a gender-neutral club." There was an eruption of applause which continued until Nora, raised her hands in acknowledgment.

"For that, I thank the National Organization of Women, the American Civil Liberties Union and CNM, in furthering the cause of women in all country clubs throughout America. Again, I thank you for your support and hope to see you all tomorrow." Nora concluded her acknowledgment, but couldn't prevent the shedding of tears, feeling vindicated by her supporters response.

The crowded dining room, once again erupted with a thunderous ovation. Nora, introduced Harvey Blackwell to George, while dabbing her eyes with a hankie.

"Those were kind remarks Nora," the CNM executive said. "As you know, we'll be televising nationally and internationally on a time delay broadcast. We need about a half hour of your time tomorrow for an interview. Considering tee off time is nine o'clock and you need what, forty-five minutes to an hour of practice time, we thought if we could meet at seven-thirty on the range it would satisfy all of our needs? We'll also be interviewing Bill Harper, Mike Grace and Louise Hopkins. George, we'd also like some insight on how you prepared Nora for the match."

Nora was pleased that George's contributions were not going to be ignored, as they easily could have been. Affectionately, she grabbed his hand in a sign of support.

"I understand Sunday's tee off time is at one o'clock?" Harvey went on. "We'd like an hour before your practice to review the first days results and some of the human-interest aspects of how this all came about. How does eleven o'clock sound?"

The scheduling was agreed upon and as she and George concluded lunch, Nora thought of how the weekend was going to be even more exciting then she had anticipated. When they departed the club, both previously agreed to meet at Nora's house to review the notes she had taken earlier. When they settled in, George congratulated her on how she had handled herself.

"I was somewhat taken aback by it all." Nora told him.

"They recognize what you've done for the club. Mike may want all of the credit, but if it weren't for you, none of this would be happening. I'm very proud of you." George said, as he postured to embrace her.

"Lets focus on the match," she told him, while gently resisting and taking a step back. "I want my head clear until this thing is over."

Giving her a quick hug, which told Nora he understood, George settled down to discuss her game.

They reviewed the notes of the morning's session for almost two hours, repeatedly stressing those holes that posed the most danger to her.

"Don't forget, this is *match play* not *stroke play*," he told her. "You can take a ten on a hole and you'll only lose that hole. Don't dwell on a bad shot or a disastrous hole, because you'll have them...and so will Bill. You put the hole behind you and move on to the next one. Never lose that focus."

After George departed, Nora curled up on the couch, exhausted. She slipped into a deep sleep, only to be awakened by the telephone. It was Bill.

"I just wanted to call before tomorrow," he told her. "I heard about the response you received in the dining room today. I think that's pretty incredible."

"It was a bit surreal." Nora confessed. "I wasn't prepared for it."

"Listen Nora," he went on. "I can't get you out of my mind and it's driving me crazy. I need to see you."

His words resonated, her heart beating faster. She wanted to see him, but considered it to be fool hardy to do so. She didn't need the emotional complications the night before the match.

"Cathy's still an obstacle," she reminded him.

"Look, I think I have a solution to the problem." Bill told her. "You and I have to eat tonight. Ask her to have dinner with you at Gino's, six o'clock tonight."

"What do you have in mind?"

"Trust me on this. I promise not to do or say anything that will put you in a position of breaking your word to Cathy."

"I don't know, Bill."

"Please Nora, it's important to both of us and I'm not going down without a fight."

"What if someone sees us eating dinner together the night before our match? We're supposed to be rivals, that's part of the hype." Nora reminded him.

"You're presuming we're going to be together and that's not going to be the case." Bill said.

Nora was intrigued. **What did he have in mind** and was it a good idea? But she gushed by Bill's pursuit and deciding to trust him, she made the date with Cathy.

After trying on several combinations, Nora finally settled on a *St. John's* sky blue tank top, white *Capri* pants accented with a *Hermes* belt and *Torre Burch* ballet slippers, prepared to fit right into the hot redhead, Bill had fantasized about.

Once at Gino's, Nora and Cathy ordered a bottle of *chardonnay* when they heard the restaurant's maitre d' say, **"Will this table do, Mr. Harper?"** And there was Bill…and…a friend.

Bill did a double take when seeing them. "Cathy Daley and Nora Cummings! What are you two doing here?"

"Well actually Bill, we're waiting for George and Laura Bush." Cathy snipped with a wry smile, determined in keeping an awkward situation as light hearted as possible, unaware of the prearranged meeting. "They want our opinion on whether we should invade *Iran* before he leaves office. What are ***YOU*** doing here?"

"Well Cathy, George and Laura asked me to extend their apologies for not joining you lovely women, but did ask me to inform you…they've decided to invade *New Jersey* instead."

Nora placed her hand to her mouth, wanting to avoid laughing at the snipping between the two. Observing them battling wits with one another, she couldn't help to ask herself, how the two of them, could ever have a compatible relationship. It certainly wouldn't have lasted the test of time she thought to herself, in a self serving conclusion.

"Please, let me introduce a dear friend of mine, Sean Mc Cray." The fair haired man who rose to greet them, was a well tanned ***Adonis***. As he bent to kiss Cathy's hand, Nora realized, this was part of Bill's *strategy*.

"Your buddy has nice manners, how come he's a friend of yours?" Cathy snipped again.

"I guess I'm just lucky." Bill said, ignoring her over zealous approach.

"Look, I have an idea." Bill started.

"That's a refreshing thought." Cathy interrupted, then raising her glass of wine, turning away with a frown.

"Bill, I think **you've finally met your match**. You're a funny lady and will be a friend if you keep beating up on this guy." Sean said,

"Why don't you both join us for dinner?" Bill continued.

Cathy, looked at Nora for a response, who shrugged, deferring the decision to her antagonistic friend.

"Okay, but on one condition." Cathy demanded.

"And that is... Cathy?" Bill reluctantly asked.

"You tell George Bush...to leave New Jersey alone and think of invading France instead. I have friends in Jersey and those bastards in France still think we still owe them for the *Statue of Liberty*, forgetting we saved their butts in two world wars."

"You have a deal." Bill replied with a grin, then glancing at the reason he was there in the first place.

Nora was struck, how easily Cathy and Sean slipped into an intense conversation, so caught up in one another, they scarcely had a word to say to either her or Bill, not that she minded. The evening passed quickly and she wasn't surprised when at the end of it, Sean and Cathy exchanged telephone numbers.

"Will you be at the match tomorrow?" She overheard him ask, Cathy. "Maybe you and I can watch together."

"Did you know that Bill and Sean were going to be at the restaurant tonight?" Cathy asked, when she and Nora were driving home.

"No, I had no idea Bill **and Sean** were going to be there." Nora hedged.

"Okay, I believe you." Cathy said cheerfully. "What did you think of Sean?"

"Seems like a real hunk. He's very good looking and an interesting guy. Did he say what he does for a living?"

"He's a Wall Street hot shot. He's Bill's broker, that's why they were at the restaurant tonight...to discuss business."

"Did you like him?" Nora pressed her friend.

"I can't remember when I talked to a man so easily without groping for conversation." Cathy said. "Do you know what I mean?"

"I know exactly what you mean."

Nora was relieved, that her fears of meeting Bill, were so easily over come and that Cathy, seemed fine with the idea."

"I see the way, Bill...looks at you." Cathy said with a coy grin. "He reminds me of a schoolboy with his first crush, he's really hooked on you."

"You really think so?"

"Please, don't pull a Laura Dicks on me." Cathy told her. "You have to be blind, deaf and dumb not to see it."

"But what about my promise to you?" Nora asked, wanting to be absolutely certain that Cathy, meant what she said.

"I've been thinking about that a lot, and…if you want to see Bill…I'll understand." Cathy said, then surprised Nora, by saying…"I realize he and I could never make it together. We'd be at each other's throats all of the time. Besides, I think Sean and I have something going."

What she said, meant a lot to Nora. She no longer had to be concerned about concealing her feelings towards Bill, while Cathy, seemed resolved her marriage was over and it was time for her to move on.

"How are you going to deal with a match against someone you're all hot and bothered over?" Cathy asked.

"Good question." Nora admitted. "A very good question."

"I have an idea." Cathy said, glancing at her with mischief in her eyes. "Have torrid sex with him tomorrow before the match. Wear him out in bed so he doesn't show up. It's a win, win situation. You both enjoy yourselves without trying to beat each other's brains in."

Nora only laughed and chalked it up to Cathy, being outrageous as usual, even though it was a very tempting idea. Not surprisingly, Bill called as soon as she arrived home.

"Nora, whatever happens tomorrow can't effect what we have going." Bill said with sincerity. "I know we'll both try to bring our best game to the course. I ask only one thing from you…please, don't wear an outfit so sexy, that I'll be completely distracted."

What an irony it was, Nora thought, as she prepared to retire for the evening, that she should have fallen in love with the man she had sworn to beat this weekend. And it was far too late for her to do anything but try her very best. But would her heart be broken by the same man and by the plotting and deceitful, Mike Grace?

CHAPTER 51
JUDGEMENT DAY

AT FIVE-THIRTY in the morning, on the day of the long awaited golf match, Nora awakened to the soft rock music of her clock radio. She lazily stretched out her arms and legs, grunting in cadence to the music. She went to the bathroom, showered, shampooed her hair and applied a coconut fragrant conditioner. This was to be a special day. Nora would be watched by millions of viewers and wanted to look her very best. She left her hair partially wet and waited until she finished breakfast before blow-drying it out.

The coffee pot cooperated with its prearranged setting, the brewed aroma acting as a magic carpet, drawing her to the kitchen. Nora took her first sip of coffee, "hum" she uttered, closing her eyes and shrugging her shoulders, sending the caffeine signal it was time for her body to waken.

She was about to pour Kellogg's Special K into a bowl when Cathy called, telling her to turn the television on to CNM. When she did, she was fascinated by the commentary of the match.

"Nora Cummings is taking an enormous leap in challenging the male champion of her club, Bill Harper," she heard the announcer say. "This story is not about war, crime in the streets or how the economy is performing. It's a feel good human-interest story for our viewers to wake up to on this August, Saturday morning. Stay tuned, as we take you to a village on Long Island, where this battle between the sexes, likened by many to the titanic match between the late *Bobby Riggs* and *Billy Jean King,* will take place."

"Holy molly, Nora!" Cathy exclaimed. "You're going to be as famous as *Billy Jean King.*"

"What are you doing up so early?"

"I couldn't sleep. After I came home last night, Fred called. He said he wants to talk… about getting back together. Oh, look Nora, the commercial is over."

"Happy Hills Country Club, located in Huntington Long Island, will be the scene of a **battle between the sexes**. A golf challenge between the club's lady and men's champion. Who thought of this Bobby Riggs, Billy Jean King like challenge and why did it come about? This will be our feature story this morning and full coverage will begin right here at CNM, starting at noon. Due to previous commitments, today's coverage will be taped delayed with the actual starting time of the match at nine o'clock this morning. Tomorrow's coverage will be live and start at noon, right here on CNM. The station that brings the world to your living room. Stay tuned and don't change that dial."

Nora would be lying to herself if she denied the sense of excitement she was feeling, as she saw images of herself on CNM. After all, who wouldn't be, she thought to herself. From simply wanting to achieve some small gains for the women at the club, Mike Grace had pushed the issue from the privacy of Happy Hills to what has turned out to be a media darling. Who would have imagined she thought, sipping on her coffee, turning her attention back to the commentator.

"You may ask yourself why is CNM covering an amateur event at a private country club on Long Island? I think you'll find the answer fascinating. It's the dramatic story of one woman's fight for women's equality at the male dominated, Happy Hills Country Club. Nora Cummings, has taken her cause to the National Organization of Women, who have embraced her efforts. Here's a quote from NOW president, Louise Hopkins." 'Our organization recognizes the brave struggle initiated by Ms. Cummings. We have addressed several issues with board president, Mr. Michael Grace and I'm pleased to say, has agreed to make substantial changes at Happy Hills, with the objective being, a gender-neutral club. It is our hope, that the example shown by the board of trustees, will encourage other country clubs across America to review their policies towards women and strive for a gender-neutral environment.'

"So there you have it folks. A struggle by one courageous woman which has bore fruit, but what still remains, is her individual battle today and tomorrow against her male champion counter-part."

"Wow Nora! Wow!" Cathy exclaimed. "You're famous baby! Suck it up and enjoy the ride."

"But I wasn't prepared for all of this hoopla." Nora told her. "I have to focus on the match. But forget that, what were you saying about, Fred?"

"I just told him I needed time to think and it would be a good idea for him to do the same. He asked me how much time and I said I didn't know. Now that I have a little freedom, it's actually not so bad. I eat when I want to, get out of bed when I want to and don't have to pick up after him. And I must admit, meeting Sean has complicated things. But don't concern yourself about my problems, you have enough of your own."

Despite assurance from Cathy, Nora was still worried about the self-inflicted issues her friend continued to face. When she approached the entrance of Happy Hills an hour later, she was surprised to find a significant crowd starting to assemble. On the way to the practice range, she observed Bill and Mike, deep in conversation, something which might have concerned her on any other day. Now however, she was focusing on her agenda, first the interview and then the match.

Harvey Blackwell did brief interviews with Bill, Mike and Louise Hopkins of NOW, a stout and matronly brunette, who wore a flowering geometrical dress. Then, interviewed George and Nora. He also explained to both combatants, they would have non-intrusive microphones attached to them, so when an announcer wanted to ask a question, they would feel a slight vibration. George wanted assurance, that Nora wouldn't be interrupted during a shot.

"We've been successful with our coverage with both the PGA and LPGA players without violating their efforts on the course." Harvey told him. "CNM crews have been doing this for a lot of years. Our experience has been, you'll have a more difficult time controlling over zealous spectators with their cameras than you will with our crews."

As George and Nora moved to the end of the practice range, she noticed Bill and Mike were talking again, but she told herself to ignore it. The one thing she could be certain of, that Mike, couldn't use Bill as a foil to cause her any more trouble...but could he?

After thirty-five minutes of hitting balls at the range, George and Nora left for the putting green, where he had her practice drills she was familiar with. She started with a series of long lag putts to a straight line of putts, ranging from two feet to ten feet, after which, he placed ten balls in a circle, six feet from the cup and had her practicing putts from different angles.

By the time they had finished, hundreds of people were lined up along the fairway of the first hole. Club pro Dave Thompson, using a loud speaker, called Bill and Nora to the first tee. It was agreed upon that Bill, would begin the contest.

"Ladies and gentlemen, **LET'S PLAY GOLF!"** Said the club pro, to which the crowd, some of whom had waited for more than two hours to secure a position on the first tee, roared their approval.

"Teeing off first, the men's club champion at Happy Hills Country Club for the past ten years, Bill Harper." Dave announced. Bill tipped his hat, acknowledging the applause. He bent down in his light blue shirt and beige pants, placing his tee and ball approximately one inch into the ground between the blue markers on the tee box. After taking two practice swings with his five-wood and looking down the fairway to set his target line, he hit a mighty drive, his ball landing only seventy-five yards from the green to the loud applause of the crowd.

"Ladies and gentlemen, the lady's club champion of Happy Hills Country Club for the past five years, Nora Cummings." Dave Thompson announced.

The crowd applauded, with some screaming out slogans of support for their lady champion, who was dressed in a pink golf shirt and matching shorts, her hair in a ponytail tied with a pink ribbon. Nora acknowledged the crowd, raising her right hand. She placed her tee in the ground between the red markers of the tee box and with her three-wood in hand, looked down the fairway to set her target line. Then…suddenly…her knees buckled and her hands were trembling.

"Nora, step away from the ball!" George cried out, recognizing what was happening.

"Look at me!" He commanded, approaching the anxious golfer. "It's just a case of the nerves. We all go through it," he whispered in a reassuring tone. "I want you to take two deep breaths before you hit every ball until you can see your hands steady and your knees are quiet under you."

Nora acknowledged George, composed herself, addressing the ball on the tee once again. She took two practice swings, then the deep breaths as instructed and swung at the ball which hit the fairway, rolling past Bill's ball by forty-yards.

As the crowd roared with approval, Nora turned to George, who raised a clenched fist. They walked down the fairway, hearing the crowd's encouragement, both waving in acknowledgement.

"Keep in mind folks, Harper hit a five-wood at a longer distance than Cummings, who used a three-wood off this first hole, the shortest of the eighteen. It won't be an unusual sight for Nora, to out drive Bill. There's a huge difference in the yardage from where he's hitting from the blue tees and Nora from the red, and she's a big hitter off the tee. To give you an idea, the total eighteen hole yardage for Harper from the blue tees is sixty-six-hundred-eighty-six-yards compared to Cummings total yardage from the ladies tee of fifty-three-hundred-eighty-six-yards. That's a whopping thirteen-hundred yards difference. This may come down to who's the best chipper and putter, the way these two can hit a golf ball."

Bill approached the ball for his second shot with a pitching wedge. When he hit the ball within three feet of the cup, the crowd roared. Nora's second shot, was one that George had her practice over and over until she had better than a seventy-five-percent rate of success in landing the ball within five feet of the flag. Once again she took two deep breaths, then hit the short thirty-five-yard shot within two feet of the hole.

"I guess Cummings, just sent Harper a message to the effect that anything he can do she can do better," the announcer commentated, over the shouts of the crowd. "This certainly has all of the prospects of being a very exciting match," remarked the CNM announcer.

Both Nora and Bill made their putts for birdie and then proceeded to the next tee box. The second hole was a slight dogleg right, the first hundred and fifty yards elevated and blocking a golfers view of the landing area. The right side of the fairway was tight and the danger side of the hole. Bill maintained honors of teeing off and drove his ball once again in the middle of the fairway. Nora's drive landed fifty-yards short of the green, after which, she and Bill, both hit their second shots within ten feet of the hole, although both missing their first putt, making the second for par.

Nora faltered on the seventh hole and was down one after the midway point. Tall pine trees lined the right side of the tenth hole fairway and several waste bunkers dotting the left side. Bill's drive landed two-hundred-seventy-yards in the first cut on the right side and Nora's in the middle of the fairway, thirty-five yards past Bill's ball.

The match was closer than most had expected, but there were still twenty-seven holes of golf remaining. Bill's second shot landed on the green, fifteen feet from the cup. Nora had one- hundred-fifteen-yards remaining and was trying to decide which club to hit when she heard George say, "hit your nine iron," now in the role of caddie.

"I was thinking pitching wedge." Nora told him.

"If I had to chose between a hard swing to get to the green or a soft swing, I'd go with the soft swing every time." George replied.

Nora decided against his advice and chose the pitching wedge. When she hit the ball, it landed five feet left beyond the hole and settled into three-inch-thick grass. She turned to George, her expression said it all. I should have listened and my emotions lost the hole. Bill made four and Nora five, now down two holes with eight remaining for the round.

Nora didn't fare well as Bill played brilliant golf the next eight holes. At the end of the day, she found herself down five holes.

When Nora and George walked to the pro-shop to hand in her scorecard, he sensed she needed some reassurance.

"You're doing a great job, Nora. You have to give the guy credit, he played a great round of golf today."

"I'll have to play more inspired, or this match is lost." Nora said dejectedly.

"Tomorrow's another day." George told her.

As they went to join Harvey Blackwell at the first tee, she once again saw Mike and Bill laughing and talking together. Nora's instincts were sending a disturbing signal that something was amiss, but she couldn't for the life of her determine what it might be.

"Here's what we're going to do guys." Harvey told them when they were all assembled.

"First, we'll do an interview with Bill and Nora, then a brief commentary by George, followed by comments from Mike and Bill. You'll be given headsets and when Sid gives you the thumbs up, you're live. When he moves his hand across his throat, you're not. This is taped and will be broadcast after the viewers see today's match, so if we're not comfortable with the way it's going, we can re-tape the response. Okay, let's start with Bill and Nora."

Harvey's first question was directed at Bill and how it had happened that he had drawn so far ahead in the match.

"The big difference wasn't in my play so much, but my opponents." Bill replied. "She faltered on the back nine while I played my usual game."

"That just about sums it up, Harvey." Nora agreed. "Bill's a great golfer and I have to play better tomorrow if I expect to make up the lead he has."

"You played a respectable game today," the CNM commentator observed. "The real question Nora, can you play much better tomorrow than you did today and make up the five holes you're behind?"

"We'll find out tomorrow...won't we?"

"There you have it folks. Nora Cummings faces a monumental task tomorrow in trying to make up what appears to be an insurmountable lead by her opponent, Bill Harper. And now, I'd like to have George Harris, Nora's coach and caddie give us his observations of today's ***battle between the sexes.*** George, do you feel Nora can overcome the substantial lead Harper's built today?"

"There's no question Nora has an uphill battle on her hands." George told him, biting his tongue, knowing in his heart it would be near impossible for Nora to overcome Bill's lead. "But she's a fine competitor with the heart of a lion and I wouldn't count her out just yet."

"Folks, I'd like to introduce Mike Grace, the president of the board of directors of Happy Hills Country Club." Harvey said into his mike, "along with our current leader in this **battle *of the sexes,*** Bill Harper."

Harvey, proceeded to quiz Mike, on the subject of how the competition had come about, which led Mike, wily as usual, to explain what the results would be if Nora, won or lost.

"It was her challenge, not ours. In fact, the board members thought the terms were too harsh and modified them accordingly," said the ***sly fox,*** painting a benevolent picture.

"So those modifications weren't forced on you by NOW?" Harvey pressed him. "Is that what you're really saying?"

"The biggest modification Harvey, was to eliminate Nora's self imposed condition to leave the club in the event she lost the match, which appears to be the case." Mike declared, with a smugness that irritated both Nora and George. "The other modifications were in cooperation with Louise Hopkins and her worthy organization."

Nora couldn't believe what she was hearing and worse was to follow, when Bill was asked to comment.

"I now have Bill Harper along side of me." Harvey told the listening audience. "Bill, do you concur with Mike's comments?"

"Happy Hills memberships are in the names of men, who reviewed the club charter and rules before joining. Most of the women in the club understand the rules which have successfully been the guidelines for over fifty years. It's my opinion you shouldn't try to fix something that isn't broken." Bill said, then curiously scurried off, seemingly annoyed.

As the CNM commentators signed off, **Nora could hardly contain herself**. She didn't understand what was happening. Had Bill's advances been some kind of ruse? Had he been duping Nora, all along? But why? The club would receive its money and the women were getting their improvements. It just didn't add up.

Once home, she paced her living room, trying to think of something she might have said or done to scare Bill off. Nothing stood out. **Why would he suddenly turn** from a potential lover to the Bill Harper, she once loved to hate?

When Cathy dropped by, Nora proceeded to tell her about Bill's suspicious behavior with Mike and his response to Harvey's questions.

"I don't get it Nora, unless..."

"Unless what?"

"Unless Mike...has something on Bill. Maybe some kind of blackmail is going on? Remember, he's an attorney and did business with Bill, before and after he sold his company."

"But why should Bill, turn on me?"

"Hey, you put two *pit bulls* in the same room and the spectators better run for their lives. **You're considered *collateral damage,*** if Mike has something on Bill. Given the way he looked at you at Gino's, Bill's either the best actor on the planet or Mike...has his *pepperoni* in a vice."

"How do we find out?" Nora asked. "I have to know, it's tearing me apart."

"Sean and I are having dinner tonight." Cathy told her. "We've made a real connection during the last couple of days. Let's see what I can find out. I'll call you before ten tonight."

But, as Nora might have guessed, Cathy did better than that. At nine-thirty on the dot, the doorbell rang and there was Cathy, with Sean at her side.

"Sean and I were talking about the match at dinner." Cathy said, after they settled in the living room. "I asked if he noticed any strange behavior from Bill in the past couple of days? Sean, why don't you tell Nora what you said to me?"

Nora tried not to show how interested she was to hear Sean's explanation, but she could tell by the look in Cathy's eye, she hadn't succeeded.

"Something seems to be bothering Bill." Sean said, leaning forward, placing his elbows on his knees while folding his hands together. "I can't put my finger on it, but he's definitely been short with me. I thought it might be the golf match, but dismissed the possibility, especially after his performance today. I do suspect it has something to do with Mike Grace. At the match today, I heard them arguing about something, but couldn't make it out."

"They seemed pretty chummy the last couple of times I saw them." Nora told him.

She placed her hand on her forehead, rubbing her fingers back and forth, trying to piece together the mystery, but again, nothing jumped out at her.

"Mike is a cunning fox." Cathy said. "I wouldn't put anything past him."

"Why don't you call Bill and ask him straight out if there's anything wrong?" Sean suggested.

"It can't hurt Nora." Cathy told her. "It's better than torturing yourself all night wondering yourself sick."

Nora was hesitant to make the call. What if Bill, thought she was seeking an edge in tomorrow's match? No, she would leave things as they were, at least for now. George had told her to concentrate and that's what she intended to do, she explained to Cathy and Sean.

Nora didn't sleep very well, several times tossing and turning, unable to dismiss the sudden turn of events. She finally surrendered, deciding on an early shower. But when she opened the door, she tripped on the ledge and fell hard, her ankle twisting under her. When Cathy arrived, Nora was unable to answer the door. Cathy let herself in with her key, calling out to her friend, who announced she was in the kitchen.

"What the hell happened to you?" Cathy asked, placing the bag of bagels on the table and removing her jacket,

Nora was sitting in a chair, her leg elevated by another, with an ice pack on her ankle and swelling at an alarming rate.

"That looks nasty." Cathy said. "You can't play with that today, you'll have to call it off."

"I can't do that." Nora grimaced, as she leaned over to move the ice pack. "Cathy, call Jack Walsh, his number is my phone book in the left hand drawer. He's only around the corner. Tell him to bring his bag...and hurry."

Doctor Jack Walsh was a friend of Nora and Cathy. His daughter was a freshman in high school and played on the golf team. Following his wife's death from breast cancer, the doctor became an active supporter of the annual breast cancer awareness drive at Happy Hills. Nora and Cathy, would occasionally have Cindy at the club to play golf and her father greatly appreciated the *big sister* role played by the two women.

When the doctor arrived, he and Cathy, helped Nora into the den and settled her on the couch. After a careful examination of her ankle, he delivered his verdict.

"Nothing broken, Nora...but I'm afraid...you're not playing golf today."

"But I have to play!" She protested. "Can't you give me a shot of cortisone, or something for the pain?"

"What time is the match?" The doctor asked, frowning as he looked at Nora's ankle.

"One o'clock," she said with a pleading smile.

"When are you leaving?"

"At ten-thirty. I have a pre-match interview with CNM at eleven."

"Well, I suppose I can give you a cortisone shot," he said thoughtfully. "We'd have to wrap the ankle, that and some pain killers might get you through the day."

"Do it!" Nora said tersely, even though she wondered if her pride was replacing common sense.

By the time she reached the golf course, Nora's pain was considerably diminished, although she still couldn't mask her slight limp. As she approached the practice range, she saw Bill, about fifty-yards in front of her and yelling at Mike, but she was too far to hear what was being said. Mike, then turned to Bill, pointing his finger towards his face, seemingly rebuffing him. It all seemed very strange to Nora and further confused her about Bill's sudden change in demeanor.

When she reached the practice range, George whispered in her ear, asking Nora, the reason for what appeared to him, a change in her gait. She assured him she was fine and didn't want to make it an issue in front of Mike, Bill, or the CNM staff.

"Well folks, today's the day." Harvey Blackwell said, as they were about to begin. "I hope everyone is well rested and ready to go. We'll do the same sequence of interviews as we did yesterday. But today we're live, so there's no re-taping. What you say is what the audience will hear at home," instructed the CNM commentator.

"Our crew will help you with the same microphones as yesterday. I suggest you leave them on at all times. Just be careful what you say, especially if you happen to hit a bad shot."

Although warned by Harvey, their mikes would be open, Mike and Bill were so infuriated with one another that the warning went unheeded. It would turn out for Mike…to be a grave mistake.

"Bill, Nora, we'll start with you guys." Harvey said. "Would you both position yourselves at the marks on either side of me."

"Here we go folks." Harvey said, as his camera man counted down with his fingers.

"Hello, ladies and gentlemen." Harvey began. "Welcome to the Happy Hills Country Club in the village of Huntington, Long Island, where the ***battle of the sexes*** continues today between club champion Bill Harper and women's club champion, Nora Cummings. I'm Harvey Blackwell your CNM commentator for the day. Yesterday, Bill Harper opened a substantial five-hole lead over his challenger in this match play format, which **may prove to be an insurmountable obstacle** for Nora Cummings to overcome."

When Nora heard the commentator's remarks, she tried to eliminate all negative thoughts of losing the match. She was as always, determine to give it her all.

"Bill." Harvey went on. "Do you think the fact that women are not as physical as men plays any part in this?"

"There are two professional divisions in the world of golf." Bill told him. "The PGA and the LPGA, and there's a reason they're separated by gender, as in professional tennis and other professional sports."

"Do you agree with that assessment?" Harvey asked Nora.

"I won't deny differences exist in the physical capabilities between men and women." Nora replied. "But there's an equalizer."

"And that is?" Harvey continued.

"The respect for one another as individuals, with equal treatment regardless of gender, after all, this country was founded on a constitution based upon one vote for each American, man or woman. True, it took time for women to attain *suffrage*, but it was when common sense prevailed."

"Very well put." Harvey said. "I hope the results of this match will bring that ideal to Happy Hills as well as other country clubs across the country. Now, I have a question for Nora's coach, teaching professional, George Harris.

George, she's five holes behind in what seems to be a *grudge match* between two people with different opinions on how a country club should conduct itself. Can she dig herself out of the hole after falling behind by five holes?"

Sitting upright, aware of his nervous lip biting on camera the day before, George showed a confident look about him, as he was about to answer the question.

"Politics aside, Nora's a fine athlete." George said, "And... if anyone can make a comeback, it's her."

"Thank you, George. And now the President of Happy Hills Country Club, Mike Grace. Mike, you heard the comments by both Bill and Nora. Share your thoughts with our viewing audience."

"Harvey, my motto has always been...**when you're in Rome, do as the Romans do**."

Today, Mike was looking even more pleased with himself than usual, Nora observed, her mind more confused than ever. What did the cagy fox, have up his sleeve? Her focus, now drifting.

Mike, continued. "I think we've all been in situations where, although the majority are content with the *status quo*, other's are not. Is it really possible to satisfy everyone on every issue? Of course not, but according to our constitution, the *majority* carries the day every time."

"Well there you have it my friends." Harvey said, concluding the interview. "This match is not only about golf, but as you've just heard, it's also about the rights of the minority, which in this case are the women of Happy Hills Country Club. Stay tuned for the beginning of the final day of the ***battle of the sexes***. We're interested in your comments. Who do you think is right? Send us your thoughts to www.cnm.com. We'll be posting some of your comments right here on CNM."

"That was great guys, thank you and good luck today." Harvey said to the four of them.

When Nora and George went to the practice range, she told him about her fall in the shower and her cortisone shot.

"My God Nora, it's bad enough to have to beat this guy, but with that ankle, you'd be lucky to finish eighteen holes."

She knew his comment was out of concern for her, but Nora, also saw a crack in his armor. The one person she could always depend upon for encouragement...was doubting she would make it.

Meanwhile, at the other end of the range, Bill was taking his practice swings as Mike, approached the stall next to him, both forgetting their microphones were still on and could be heard by the national viewing audience.

"Well, Billy boy, it won't be long now." Mike glowed. "You'll have your championship and I'll see Nora, disgraced in as public a forum as you can get."

"Harvey, are you getting this?" Said one of the CNM crew. "Do you want me to cut them off?"

"No!" Harvey said. "Let's see where this is headed, it could be dynamite. Keep it going and get the video feed from the practice range to focus in on Harper and Grace."

Mike could see that Bill was faltering in his support and resented he was putting aside their long term friendship for the love of a woman and of all women…Nora.

"Don't you have a single shred of decency?" Bill said, showing his displeasure. "First you ask me to defraud Nora, with your phony invisible ink scheme. Of all the birdbrain ideas, having her sign a legal agreement, only to have the terms disappear. You're an attorney for Christ sakes, and for my money…you should be disbarred."

"Oh come off of it!" Mike replied. "You once understood she's a menace to this club. But then, you had to go and fall in love with her."

"You're right, Mike. I didn't like her at first, but I've seen a different side to the woman. She's a beautiful person in and out. You're a fool to think there's any excuse **to tarnish her dead husband's reputation** in order to win." Bill said, throwing his club on the ground. "But what did you win, Mike? The club is going to be gender neutral in spite of you, NOW will make sure of that."

"Those fools at NOW will never dictate the rules of our club!" Mike snapped. "Happy Hills will never be gender neutral and you know why? Because the money deal I made with CNM makes me a hero. That's' what it's all about in the end, Bill. It's a thirteen million dollar bonanza against a loud mouth broad."

"No Mike, it wasn't just Nora, you hurt. You also lost a friend by blackmailing me into turning against a woman I care for. **I don't play ball and you tell Nora and others about a onetime mistake her dead husband made in a weak moment**. I couldn't let you do that."

"You're a sap, Bill. In the end, you turned out as weak as Nora. Just do your part as we agreed and I'll let her husbands secret stay in his grave." Mike snarled.

"This is unbelievable!" Harvey said. "They don't even know they're live. This is better than the Rosy O'Donnell and Donald Trump bashing."

"Boss, the center is saying the phones are ringing off the hook…all against this Grace character," said one of the crew technicians.

"I'll bet they are." Harvey said with a smile. "I'll just bet they are…"

Nora, George, Bill and Mike, walked from the practice range to the first tee, unaware of what a national viewing audience had just witnessed. Most of the crowd attending the match hadn't heard either. They were gathered along the first fairway and CNM hadn't installed video screens on the course. But the few fans who had brought portable television sets or videophones, heard the exchange, as did many members of the club who were huddled around television sets at the bar and in the dining room, where a large screen had been installed by CNM. As a result, word spread quickly to the fans gathered at the first tee and those lined along the first fairway.

Harvey Blackwell glowed. He captured a bonus *coup* in broadcasting, an unrehearsed television reality, thanks to a **gigantic** ***faux pas*** by Mike, which the crowd would ensure a proper greeting when the embattled president was introduced at the first tee.

"Ladies and gentlemen." Harvey declared. "Before we start our second day of the ***battle of the sexes*** challenge between Bill Harper and Nora Cummings, I would like to introduce the man responsible for bringing this telecast to Happy Hills Country Club, the president of the club, Mike Grace." Harvey Blackwell commentated, the grin on his face couldn't be disguised.

Mike stepped forward, smiling like a conquering hero with arms high above his head, only to be greeted with a thunderous round of *boo's*. He was dumfounded, looking perplexed, he glanced at Blackwell for an answer. Instead, Harvey introduced Bill, who received a prolonged and deafening roar from the crowd. But the best was yet to come.

"Ladies and Gentlemen." Harvey announced. "I would now like to introduce to you a brave combatant who was willing to put it all on the line, by holding the torch high in her efforts to make Happy Hills Country Club, a kinder and gentler place for her fellow women golfers. A woman who, her coach tells me, suffered a serious fall in her home this morning, yet, is willing to be your *Joan- of-Arc*. I give you your lady club champion, Nora Cummings."

The reception by the fans was deafening. Soon shouts of **"Nora, Nora, Nora,"** echoed through-out, deeply touching the lady champion, as she acknowledged her admirers with a wave of both hands, tears flowing freely. She glanced at Bill, as he too joined in the applause, Nora nodding, but still unsure of his position.

Cathy was sitting at a table in the dining room with Sylvia, Laura and Sharon, who planned to watch the match on the big screen until the last nine holes, then following hole-by-hole.

"That son-of-a-bitch Mike, he's going to get his after this thing is over," a joyous and teary eyed Cathy announced.

"What's he going to get, Cathy?" Asked Laura. "If you want my opinion, he's too mean for us to get him anything."

Everyone at the table looked at Laura, bewildered as usual and not believing anyone could be so deliciously entertaining, while void between both ears.

"Laura, please don't ever change." Sharon said with a wry grin.

Nora was humbled by the crowds reaction to her introduction, yet completely in the dark as to what had transpired just a few minutes earlier between Mike and Bill.

Bill was about to address his ball at the first tee, when someone cried out, **"MIKE GRACE, YOU'RE A DISGRACE! MIKE GRACE, YOU'RE A DISGRACE!"** Soon, that call was being echoed by everyone, not only on the course, but soon resonated in the clubhouse as well. Nora glanced at the crowd with a blank expression, baffled by the antagonism towards Mike.

"Folks, I have to apologize for the delay." Harvey said to his listening audience. "Evidently, the dialogue you first heard between Mike Grace and Bill Harper has now spread to the fans here at Happy Hills and I can tell you that they're not happy with their president."

Neither Bill or Nora, understood why the crowd was so aggressive in booing Mike.

Bill approached the tee box and promptly swung his three-wood, driving the ball down the fairway, one hundred yards short of the green. Nora hit her drive seventy-yards past Bill's ball and thirty-yards short of the green. When they walked down the fairway, Bill mentioned her limp and asked if she was all right, to which Nora, simply nodded. After all, right now, he was her opponent.

Meanwhile, as Mike walked along the fairway, he was subjected to constant ridicule, with the result, he immediately returned to the first tee to inquire from Harvey, what had prompted the crowd's derisive reaction. When Harvey played back the tape of his conversation with Bill, the board president ripped the mike from his sweater and threw it on the ground.

"I'm going to sue you bastards for defamation of character, slander and whatever else I can come up with!" He shouted.

"Mike, from what I can gather, you're finished at this club. You may be brought up on charges with the Bar Association, as it appears they may have grounds to take away your license to ever practice law again. You may even be arrested for conspiracy to commit fraud. You're going to need all the friends you can get and I think you better start with Nora and Bill. And as far as suing CNM? You sue us and the club's fee will be held up until the suit is settled. As an attorney, you know that can take years, especially with the appeal process. Your only bargaining chip is that fee and sucking up to Nora and Bill. That's all I have to say. Now, I have a golf match to cover."

Mike stormed from the television booth, seething from his own indiscretion. How would he regroup? He seemed to have run out of options. But, was there one more *rabbit under his hat*?

After Bill's second shot landed twenty feet from the hole, Nora hit her wedge twelve feet closer. Bill was away and putted first, his ball stopping inches from the hole.

Nora, conceding the putt to Bill, for a par four, limped behind the hole to view the break in the green. She took out her spiral pad containing the notes she and George compiled when they walked the course, diagramming the various breaks by the ball on each green. The eight foot putt confronting Nora, had a slight left to right break. She addressed the ball, striking it towards the left side of the hole. She held her breath, while the ball did a three-hundred-sixty-degree turn before falling into the small cylindrical pit in the green, the gallery responding in cheers. Nora had won the hole with a birdie three to Bill's four and reduced his lead from five holes to four.

They both parred the next three holes, Bill still leading by four. On the fifth hole, Bill drove his ball in the fairway, one hundred thirty-yards from the green, while Nora's drive went left of the fairway into a clump of trees, at almost the exact place of a previous practice round with George, the crowd sighing with disappointment.

Nora saw two alternatives. One, a narrow opening of three feet between two trees and the second, to chip out to the fairway and have a hundred and fifty yard third shot to the green.

"I think we've seen this before Nora." George said, handing her a nine iron to chip out to the fairway.

"We're behind four holes," she reminded him, at the same time challenging his conservative play. "George, I've got to take a chance in order to cut into his lead?"

"Nora, take the nine-iron." George advised her. "Chip out and hope for a one putt. You never know what he's going to do. We can't afford to fall behind any more holes."

She reluctantly took the nine-iron from George and chipped out to the fairway. Bill hit a nine iron, his ball landing on the top slope of the green, with a remaining tricky downhill putt of about twenty-five feet, for a birdie three.

Nora took an eight iron from her bag. It was a hundred and fifty yards to the middle of the putting green, the red flag indicating that the hole was in front and below the two tiered green.

"You want to be short on this green, Nora." George told her. "Don't take it to the top of the slope."

She hit a high lofted shot which landed on the top rim of the green, Nora lowering her head. The hours of practice, she thought to herself, seemed to have failed her when she needed it most. Suddenly, the ball moved forward, rolling ever so slowly and then picking up speed as it descended down the hill and towards the flag, landing in the cup for a birdie three. The gallery was delirious, as Nora kissed George on the cheek. As for Bill, always the sportsman, he clapped for her achievement...but now...with a twinkle in his eye.

Bill addressed his ball for a difficult twenty-five foot downhill putt. He tapped his ball ever so slightly for the putt that would tie the hole. He watched it pick up speed as it descended down the slope, heading for the middle of the cup and dropping into it...before...inexplicably, bouncing out, the gallery of fans shaking their heads in disbelief. Bill's lead, now only three.

Nora's limp was more pronounced, her pain intensifying, as she completed the first nine holes, still trailing Bill, by three holes. By now, the entire gallery was aware of the pre-game drama played out by Mike and Bill, particularly since Harvey Blackwell, repeatedly referred to it, adding to his viewers interest in the outcome of the contest, now picked up by several radio stations.

"I find it ironic Tony, everyone but the two players know that an ethical drama is being played out here." Harvey said.

"Being a former professional golfer," Tony replied..."at a time like this, you're so focused that nothing else penetrates."

"And then there's another factor." Harvey told him. "Given the fact this man is clearly head over heals in love with his opponent, together with the obvious, the pain she's enduring, isn't it possible he has mixed feelings about beating her?"

"Harvey, if Bill Harper is any kind of athlete, he's focusing on his golf game and his instinct to perform well. The time for niceties is when the match is over and he wins."

"Nora Cummings still has a monumental task ahead of her. Tony, do you think she can do it?" Harvey asked.

"Impossible, no Harvey. Probable? I don't think so. She can't lose a hole on this back nine and all Bill has to do is keep making halves to win this thing. He's definitely ***in the cat birds seat,*** Harvey."

"Well Tony, it's time to see if your observations prove to be a correct forecast, as Bill Harper is about to tee off on the **tenth hole**."

"Looks like Nora, will be playing the back nine from a golf cart." Harvey observed. "That ankle must be really hurting her. One has to question why see didn't use the cart from the beginning of the round."

"Nora Cummings is a walker." Tony said. "It allows her to maintain a rhythm which is very important to a golfer. Playing from a golf cart will be to her disadvantage."

"I'll tell you Tony, if Nora pulls off a miracle and wins the match, this place will go bonkers."

Bill's next drive was in the middle of the fairway again, his second shot landing twenty-feet from the hole. "Boy is he consistent for a club duffer." Tony remarked.

Nora limped to her ball, selected a pitching wedge and hit a high lofted shot which landed five feet from the hole. Bill missed his first putt but was close enough to the hole that Nora, conceded his next putt for a par.

"If Nora makes this five foot putt, the lead will be cut to two." Harvey said. "And it's not that they're against Bill, because he's their ***knight in shining armor***, it's simply Nora…is their ***Joan of Arc.***"

The fans let out a resounding cheer, as Nora sank her putt, now trailing Bill by **only two holes** with eight remaining. They halved the next three holes leaving her still down two with five holes to play.

As Bill readied for his tee shot at the fourteenth hole, Cathy, Sylvia, Sharon and Laura, pushed their way through the crowd in time to see Bill's ball sail far left and nearly out of bounds, as he slammed his club to the ground in disgust, while Nora's drive landed in the fairway, just seventy-five yards from the green.

"Nora has an opportunity to win this hole, Tony." Harvey observed. "It would cut Bill's lead to one, which seemingly is getting to the club champion."

Bill had no clear shot and had to chip out to the fairway, leaving him a third shot of one- hundred-thirty-yards. Nora's ball was seventy-five-yards from the green. She was in noticeable discomfort now, when she reached for her pitching wedge.

"Remember those wedge drills we did?" George reminded her. "I want you to stick this within ten feet."

Nora looked at the slightly elevated green and pictured where she wanted her ball to land. To her fans delight, the ball floated towards the green, hitting the flag pin and landing three feet from the hole, the gallery, now in a state of delirium.

"Oh baby! What a shot by Nora." Tony said, jumping up from his seat.

Bill approached his ball with his nine-iron in hand, then swung, his ball landing within one foot from the hole.

"Can you believe those two shots, Tony?" Harvey asked. "These two warriors are putting quite a show on…and the fans are loving it. It appears Nora, will win this hole and will be down only one hole with four to go. What a turn of events. It's now conceivable, she could overcome Bill and win this thing."

Nora and Bill approached the green to a prolonged applause and sunk their putts. Bill for a par and Nora for a birdie, leaving her **one hole behind**. Then, after halving the fifteenth hole, they prepared to play the sixteenth, the second shortest hole.

Bill placed his tee in the ground with his five-wood in hand and although Nora had won the previous hole and had honors to hit first, it was agreed he would take her place because of her injury and the difference in the location of the tee boxes.

He drove his ball two-hundred-forty-yards straight down the fairway with eighty-yards remaining to the green. Nora hit her drive right of the fairway, with no shot to the green, her ball landing behind a large pine tree. She chipped out to the fairway and was sixty-yards from the green. Bill hit his second shot fifteen feet from the hole. Nora hit a poor third shot, landing twenty-five feet from the cup and on the upper level of the two tiered green. The flag was red and located at the front of the green.

Nora was first to putt. She presumed Bill would at least par the hole. If she missed her difficult putt, she would fall two holes behind with two remaining. Nora took out her spiral pad to review the breaks of the green, which she and George, had meticulously diagrammed. She limped around the hole, looking for the break that corresponded to her notes. A straight twenty-five-foot putt was difficult in itself, but this one had two different breaks and…was downhill.

"This putt could be the tournament end for Nora." Tony told the listening audience. "Bill will have a two putt for a par and could possibly one putt for birdie. If Nora misses for a five, she'll fall two holes back with two to play. She'll be lucky to stop the ball two feet from the hole, because it will pick up speed when it comes down the slope."

"Take two deep breaths and trust the read," she reminded herself. Nora drew her putter back and then struck the ball hard enough to barely reach the edge of the slope. She watched the ball turn in one direction, then another, as it picked up speed heading directly towards the hole, then…miraculously falling in the cup. The crowd erupted, while Nora, raised both her arms in triumph.

"Oh my goodness! Oh my goodness! I don't believe she made that putt." Harvey said, standing from his chair and looking at Tony. "If the ball doesn't go in the hole, it rolls ten, maybe fifteen feet past and the match is all but over."

"Look at Bill." Tony said. "He's shaking his head. He can't believe it went in the hole, neither can his caddie, there're both in shock. However, if he sinks this fifteen footer, he wins the hole and Nora's miraculous putt will mean nothing."

Bill stood over his ball, then struck it firmly. The crowd drew a collective breath, as the ball rolled straight towards the hole.

"He's got it Harvey." Tony said. **"That balls going in the hole!"** Both announcers, now standing from their chairs and waiting for the inevitable.

Bill started towards the hole, pointing his finger down, presuming he had sunk the putt, when the ball…went in the hole and abruptly came out. The crowd reacted with shock, Bill raising his hands to the heavens…seemingly appealing to the Gods for some relief.

"My heavens! My heavens! Bill's got to be thinking the golf Gods don't want him to win this thing." Harvey commented, as both golfers moved on to the seventeenth hole, Nora **only one behind.**

The seventeenth hole was a par three, two-hundred-seven-yards from the blue tees and one- hundred-sixty-five-yards from the red tees. Bill's ball started high, straight toward it's intended target…when a sudden gust of wind carried it astray and into a greenside sand trap.

Nora's tee ball started right, then drawing left, hitting the flagstick and falling six inches from the cup. For a full minute, the reaction of the crowd drowned out the voices of the commentators.

"Unless Bill…can hole out his next shot, this match will be tied." Harvey said, when he could be heard again.

Bill stepped into the sand trap, fully aware that he had to sink his shot to tie the hole, as Nora, had a tap in birdie. Blasting the sand, he sent the ball towards the hole, only to see it stop short, for a conceded par. **The match was now tied**.

In the meantime, Laura, who was standing with Cathy and Sharon on the sidelines, insisted Nora be informed about Mike, blackmailing Bill.

"You can't just interrupt the match." Cathy insisted, as they moved closer to the CNM announcers.

"Who would have believed we would still be announcing this match on the eighteen hole?" Harvey observed.

"You know how many PGA and LPGA matches you and I have covered." Tony pointed out. "This battle between Bill and Nora is right up there as the most exciting and dramatic for me."

"Given the melodrama played out before the match between Bill and board president Mike Grace, it just doesn't get any better." Harvey agreed.

"What's also fascinating, Tony…is neither Bill or Nora, apparently know about the conversation that millions of our viewers overheard."

"Bill is ready to tee off on this three-hundred-ninety-five-yard par four, eighteenth hole. You have to wonder what's going through his head." Harvey said. "Incidentally, while I'm at it, we'd like to thank our viewers for their e-mails, most of which, want to see Mike Grace go to jail and the others, hoping Bill and Nora get together after this match and live happily ever after.

Harper's teeing off and oh, it's another beauty, straight down the fairway. He's going to have about a hundred-thirty-five-yards to the green for a second shot."

"Nora is about to hit her drive. That ankle must really be barking, her limp is really pronounced." Tony observed. "This hole is only three-hundred-fifty-yards long for her. Boy, she's in obvious pain. I don't know how she can get any leverage with that ankle. I'll tell you Harvey, win, lose or draw, this woman is **one *courageous dude.*"**

"She sure is Tony…and the members of this club owe her big time, both the women and the men."

Nora limped to the tee box. She leaned on her left leg while using her driver for support, placing her tee in the ground. Forgoing her practice swings, she swung weakly at the ball, sending it down the fairway, but not very far, about one-hundred-eighty-yards from the green.

Nora's body surrendered. She could no longer put pressure on her right foot during the swing. Frustrated, she limped into the seat of the cart and forced herself to admit…she could no longer go on. George, put his arm around his brave protégée, Nora, sobbing, not in pain, but in being so close to achieving the impossible, yet falling short on the last hole of the match.

"Tony, I think Nora has retired from the match? She's in obvious distress, sobbing in her teacher arms, George Harris."

"Harvey, I have to say…for her to stop this match on the eighteenth hole, perhaps with one or two shots to go…tells me, our brave lady is really hurting. My hat's off to her." Tony said, his elbow sliding across his eyes.

"Holy mackerel! Tony, do you see what I see running towards Nora's golf cart?" Harvey declared.

"Harvey…I do believe…I see a half naked lady running on the golf course. Are my eyes playing tricks on me? **Man…is that woman stacked or what!"** Tony said, forgetting his mike was live, then apologizing to his listening audience, Harvey holding back an inclined burst of laughter.

"WHO'S that *half-naked ditz?* Doesn't she know we're on national television?" Blackwell asked.

"Harvey, just when you think you've seen it all something else comes along to top it."

"Laura, what are you doing!" Nora cried out, George wide-eyed and startled, drawing the cart to an abrupt halt.

"Now the woman's whispering in Nora's ear." Harvey, breathlessly announcing the play-by-play extra activity. "Whatever she's telling her is obviously taking her by surprise. Now, Nora is hugging her and thank goodness giving her a sweater to put on. What in the world is happening here?" Harvey asked, turning to his co-anchor.

Nora spotted Cathy, standing among the gallery of fans, nodding her head in validation of Laura's story. Suddenly, it all began to make sense to her, the odd behavior by Bill and the chants at the beginning of the tournament chastising, Mike.

Laura strutted back towards her friends with a grin from ear to ear amongst the loud whistles, cat calls and applause, showing their approval for her bold action and...**exposed boobies!**

"Look at Bill." Harvey said. "He's coming toward Nora's' golf cart and she's...limping toward him. **Oh! Oh!** Her ankle just gave out, she's down! Bill dropped down to his knees and is holding her in his arms."

"Nora, darling. I couldn't say..."

"I know Bill, you don't have to say anything." Nora said, putting two fingers to his lips, Bill, kissing them gently.

"Folks, this is incredible. These two seem to have forgotten all about the contest. But the gallery doesn't seem to mind. You can probably hear them **OOHING** and **AHING** in the background. Now...he's picking Nora up, he's carrying her down the fairway. Tony, he's going to finish the eighteenth hole with Nora...in his arms.

What symbolism folks, we have our Sir Lancelot in Bill Harper, carrying off his Lady Guinevere, Nora Cummings, it just doesn't get any better than that. Listen to the gallery, they're going bonkers!

Tony, this match is over and a great love affair has begun." Harvey said, slumping back in his chair and tossing his head-set to the floor.

EPILOGUE

Harvey Blackwell quit CNM and started his company specializing in reality television.

George Harris, enamored with Laura Dicks' boobies, gave her a series of *FREE* golf lessons.

Laura Dicks opened her own sex shop with **Sylvia Gibbs,** naming it *Sylvia's...*

Fred Daley moved in with Sylvia Gibbs and Tammy moved in with Bob Gibbs.

Marion Blake got her boob job! Then left her husband.

Mike Grace was disbarred and prosecuted for attempted fraud, but was given community service, his final scheme never executed. He served as a counselor to women inmates...who killed their husbands. He married the warden...who shortly afterwards became an inmate of the prison she once ruled.

Happy Hills became gender neutral. Few members resigned as predicted by the infamous, Mike Grace.

The New Board of Directors consisted of four men and four women with co-presidents Jerry and Laura Dicks.

Judy Feinstein joined Happy Hills and became the co-social director with **Maggie Howser.**

Bagels and lox are now served daily at the halfway house and gas masks are provided for all caddies.

Ralph Cipriano and his partner **Herb Blake**, opened a dress shop for cross-dressers.

Dr. Jack Walsh took up golf after his daughter Cindy, became a top LPGA golfer.

Nora Cummings, Bill Harper, Cathy Daley and **Sean** married on March 17th in commemoration of continued Irish luck.

Oh, Ramon, "Tomatillos." He opened his own topless bar featuring non other than...**Marion Blake...and...her new 42 double D pistols.**